Shear Deception

A Melanie Hogan Mystery
Book Two

Rhonda Blackhurst

Shear Deception

Published by: Lighthouse Press, Colorado
Cover design by: Isabel Robalo
Edited by: Sandstone Editing
Library of Congress Control Number: 2016903030

ISBN-13: 978-0991353231
ISBN-10: 0991353234

First Edition

Printed in the United States of America
www.rhondablackhurst.com

Praise for Rhonda Blackhurst's Books:

The Inheritance

I really enjoyed this book! Rhonda has created some highly relate-able characters and I found it easy to hear the different voices as she switched perspectives. Very worthwhile purchase!

I rarely review a book but this one hit home for me. Each character spoke to me and had a purpose. Thank you Rhonda for writing this book. It is now one of my favorites!

Very good story! I highly recommend buying this book!

Loved this book! What a wonderful debut for this newly published author. Can't wait to see what else she writes.

What an awesome book...It really makes you understand what's really important in life, the love of family.

Shear Madness, **A Melanie Hogan Mystery (Book One)**

Great story - Took a twist at the end that I hadn't anticipated! Rhonda writes in a way that helps the reader visualize the scene - makes it a very fun read and even more suspenseful. I'm ready for the next one in the series!

Loved this cozy mystery and can't wait for the next one in the series. Melanie is a charming character, the dialogue is witty and funny, and the mystery has a twist I didn't guess.

For Ben, Alex, and Clint, the wind beneath my wings.

and

For my parents, who gave me the foundation of family and faith.

Acknowledgments

Special thanks go to the following:

To my husband, who has given me endless support and encouragement in pursuing my writing dreams. You have been my most avid cheerleader in this amazing blessing called life. This journey is all the better, all the richer, because I share it with you.

To my boys, Ben and Alex. Keeping journals for each of you while you were growing up kept my love of writing alive. Writing to, and about, both of you in those journals, was pure joy. Being your mother has been my most valued role in life. You influence many of the characters I write.

To my grandchildren – whatever I write, I write it with you in mind, hoping to share with you my love of story.

To my parents who put up with so many years of locking myself in my room so I could write and giving me the time and space to sit on the dock by the lake or float in the boat on the water writing, dreaming, and dreaming about writing.

To Becky, my beautiful angel who waits for me in heaven. Your warmth, your beautiful spirit, and your gentleness are so missed. I hope that someday we can co-author a book on the beauty of heaven.

To my "Brighton Group" (you know who you are) for accepting me just as I am, broken and flawed. It's because of your experience, strength, and hope that I have the drive, determination, and ability to keep writing.

To Sarah and Jade. Your time, insight, and suggestions were priceless.

To Rachel with Sandstone Editing. Your knowledge and leadership in the Colorado Writing School Critique

Group has helped me grow as a writer, pushing me to do my best work and settle for nothing less. And to all the members of that critique group, you play an important role in my writing life.

To SinC Colorado, my sisters in crime. Being part of such a talented group of writers is such a blessing. Not to mention a fun blessing.

To Rocky Mountain Fiction Writers. You are all such a warm, welcoming, helpful group of writers. What a gift you are to this writer.

And most of all, to my Father in heaven, who has given me a thousand chances to get it right. Thank You for strategically placing each and every person in my life exactly when and where I needed them most, and for planting in me the love of writing. May I always strive to honor You in all things and be Your hands and feet in this life.

Also by Rhonda Blackhurst

- ➢ The Inheritance

The Melanie Hogan Cozy Mystery Series
- ➢ Shear Madness
- ➢ Shear Deception
- ➢ Shear Malice
- ➢ Shear Murder
- ➢ Shear Holiday Mayhem
- ➢ Shear Camping Caper
- ➢ Shear Fear
- ➢ Shear Misfortune

The Whispering Pines Mysteries
- ➢ Finding Abby
- ➢ Abby's Redemption

Chapter 1

THERE ARE SOME DAYS that I wish I could reverse time back to when I woke up that morning and retreat under the covers, head and all, like a turtle in its protective shell, and not come out for a good long time. At least, until I was sure the horizon was clear or I realized what was happening was only a dream. Either would work at the present time; this was one of those days.

Unable to speak, I stared at my grandmother after she delivered the bombshell news to me that my birth mother, Violet, was coming for a visit. All of my old insecurities came rushing back in, my ears pulsing with a deafening whooshing sound as everything around me seemed to fade away. I was sure I was about to faint.

I sat tucked into the corner chair of her little breakfast nook, my gaze stubbornly fixed out the window at the droplets of water dripping off of the icicles that hung from the overhang of her porch. I'd once seen on a TV show, one of the rare times I watched TV, that using an icicle to kill someone is the perfect crime. The murder weapon melts and presto! No fingerprints, no proof. The alarming realization that I was even thinking about that right now snapped my attention back to my grandmother who was closely watching me.

"Why does Violet really want to come visit, Nana?"

"She said she misses you."

"Why now? Isn't it about thirty-six years too late to miss me?"

"A child is never far from a mother's heart, dear." Her cornflower blue eyes looked misty.

"Yes, but she's shown no signs of missing me since she dropped me off here at the ripe old age of four, so why now?"

"Maybe she's hoping it's not too late to be a mother to you."

That thought was almost laughable. I knew she was trying to make this easier on me, but it wasn't working.

"She's not a mother, Nana. Violet missed that day of class when God was handing out job descriptions."

"God doesn't make mistakes."

"To think I spent all those years scared she'd come back and take me away from you and granddad. What was I thinking?" Nana's gentle smile remained in place. It was that constant smile that got me through many trials and tribulations in my life. I was counting on it getting me through this one. "Did I ever tell you that when I was about ten I sneaked into your room one night when you were sleeping to see if you smile even in your sleep?" Her eyes twinkled, and her rosy cheeks deepened a shade or two. "Wouldn't you know there was the tiniest trace of a smile on your face even when you sleep? I remember thinking you must have been having a delightful dream because no one looks that happy when they're sleeping. No one except you, I learned." She chuckled. I sat back in my chair and sighed, leaning my head against the back of the chair, the edge resting on the nape of my neck. I stared up at the ceiling, noticing the fine strands of a cobweb in the corner. "There's something she's not telling us."

"You have every reason to be skeptical—"

"Good, because I am. I've earned that right."

"Melanie Hogan!" She was the only one who could pass off a stern reprimand as loving.

"Well?"

"Well is a deep subject."

"Nana," I scoffed. "You say that every time." And yet her old sayings I've heard time and time again brought comfort. "Don't you think I have a right to be skeptical?"

"We never have a right to be anything. Don't get all entitled on me, dear. I didn't raise you that way." She took my hand in hers and gave it a gentle squeeze.

"You said I have every reason to be skeptical."

"Every reason, yes, because of Violet's past promises. But that's entirely different than thinking you've earned the right."

"As usual, you're right," I groaned. "But the answer still remains a mystery. What that woman really wants."

"She said she wants to celebrate your birthday with you."

My eyes about bugged out of my head. I couldn't believe what I was hearing. "Well, the irony in that is enough to knock me right over. My actual birth date was probably the only day Violet was ever there for me. And that's only because she didn't have a choice." Nana once again took my shaking hand in her own steady, warm one. "I guess I could feel grateful that she left me with you instead of on the steps of a church or fire station right after she gave birth to me."

"She chose to have you, dear. I believe she really wanted to be a mother. At one time, anyway."

"You give her far too much credit." My cynicism was screaming. I searched her eyes trying to understand. "How can you be so calm about this? How can you—how can—can you honestly tell me you're okay with her coming? Aren't you mad at her?"

"Not angry, no. Sad. Just very sad."

"How can you not be angry?" I desperately wanted the peace I saw in my grandmother.

"I forgave your mother a long time ago. And that is the only thing I can do. What your mother does is in her own power and control. Not mine."

"And that's it?" I was dumbfounded. "I could sit here and say I forgive her ten thousand times and I would still hate her."

"Hate is—"

"—a strong word," I finished for her and sighed. I'd heard that statement more than a dozen times over the course of my lifetime. "I just don't get it. How can you just forgive her after what she put you and granddad through?"

"Forgiveness isn't about a simple statement. It's a condition of the heart. You'll get there. I'm sure of it." She patted my hand and then held it tight. The warmth of her firm grasp felt like a security blanket right now.

"You seem more sure of that than I am."

We sat in silence for a moment as my grandmother let me absorb the shock of it all. I love a good mystery, but what Nana just put on my plate wasn't going to be a mystery. This was going to be nothing other than a nightmare. One I hoped I could survive.

"Nana?"

"Hm?"

"I used to feel so humiliated that my own mother rejected me like a mechanical inspection device rejects a piece of flawed merchandise. But I just want you to know that the day Violet left me here with you and granddad was actually the best thing she ever did for me. I didn't realize it at the time and I know I wasn't always an amiable child to raise, but in case I haven't told you lately, thank you."

"You weren't so bad," she said, giving me a wink.

"And you're a terrible liar. You know, she probably never even got all those big acting roles she told me she got. In fact, those movies probably never even existed."

I leaned over and lay my head on her lap as she stroked my hair. Here I was, an almost-forty-year-old woman melting into the insecure four-year-old I'd once been.

Did Violet still hold that much power over me? I had to reclaim that power. Fear had been my constant, unwanted companion for far too long. I knew the only way I could dump the fear for good and reclaim my power was to agree to see her. If nothing else I needed to know her agenda. Because there was no doubt in my mind that there was definitely an agenda.

Chapter 2

BY THE TIME WE finished dinner and I drove home it was after nine o'clock. It was cold and dark, and as I pulled up and parked in my detached garage, my eyes darted down the path to the house, looking for any movement. Before I dashed the hundred yards between the garage and the house, I peered at what snow was left, looking for footprints. My all-too-recent stalker could have avoided the snow patches. He was that smart. He'd gotten into my house nearly a year ago, and I'd still not gotten back to feeling completely safe.

In my rush, I nearly slipped on a patch of melting snow that had turned to ice once the sun went down and the warm air turned cooler. Regaining my footing, I reached the door, fumbled with my keys, slipped inside and locked the deadbolt behind me. My small, humble log house just yards away from the lakefront had always been my haven, my place to get away from it all, to find solace and stillness after being surrounded by customers and noise all day. A time to put my feet up or sprawl on the floor after being on my feet for ten plus hours.

I quickly called my grandmother, as I promised I would, to let her know I'd arrived safely. I knew she would love for me to move back in with her, especially after the events of last summer, but I think she's come to terms with my stubborn determination to stay put. I wouldn't be chased from my own home by some bully of a stalker.

It was last summer that I decided I was craving some excitement in my life rather than the usual run of the mill day-to-day life stuff. While that desire nearly got me killed, not to mention my best friends Claire and Jack, it set a fire under me to find mysteries to solve. I began watching more of them on television, something I never did before, paying close attention to how they figured out the clues. Samantha Kinsey from the Hallmark Channel's *Mystery Woman* series quickly became my virtual mentor. I even roped Claire and Jack into playing the board game Clue with me nearly every time we got together at my house. The good sports they are, they even agreed to watch the movie *Clue* with me. Asking them to watch it the second time, though, was met with a resounding no! from Jack. They both think I'm a little obsessed but truth be told, they enjoy it all as much as I do. As long as it doesn't hit too close to home as it did the first time.

I went through each room, closing every blind and curtain in the house, something I used to think was almost sinful less than a year ago. But since then I've decided covering the beauty of the great outdoors at night, when it was too dark to see it anyway, was a small price to pay for shielding myself from a peeper. I went upstairs to the loft where my bedroom was and slipped out of my clothes and into a pair of sweat pants, a sweatshirt, and my warm fuzzy slippers, pulled my hair back into a ponytail and headed back downstairs to make a cup of salted caramel hot chocolate from my Keurig.

Circling the steaming cup with my chilled hands, I turned off the lights with an elbow and headed back upstairs and slid beneath the covers in my sweats. It may be spring, but springtime in a log house could get downright cold. Especially with the humidity this time of year brought with it in Minnesota. Sometimes it felt like the wind that blew off the iced over lake came right through the walls. Someday I would get around to winterizing better, but for right now I was content with the way it was.

I had just settled back against my propped-up pillows with a book when my phone rang. I looked at the caller ID and smiled.

"Hey, Jack."

"Hey. Just checking in. Everything going okay?"

"Yup. Still coming up tomorrow?"

"That's the plan."

"Bryce coming too this time?" Bryce was Jack's significant other. Personally, I think Jack could do so much better, but it's not me that has to live with him. As long as he was good to my friend, I bit back my complaints.

"No. He's got something else going on."

"Yeah?"

"Yes. Why do you say it like that?"

"Cause I think Bryce is avoiding me."

"Now why would he be doing that? And where would you even get such an idea?"

"Come on, Jack. I'm not dense."

"No, you're not. But you have one heck of an imagination."

"I just get the feeling that he's a little miffed that you nearly got killed because you were here trying to protect me." Okay, so I usually bite back my complaints.

"First of all, it was a hit on the head. I'd hardly call that nearly killed. Second, I wasn't trying to protect you, I *did* protect you."

"Of course you did." I chuckled.

"He might, however, be a little jealous."

That admission shocked me. "Of what?"

"You."

"He realizes I'm not your type, right? I mean, he's met me many times. I really am a woman, not a wanna-be."

"Not that kind of jealous, silly girl." I grinned. Sometimes he sounded so...feminine. I loved that about him. "He's just not so sure I would put my life on the line for him like I would for you."

"And?"

"And what?"

"Would you?"

"What is this, a competition between you two?" His voice scolded over the phone, and I laughed. "I don't know which of you is worse."

"Duh!" I sang. "He is. I'll see you tomorrow, okay? Love you."

"Love you, too."

"Don't let Bryce hear you say that," I teased.

"Girl, you are insufferable!"

I laughed, and we hung up. I had just gotten settled back against the pillows when my phone rang again.

"Grand Central Station. Hi Claire."

"Melanie, I hope you don't mind, but I'm—wait a minute! What do you mean, 'Grand Central Station'?"

"Wow, you're a quick one, my friend," I laughed. "I just hung up from Jack before you called."

"Cool! How's he doin'?"

"Jack's Jack. He's coming up tomorrow. Wanna come by after work for our usual 'Jack's here' gathering?"

"Can I bring Syd? That's what I was calling for. I'm going to be a little late getting in tomorrow. I need to talk with her teacher tomorrow when I drop her off at school."

"Uh-oh. Everything okay?" I frowned and bit my lower lip. Sydney was Claire's daughter of seven going on sixteen. "Is there a little girl—or boy—in her class that I need to talk to? If anyone is picking on my girl, I'll take care of it."

"Everything's fine. Well, mostly fine. She hasn't been turning in her homework for math."

"Since when does a seven-year-old have math homework she's supposed to turn in?"

"It's called school. She has to be responsible, Mel."

"Exactly the point. She's seven, for crying out loud."

"A seven-year-old who needs to learn responsibility."

I knew I wouldn't win this one. "Fine. But Claire?"

"Yeah?"

"Give her the benefit of the doubt. Maybe she has a reason."

"Oh, she has a reason alright. I asked her."

"See?" I crowed. "What is it?"

"She doesn't like math and doesn't know why I'm being mean and making her do it."

"Oh." I snickered. "Well? Why are you?"

"Why am I what?"

"Being so mean?"

"Melanie!" I jerked the phone away from my ear to prevent hearing loss.

"Well, what do I know? I'm not a mother." I felt a pang of envy slash through me. One would think I would be used to that fact by now, but my inability to be a mother continued to haunt me. Sometimes I wondered if the reason I wanted to be a mother was to prove I could do what Violet had proved she couldn't. Maybe it was God's way of saving a poor child from having me as a mother in case I was just like Violet. "Guess who's coming to visit?"

"Besides Jack, you mean?"

"Violet."

"By the sounds of it, you're less than thrilled."

"Good catch," I said, rolling my eyes.

"Why is she coming to visit?"

"That, my dear friend, is the million-dollar question."

"Maybe it's nothing."

"No, it's something. I just can't imagine what it is." The line was quiet for a minute. "Whatever it is, though, I guarantee you it's not good."

Chapter 3

I SLEPT FITFULLY THAT night, tossing and turning until I woke up sweating and completely tangled in my sheets. Dreams of Violet, my grandmother, an old nemesis from last summer, and even Cain, my ex-husband, intersected. I felt anything but rested, but nevertheless, I needed to get myself out of bed and in the shower so I wasn't late for work.

Claire and I co-own a hair salon, A Cut Above. After one of our stylists, up and quit last summer we tried to make do with the current staff, that being Claire and I, Connie, and Gina, a part-time nail tech. Finally, we'd agreed to take in another stylist, Rubie, which gave us the flexibility to be gone a day here and there without being a complete inconvenience to everyone else. Gina didn't come in very often, part-time at most, but she paid her monthly rent and scheduled her own appointments, as long as they were during normal business hours.

Today, for no reason I could put my finger on, I didn't want Rubie alone at the salon, and since Claire was going to be late, Connie had the day off and Gina was hit or miss, I needed to be there plenty early. I had the never-ending paperwork that needed to be done anyway. It was the one thing that was always the same that I never tired of. It kept me grounded.

I was well into the application process of the hair color concoction on my second client when Claire came through the door, the usual bounce in her step absent.

"You okay there, Tigger?" I asked. She met my attempt at humor with a scowl. Well, as much of a scowl as was possible for Claire.

"So it turns out that not only is she not turning in her math homework, but she also punched a boy on the playground."

My client, Mrs. Sorenson, swiveled to look at Claire. "Oh dear," she crooned. I was wondering if I was going to have to hold her down. It looked like sweet Mrs. Sorenson was going to jump right out of the chair to comfort Claire. "Honey, maybe he had it coming to him."

"Mrs. Sorenson," Claire explained sounding much more like the confident mother than she actually was, "Sydney cannot just go around punching people. If he said something that wasn't right she has to use her words, not her fists."

I did my best to stifle a giggle. I wouldn't tell Claire this, but I was proud of my little slugger. "Did you ask her about it? Maybe she has an excellent explanation. He's probably a bully."

"Melanie, you're no help at all! I swear sometimes you're worse than she is."

"Well, did you?"

"I asked her why she didn't tell me. Know what she said?" She continued without waiting for me to answer. "She said, *You didn't ask me, mommy*. Seriously?"

"Can't blame a girl for not wanting to rat on herself," I said.

Mrs. Sorenson let out a hoot, and Claire shot us both a menacing look, which for Claire was simply the absence of a smile. Come to think of it, she and Nana were two peas in a pod. But for Claire, that look made both Mrs. Sorenson and I sober up. On the surface anyway.

Rubie swiveled her client around so they were both facing Claire's direction. Claire looked at them and started giggling. I looked to see what was so funny and the sight that met my eyes was indeed a sight to behold. Rubie's blonde bouncy curls were in sharp contrast to the hair color she was applying which turned her client's hair fire-engine red. A dollop of color had worked its way onto Rubie's chin. She spun around to look in the mirror.

"Looks like I'm sprouting a beard," she grinned. "Y'all can just call me Ruben," she drawled in a low voice.

And that set the course for the rest of our day. A day I so desperately needed after my grandmother's news the evening before and my night of sleep. Or lack thereof. Claire and this salon, and even Rubie, were exactly the medicine the doctor ordered. In fact, I almost forgot about Violet entirely. Almost.

"So have you found out why Violet is coming to visit?" Claire asked.

"No. And my anxiety is alive and well trying to figure it out."

"Who's Violet?" asked Rubie.

"Someone who's not important," I said.

"Sounds like she is," Rubie said. "If someone has that effect on you," she said, pointing at me with her shears, "she's important whether you want her to be or not."

"I just wish I could put my finger on what's bothering me so much," I said, looking at Claire. "Probably the fact that she has the nerve to think she can pop up after all these years to celebrate my birthday. Whatever would make her think that I even want her here for my birthday? Birthdays are a time for family and friends. She's neither one."

"Then who is she?" Rubie asked.

"No one," Claire and I said in unison."

"Whatever," Rubie said in a sing-song voice. "If you don't want me to know, then don't talk about it in front of me."

"Good point," I mumbled.

Jack arrived an hour before closing. He liked to time it that way so he had enough time to get his business done and then head to dinner with Claire and me. I met Jack at a hair show I had attended in Minneapolis several years ago and we hit it off immediately. I wear little jewelry, but there was something about the pieces he makes that attracted even me. His business, Jack's Originals, made a killing in the metro area, and it isn't necessary for him to travel as far as he does for me, but it's an excuse to see each other more frequently. And Claire and I love it because we get to offer an accessory line unique to the area.

After the last clients of the day had gone, and Gina the nail tech, who showed up for a few hours, had finished up and left, the rest of us headed to my house.

As I drove home, thoughts of Violet flooded my mind again. By the time I reached my driveway I could feel my mood had soured. I scolded myself for letting her have that power over me yet again. Or still. I couldn't decide which.

I hadn't even gotten the door unlocked when I saw headlights coming up the drive. I couldn't say I was sorry. I didn't want to be alone with myself and my thoughts a moment longer. Violet's impending visit was turning me into a Negative Nellie.

I turned and watched as Rubie's long legs uncurled from her car and she stood, a fawn in her lanky innocence. Her blonde shoulder-length curls bounced as she strode toward me and up the front porch steps all smiles. I held the door open for her and she gave me a half hug as she passed, leaving me with the powdery floral scent of Loves Baby Soft. I didn't even know they still made that stuff until Rubie started working with us. It brought a blast from my past as I remembered many a night with that as my fragrance of choice.

"I'm gonna run up and change. Will you watch for Claire, Sydney, and Jack?"

"Of course." She beamed.

Geez! What was it with these chronically happy people I had in my life? Maybe if I was lucky it would rub off on me. Although, Jack had accused me once of being eternally optimistic. It must have been on one of his pessimistic days where anyone that didn't match that pessimism qualified as eternally optimistic.

Comfortable in my usual sweat pants and one of the dozens of free t-shirts I got from sales reps, I came back downstairs at the same time the three of them walked through the front door, Claire and Jack each giving Rubie a hug. You'd think we hadn't seen each other for months.

"Let the party begin!" I called and joined in on the hugging, knowing they were fully aware I was being my typical sarcastic self. Sometimes I thought about working on that but why do today what can be put off until tomorrow.

Jack began dishing up the pizza, Claire poured the wine and Rubie helped me get a fire going in the fireplace to help take the damp chill out of the room.

"Don't make it too warm in here or we'll all be sleeping," Jack called out to us.

"There will be no sleeping!" I called back.

"I love your house, Melanie," Rubie said beside me. "It's so beautiful. So...you."

What did that mean? So...you. Hmm.

"I've always wanted a log house like this. Maybe someday," she said.

"Yeah?" I asked, intrigued. We'd never been to Rubie's house. Not because we didn't want to but because she'd never extended the invitation. "What's your house like?" I asked as I struck the match and lit one of the logs.

"I live in an apartment on the north side."

"Hm." The north side. I once knew someone who had stayed at a hotel on the north side. Or so he said that's where he was staying. Who knew? It wasn't a pleasant memory and I pushed it aside. "Maybe next time we can go to your apartment."

"Maybe."

I waited for her to say more, but she didn't. In fact, she was oddly quiet for Rubie. Satisfied with the fire, I closed the curtains and blinds.

"Do you need to close those out here?" She finally spoke. "Who would ever see in? You don't have any neighbors."

"We make her close them," Claire said as she came in and reached up to close the curtains on the bay window that faced the patio and the lake. "Melanie had an unwanted visitor recently. It was the scariest thing ever."

"I wouldn't say ever."

"You're not the one who someone hit over the head and knocked out," Jack joined in.

"No, but I can protect you now."

17

"How's that? With your high heels you always wear? What are you going to do, take one off and club someone?" He looked at me over the top of his glasses, the black frames making his eyes appear even deeper brown than they actually were.

"It worked before, didn't it? But that aside, I got my CCW."

"CCW?" Rubie asked, brows knit. "What's that?"

"Concealed carry permit," Claire explained. Noticing Rubie was still confused, she added, "A gun."

"A gun?" Rubie's eyes went wide.

"Yeah, that should scare everyone statewide," Jack said.

"Shut up!" I threw a pillow at him. "I took classes with a certified instructor just like I was required to do. And I must admit I'm darn good."

"Yup, she is!" Claire backed me up. "We go to the range sometimes and she's a great shot."

"You girls scare the crap out of me," Jack muttered and shook his head.

But I knew he was secretly glad I had it. He worried about me living out here by myself. Granted, I'm not completely alone. There are other people who live in the area year-round, but our houses aren't on top of one another like they practically are in town.

"Don't worry. I only got it to keep here in case another crazy person visits. Other than the three that are here tonight," I added.

"There's four of us here, Aunt Mel," Sydney corrected me, snuggling in beside me for a split second before she tuned into a game on Claire's iPad.

"Yeah, but only three of them are crazy. You and I are normal." I put my arm around her shoulder and gave her a squeeze. Her giggle made my heart happy. But then anything Sydney did made my heart happy. I just love that girl. "Have you been leaving the boys at school alone, Syd?"

"She wanted you for her mother by the time I got done scolding her," Claire said, wrapping a protective arm around Sydney.

I felt a painful pang in my gut. "I wish I were, too," I said, my voice barely audible.

"Do you ever want kids, Melanie?" Rubie asked.

"Can't."

"Unmarried people have kids all the time," she said.

"No, I mean I can't."

"That's why she's divorced," Jack explained. "Her jerk of an ex-husband found out and got someone else knocked up before they were even divorced."

I saw Rubie's look of pity and I bristled. "God's way of making sure I don't repeat what Violet did." I looked at Rubie. "Yes, I'm still bitter."

"Who is Violet?" Rubie said in utter frustration. "And don't say no one."

"She's my birth mother. One who failed at the mother part." I filled her in on the basics. "And now she's decided she wants to come and visit."

"Why? What does she want?"

"That's what I want to know," I said. "Because if there's one thing I've learned, it's that Violet does nothing unless something's in it for Violet. I, for one, can hardly wait to find out what that is."

Chapter 4

THE NIGHT BEFORE I was to pick Violet up, I called my grandmother to be sure I had the airline, flight number and time correct.

"Did she throw a fit when you told her I wasn't picking her up at the Minneapolis airport?" I asked.

"I wouldn't say a fit, exactly, but she didn't understand why."

"Of course, she didn't. She expects everyone to rearrange their lives to suit her. She's a prima donna."

"I think she's just relieved you've agreed to see her."

"Nana, I love you to death. But you're a terrible liar."

She chuckled. "Positive thoughts dear."

"You have enough for both of us. How about I keep us balanced by harboring some not-so-positive thoughts?"

Another chuckle. "Just a reminder that I can pick her up if you need to work."

"No, no. I've rescheduled my appointments already. Besides, if I pick her up I can find out sooner what her motivation is for coming here."

"Good night my sweet girl. Get some sleep."

"Probably not going to happen. But I'll try. Hey, Nana? It just occurred to me. She better not be coming to ask for money. And if she does, I hope you don't even think about giving it to her. Not that I'm telling you what to do."

She laughed softly. "Of course, you are. Nevertheless, I don't have any to give."

"Nana, do you need money? If you do, all you have to do is let me know."

"I'm doing just fine. Now go to bed. And say your prayers."

"I will. I love you, Nana."

"I love you too, dear."

I turned out the lamp and lay back in my bed staring at the barely visible reflections the moon cast on the ceiling through the windows that occupied much of the wall beside the stairs that led to my loft. The only windows in my house I didn't have curtains to cover these days. Not because I didn't want them so much as it would take the time to get someone out here to measure and get them custom made since the large windows are at an angle that follows the wall beside the stairs. On the bright side, at least, the glass in those particular windows is thick and doesn't let much in as far as cold air goes. Just moonlight, sunlight, and a breathtaking view of the lake.

The fresh snowfall from earlier that day and the white ground made it look almost like daylight outside. I stared through the skylight above my bed at the stars that glistened and twinkled in the chilly night sky like little crystals. I watched as one shot across the sky leaving a trail of light in its wake. A shooting star. I reached my arms above my head, laced my fingers, and rested the back of my head on my hands. If I could make a wish on that shooting star and believe it to come true like I used to when I was little, I would wish for tomorrow to be over. For the whole awkward reunion thing to be behind us.

I was contemplating calling Claire to take her up on her offer to go with me when I heard a thump outside. It sounded like it was just outside the patio door. I pulled the covers up to my chin and held my breath, listening closely, hearing nothing more than the wind howling outside. I breathed with relief. This entire visit had my stomach in knots. It was time I stop being afraid of all the what-if's, put on my big girl panties and face this head on. If for no other reason than to let Violet know I'm not afraid of her.

The ring tone on my cell phone startled me awake. "Wind Beneath My Wings," the one that played only for my grandmother. I stretched my fingers, grasping the covers, fumbling for my phone with one hand, my other arm thrown across my eyes hoping to delay the light of morning by any means I could.

"Morning Nana," I mumbled.

"You're not still in bed are you, dear?"

"No," I lied. But she was too smart for me.

"You need to get a move on if you're going to make it to the airport on time."

I groaned. "Waiting for a while will be good for her. She made me wait years."

"Melanie Hogan!" she said in a failed attempt to scold me. "Are you sure you don't want me to come with you?"

"No need for both of us to be miserable. Unless you think you should referee?"

"You betcha I will." She chuckled. "She can only make you mad if you allow her to. Are you going to give her that?"

"Not on your life."

"That's my girl. Call me when you're on your way back home so I know you're okay."

I tapped the end call button and tossed it to the foot of the bed. I heard it thud onto the floor and clatter a few feet away, a sound that let me know something was no longer intact. I let out a sound that started as a groan and ended as a primal scream I didn't even recognize. "Off to a good start today, Melanie," I muttered. *God give me strength. And lots and lots of grace.*

I stayed in bed for just a moment longer before forcing myself up, my breath catching as my feet touched the cold hardwood floor as I remembered the missing rug. I needed to remember to pick it up from the cleaners today. The cold shock was, however, a moment's reprieve from the anxiety that was doing its best to take control.

An hour later I was on the road with a cup of coffee in my travel cup, the radio blaring, and the airline, flight number and flight time scrawled on a slip of paper that lay taunting me on the passenger seat. The seat that would soon carry my guest. Oh goody.

The drive to the airport went too fast as I processed numerous scenarios of 'what if' through my overstressed brain. What if she decided not to come and I made the trip for nothing? What if I wasn't what she expected me to be? And what, exactly, did she expect me to be? What if I wasn't pretty enough, smart enough, good enough...just simply not enough? And did it really matter what she thought or if I was enough of anything for her?

Obviously, it did or I wouldn't be a breath away from a panic attack.

After driving up and down rows of cars in the parking garage, I finally found a parking spot between a panel van and a one-ton truck, my little Nissan 350Z swallowed up between them. I fumbled with my key fob until I heard the chirp showing I'd clicked the button I was looking for. The one that announced my car was secure from any honest thieves since the dishonest ones could care less if it was locked or not.

Once outside from the parking garage, I stepped tentatively through the melting snow, nearly slipping more than once. I cursed myself for having insisted on wearing my typical high heeled black boots rather than something more sensible. But now, more than ever, I needed comfortable and familiar terrain. And that included my chunky heels or wedges, jeans, and hoop earrings. No doubt if Claire saw what I was wearing she would have begged to dress me up as she had a time or two in the past, or to at least expand my color choices beyond various shades of black, and an occasional dash of color, graduating to color with an occasional dash of black, but to no avail.

"Please!" she'd begged. "Let me add some versatility to your wardrobe."

"Claire, I'm not your doll. I'm a real person. An adult even. I can dress myself. Dress one of Syd's dolls for crying out loud," I'd said. More than once. Every. Time. She. Asked.

I reached the terminal and went in as far as I could go without having to go through security. I looked around, not knowing exactly what I was looking for. I couldn't remember what she even looked like. She'd sent pictures over the years, but they were always more like paparazzi shots that were unclear. For all I knew it wasn't really her at all. She probably hired her own paparazzi to make us think she was some big star, I thought cynically, feeling a twinge of guilt. Her impending presence was bringing out the ugly in me and she wasn't even here yet. Yikes! This could be a long visit.

I was leaning against a big cement circular pillar, hands in my jacket pockets, watching all the people pass by and wondering how long she was planning on staying when my breath got caught in my lungs. I knew the minute I saw the woman walking toward me it was her. Our eyes met and locked for a moment. A very uncomfortable moment. She was one of the most beautiful women I'd ever seen. In a not-anything-like-me sort of way. I felt an odd wave of relief. As she turned her head I could see her coal black hair pulled back in a tight bun at the nape. She faced forward again and I noticed her lips were the brightest red, a color I'm certain I've never seen before, her skin flawless from afar, a touch of color on her cheeks. And who could miss the white fur coat? She looked like she just stepped off the pages of a Cosmo magazine.

Suddenly she marched toward me and swept me in her arms. "Melanie!" she cooed. "It's so beautiful to see you, darling."

Darling? I stayed stiff, arms at my side, not knowing how to react. My body was frozen, rejecting a reaction even if I'd wanted to. I was surprised to feel part of me yearn to put my arms around her and hold on for dear life so she didn't disappear again. To pretend like this was real and we were like every other mother and daughter. But the stronger part of me held to reason and finally pulled back so I could look at this stranger whose blood filled my veins. When she released her grasp and took a step back, her fingers curled around my upper arms holding me in place, our faces mere inches apart, I saw she wasn't nearly as beautiful as from afar. Her dyed hair was graying at the roots, her skin caked heavy with makeup, her lips creased and wrinkled around the edges, red lipstick seeping into the creases. And I could smell why. She was definitely a smoker.

I broke free from her clutches and pulled completely out of her reach, grabbed for her suitcase which felt like she had bricks in every pocket, and offered a stiff smile. I knew it must have looked stiff to her as well, because it felt like my face was going to crack.

"Shall we?" I asked, turning to walk before I waited for an answer.

She was kind enough to remain silent until we reached my car. She watched as I struggled to hoist her suitcase into my trunk. "I would appreciate a little help if you are so inclined," I said just loud enough for her to hear.

"There you go," she said lightly as I finished cramming it into my trunk.

I bit my tongue from saying, "And there you go."

Violet talked incessantly about everything and about nothing for the first half hour. I don't think she even noticed that I hadn't said a word. I didn't have the chance even if I'd wanted to.

Finally, she stopped and came up for air. "I can't wait to get to your house and see where you live, darling." Her voice was more raspy than smoky from talking so much.

"My house?" Oh, crap! I hadn't even thought of where she would be staying.

"Yes! I am staying at your house, am I not?"

"I just assumed—well, I just thought you'd be staying at a hotel. You'd be much more comfortable there." I knew I was grasping but it didn't hurt to try.

"Oh, nonsense! Why would I stay at a hotel?"

"Because you can't stay with me." The minute the words were out, it shocked me into silence from saying anything more. Where on earth did that come from? Good thing I was past grounding age.

"And why not?"

I briefly glanced at her from the corner of my eye, but long enough to see her cold, emotionless eyes watching me. Yet, I could tell my refusal to let her have her way stung her. "It just wouldn't work. I have a small place and—well, like I said, you would just be more comfortable at a hotel. It would have all the—the— amenities you're accustomed to."

"I can see this will not be the homecoming I expected from my daughter."

"You don't have a daughter," I answered coolly. "You gave up that privilege a long time ago. In fact," I looked at her and back at the road, "it's been about thirty-six years now." There was a pregnant silence that fell between us. Until I birthed the virtual baby, that is. "And what do you mean by homecoming? How long are you staying?"

"I was planning to stay as long as it takes for us to work things out. To get our mother-daughter bond back."

I blanched. "That long? Because—well, I just don't see that happening at all." I stopped at a stoplight and glanced at her, trying to read her expression. "Besides, we never had that bond you're referring to. You left me, Violet."

"Mother."

"Excuse me?"

"I'm your mother. Please don't call me by my name."

"To me you're Violet. Just Violet. So that's what I will call you." Silence threw its hot, uncomfortable blanket around us again until it was nearly suffocating. We were almost back to town when I realized I had forgotten to call my grandmother. I picked up my phone and dialed her number.

"You shouldn't be talking on the phone while driving, darling," Violet said.

"Don't be getting all parental on me. You're about thirty-six years too late to play mommy. Actually, make that forty."

I finished talking with my grandmother and hung up the phone, laying it on the center console. Violet reached for it. "Don't touch that please," I said, stopping her. "Here we are. This is a nice hotel and you'll be comfortable here."

I pulled up in front of the doors and got out to retrieve her suitcase from the trunk, this time with no expectation that she might help. Wouldn't want her to break a nail. I finally maneuvered the thing out and set it on the ground and looked up to see Violet standing and watching me. Her red lips, no doubt filled with Botox, were now fully pouting.

"You're really going to just leave me here?"

"I really am." My heartbeat quickened with guilt I didn't want to feel. I swallowed hard, hoping it would disappear.

"What if they don't have any rooms available?"

I pointed to the billboard sign by the entrance. "That vacancy sign tells me they do."

Her eyes stayed locked on me, her jaw hanging open, showing a smudge of red on one of her front teeth. Finally, she huffed and turned to walk away, pulling her suitcase behind her. I watched the back of her white fur coat until she was at the revolving door. I studied that coat from the corner of my eye in the car and was relieved it was fake. I have a particular dislike for people who killed animals just to sport the fur, and I really didn't need yet one more reason to dislike her. Yet the irony that the coat was as fake as she was caused a smidgeon of something I couldn't put my finger on. Sadness perhaps.

She stopped and turned around to face me as I stood frozen in place. "How shall I reach you?" she called.

"I'll see you at Nana's house later. She said she's making dinner. One of us will be by to pick you up."

I found the strength to move, got in my car and drove away without waiting a second more. I looked in my rear view mirror as I pulled out of the parking lot and saw Violet in her white ball of fake fur disappear through the hotel lobby doors. I hadn't realized I'd been holding my breath until I could no longer see the hotel behind me. Cold as it was, I opened my window so the fresh spring air could permeate the staleness of what the inside of my car had become. The air felt heavy and stifled, and Violet's perfume, combined with stale cigarette smoke, lingered. I wasn't a perfume person anyway, and the smell of it was just adding insult to injury.

I hadn't realized until I could see the shopping plaza that my car seemed to direct itself toward the salon. Talk about auto pilot. It's probably the exact place I needed to be right now anyway. Being at home alone with my thoughts and emotional chaos wouldn't be good for anyone.

I zipped my little black car into the parking space at the end of the lot and walked across the lot, heels and all, the slippery patches the least of my worries right now.

The cold air felt like a much-needed drink of water after an intense workout. Not that I would know how that felt for a good long while. A good workout, that is. I really needed to get back in shape. But there's always tomorrow. Despite being exactly what I needed, today didn't work for me. I was too busy staying in my little black box of resentment.

I walked into the pungent smell of chemical hair straightener Claire was in the middle of applying on her client, and to Rubie applying permanent wave solution. Connie was doing an up-do, and Gina was applying a set of acrylic nails, adding to the aroma. Most people thought they stank to high heaven. For me, it was like comfort food. It just made me feel like I'd come home.

"Mel!" All but Gina chimed in unison. The old TV show *Cheers* came to mind when Norm would walk into the bar and all would say together, "Norm!" I had always loved that show, and the likeness of a bartender and a hair stylist had always intrigued me. Both were in the same category as a shrink with people telling them their woes and confessing their deepest, darkest secrets. As long as I didn't have to share mine, I was all for hearing others'. I glanced at the plaque that hung on the wall behind the front counter. *If these walls could talk.* Jack brought that with him last year when he overheard one of my clients spill the town's gossip. Yes, indeed, if these walls could talk. These salon walls would have quite the story to tell.

"Where's Violet?" Claire asked as she looked behind me expecting to see her.

"At a hotel."

"Why—"

"She thought she was going to stay with me but I nixed that idea quickly."

"Good for you!" she exclaimed. "She needs to know she can't just waltz in and pretend like nothing happened."

"What did happen?" Rubie asked, turning her client so both were facing me.

Connie and her client watched me expectantly.

"Long story," I murmured. "I'll be in the office."

"I'll be back there in just a sec," Claire said and focused back on her client.

As soon as I got in the office I reached for my phone and called my grandmother to let her know where I'd dropped off Violet.

"Hi, dear," she answered. Her voice sounded off. Just the tiniest bit. But I know my grandmother. Then I found out why she sounded different as I heard Violet's voice in the background asking what time dinner was going to be.

"I'm famished!" I heard her dramatic voice in the background.

My blood froze. "Nana, what is she doing there?"

"She's staying here, dear." Her voice was quiet, no doubt trying to answer my question without Violet's knowledge.

"Why?"

"Because she asked, of course."

"Nana, I dropped her off at a perfectly acceptable hotel. She should have stayed there."

"She said they didn't have any available rooms."

"She is standing right heerre," Violet's previously smoky voice sang in a screech from the background.

"Yes, they did. The vacancy sign was well lit."

"Maybe it was an error. It's nothing to concern yourself with."

Maybe Violet was telling the truth. It was possible, I guess. I let it go. "How long is she here for?"

"I'm not sure."

"Well, I'll take my turn and let her stay with me part of the time. I don't want her to take advantage of you."

"You don't need to protect me, don't cha know."

"And how would you feel if I told you that? Don't cha know."

"I wouldn't like it one bit."

I could hear her smiling right through the phone line. "Is she still in the room?"

"No, dear, I left the room. I couldn't very well have this conversation with you while I was in it."

"K." I knew I was sulking but I didn't like Violet being there. Exactly why, I wasn't sure. Maybe it was motivated by guilt because I wouldn't let her stay with me when that's what she had wanted to do. Or was it because I was harboring resentments toward her as deep as the ocean is wide? Maybe it was a legitimate concern for my grandmother. What I knew was that I didn't trust Violet one bit. She was already weaseling her way in through lying to my grandmother and I wasn't having it.

I stood and picked up my jacket, determination taking root. It was time to find my voice and stand up to this woman.

Chapter 5

"WHY THE LONG FACE?" Claire asked. "I thought you were coming back out there." She jerked her thumb toward the work area. "Where ya going?"

"Violet's staying with my grandmother."

"Is that a bad thing?"

"I don't know yet."

"Because?" She probed.

"I don't know that yet either." I sat back down at the desk, my elbows propped on the desk, my chin resting in my hands.

"Well then here's a suggestion—"

"I can hardly wait to hear it."

"Stop worrying about it until you have a reason to. How does your grandmother feel about it?"

"She told me it's nothing to concern myself with."

"Well, there ya have it." She beamed. "Nothing to worry about."

"Says you."

"And Nana."

"You two are in cahoots," I grumbled. Claire laughed that silvery sound that reminded me of beautiful colored glass bottles tinkling together in a gentle wind.

"Come on, Eeyore, get your happy pants on and let's go mingle with the guests." She took me by the arm and pulled me up from the chair.

"I need to go."

"Where?"

"My grandmother's."

"And do what? Start a fight before the first day is even over?" She put her hands on her hips. "Look, Mel. Go home. Promise me you'll just go home and not do or say anything until you've processed it all."

I sighed. "Fine."

I followed her out to the salon. Gina was in today and in an unusually good mood. She typically didn't talk a whole lot except to the clients she knew well, and her demeanor was always so sober. Not so today. I wanted to ask her why she was so happy but thought better of it. It could be—and likely would be—taken in the totally wrong way. I could already hear her spout, *Are you saying I'm usually grumpy?* I didn't want to ruin this moment. Given all the crazy that was going on in my life right now, I wanted all the happy around me I could get.

"Claire, you and Sydney are still coming to Nana's for dinner, right?"

"Wouldn't miss it," she said, grinning.

"What am I, chopped liver?" Rubie asked from across the room.

I assumed she was joking, but just in case I said, "Rubie we would love to have you come, too. Would you do us the honor of sharing your company?"

"Can't, I'm having dinner with my boyfriend." She looked at me and laughed. "I just wanted the invitation."

She was going to fit in around here just fine.

"What about me?" Connie asked, her voice gravelly from a cold she was finally getting over.

"Consider yourself invited."

"Kidding. I have plans." She laughed.

"Quit feeding off Rubie." My voice reminded me of a five-year-old child's.

"What are you having?" Connie asked. "My mind could be changed."

I looked at the woman in Claire's chair, hair slicked with another application of straightener, then back at Connie. "My grandmother is making her famous meal called, appropriately, Melanie's Birthday Dinner. It's seven-layer lasagna and French bread, complete with cheesecake oozing with cherries." I smiled, closed my eyes and moaned. "Just thinking about it adds about two inches to my waistline and ten pounds on the scale."

"Is she staying with your grandmother?" Rubie asked.

"Who are you all talking about?" Gina asked, reminding me she was there. She may have been in a good mood, but it was so rare I had forgotten already.

"Just someone who's staying with my grandmother."

"And you don't like her?"

"Nope."

"Then take your grandmother out somewhere and leave the woman at the house," Gina said and shrugged.

"If only it were that easy," I said, before quickly changing the subject. "What's your schedule like tomorrow during the day?" I asked Claire. "Oh! By all means, you too, Rubie and Connie. Wouldn't want to leave you guys out," I said with more than a little friendly sarcasm.

"Why thank you," Rubie smiled and curtsied. "Thought you wouldn't ask. I'm wide open for a long lunch. And what's that Claire?" she asked, cupping her ear with one hand and leaning in Claire's direction. "You are too?" she turned back to rinsing the permanent solution from the head she was working on. "Guess that says it then. Long lunch at Grizzley's Tap House."

"Gina? Connie? Would you like to go?" I asked.

Connie politely declined. Gina's answer was short and quick like usual, my request for bonding denied as usual, but hey, at least she smiled this time and said thank you, which was so not as usual. Claire noticed too, because she turned to look at me, eyebrows raised in wonder.

"Gotta go, ladies. I have some processing to do," I said and made a face at Claire. "The sooner I process the sooner I can do something about this situation. Right, Claire?"

I waved and headed out the door before I could hear her answer.

Chapter 6

BY THE TIME I got home I'd decided to go for a walk in the woods by my house. The freshly fallen spring snow was melting furiously in the warmth of the sun, and the air smelled of spring in all its glory.

I slipped out of my heels and into my Sorel boots, pulled a hoodie on over a long-sleeve t-shirt, some light gloves, and headed out the door. The snow crunched beneath my feet leaving the familiar boot tracks in my wake. It was cold enough that I could see my breath and feel my cheeks flush from the cool air, but warm enough that I could feel the promise of summer looming in the foreseeable future.

As I walked I felt renewed energy and enthusiasm for the evening. Despite Violet being there, I was going to make the best of it. After all, Nana, Claire, and Sydney would all be there. How bad could it be?

I walked a little further into the woods and saw squirrels scamper from the giant intruder in their home. It was so clean and white and untouched in the woods. Patches of dark earth peeked through here and there. Everything looked so pristine and so natural. I put my gloved hands in the pocket across the front of my hoodie and looked down to step over a fallen tree, stopping to examine a footprint. Apparently someone else had the idea for a walk in the woods today too. The problem was these secluded woods were private. I've never noticed anyone else out here. Ever. In fact, most of the entire area this side of the lake remained deserted this time of the year. Panic sizzled beneath the surface but fizzled when I remembered my stalker was no longer walking this side of prison bars. And as much as I wanted to feel sorry for the person, I couldn't. Instead, I was glad. It wasn't until iron bars separated us did I feel safe in my home again. And yet, I was still jumpy as could be, thanks to Violet's presence.

I squatted down by the prints, trying to make out the size and shape. Because they were partially melted, it was difficult to determine significant details. I reached in my back pocket for my phone to snap a picture and realized that in my haste to change and get out in the fresh outdoors I had forgotten it on my bed. I stood and traipsed through the brush and snow another ten minutes before making a u-turn and heading back toward home.

Not more than ten steps into my trek back I spotted more footprints, the tread the same pattern as the others I'd seen. These, however, looked more recent and led the same direction as I was going. And since I was going to my house, I saw a potential problem with that. The hair on the back of my neck stood on end. It was as if the person who made these steps was one step ahead of me on the way out and then again on the way back to my house.

I scanned the entire area as far as I could see in all directions. Nothing. Not a soul in sight or any sign there was anyone else in the vicinity save for the mysterious fresh footprints. "Good thing you don't believe in ghosts," I muttered. But what other explanation could there be? One more scan of the area and I shrugged, moving along.

The sound of a twig snapping somewhere in the distance stopped me in my tracks. I inhaled sharply. I took a moment to take a deep breath and rationalize the likelihood that it was probably just a squirrel or even a clump of snow falling off of a branch to its demise below, soon to melt into the earth. Silently I scolded myself for being so jumpy. I used to walk these woods all the time and found such peace and solitude. At the very least I could take comfort that unless my stalker broke out of prison, I had nothing to fear. And yet I felt an uncomfortable prickle of fear. I chalked it up to lingering feelings of vulnerability and hurried my pace toward home.

I'd no sooner gotten into the house and locked the door behind me when my phone began its ring tone, "The Wind Beneath My Wings." I didn't even get a hello in before her voice came across singing Happy Birthday. I grinned like a little girl until the very last word.

"I don't know what I would ever do if you forgot to do that," I smiled, warmth and love saturating my heart. Until I heard Violet's voice in the background.

"Let me say happy birthday to my daughter."

"Tell her I'm not her daughter," I grumbled.

Violet's voice was on the other end before I knew what happened. She began saying something but I quickly cut her off.

"Violet, I was talking with Nana."

"Darling, don't you think you're a little old to be calling her that? Besides, you're my daughter, and I have a right to wish you a happy birthday."

"I saw you earlier, you could have said it then. But whatever, you said it now. Now can I talk to Nana again, please?" Who was this woman to waltz in here like she never left and criticize what I call the woman who raised me as her own.

"How long are you going to make me stand in the corner, Melanie?" she asked, her voice cool.

"I'm not making you do anything," I said, competing nicely with the chill in her tone. "I simply asked you to give the phone back to Nana."

"Very well. I'll see you this evening for dinner. What time will you be here?"

"We'll be there about five-thirty."

"We?" She asked with sudden interest. She sounded like a bird chirping the way the last part of the one-syllable word went up an octave.

Careful Violet. Curiosity killed the cat. "Yes, we. Claire, Sydney and me."

"Who're Claire and Sydney?"

"My friend and her daughter."

"Oh." I could almost hear the wheels creaking and churning in her head as she remained silent for a moment. "Are you—are—"

"No, I'm not gay," I said, disgusted that she even went there, but more so that she had that disapproving tone. "But one of my very dearest friends in the world is, so don't even think about going there with me on that one."

"I was simply wondering—"

"Let me talk to Nana, please," I said, a knot in the pit of my stomach. I had all I could do to hold it together. I was going to have to do some serious work with myself on getting my emotions under control before this evening. I wondered if a convent could give me a crash course in finding peace and self-control.

"I think we should just stick with family for dinner. Don't you think that—"

"If that were the case you wouldn't be there either. This is the last time I'm going to ask you, Violet, put Nana on the phone. Now." My mood had made a serious nosedive.

When I got to my grandmother's house at 5:30 sharp, her garage door was open and her car was gone. I let myself into the house, concerned to find the door unlocked. I'd asked her time and time again not to leave her door unlocked whether or not she was home, which now brought fresh concern. She might feel safe in her neighborhood but these days one just never knew. Of course, I didn't listen to her about safety measures until recently, so I hardly had room to talk about her not listening. I sighed and closed the door behind me, the aroma of garlic, hot bread, and lasagna making me forget everything except the fact that I should have brought a bib. I was practically drooling.

"Nana?" I hollered. She nearly scared me half to death when I turned the corner to the kitchen and almost knocked her over. "Oh, my heck!" My hand flew to my chest. "Nana you scared me half to death! I thought you were gone."

"Guess you found out I'm not." She smiled and folded me in a hug. "If you thought I was gone why did you call my name?"

"Your door was unlocked. Where's your car?"

"Your mother's using it. Said she had to run some errands."

"I wish you wouldn't call her that."

"Call her what?" Her eyebrows rose.

"My mother. She's not my mother. She relinquished that title when she abandoned me. What she didn't count on," I added, "was that leaving me with you and granddad was the best thing she ever did."

"It was good for grandpa and me, too."

"But not easy. And don't even try telling me it was. I know I wasn't an amiable child."

Nana chuckled. "You were absolutely perfect."

"Liar." I nudged her with my shoulder. "So what errands did Violet have to run?"

I watched her butter the French bread and sprinkle plenty of garlic on it, exactly how I liked it. I inhaled deeply, finding comfort in the smells that surrounded me.

"She didn't say what exactly. Just that she had some errands to run."

"She just got here. What in the world kind of errands would she have to run?"

"I didn't think it wise to press."

"She's driving your car. You're darn right it would have been wise to press."

"Put your sass to work and finish these cherries for the cheesecake."

"I'm not supposed to work on my birthday. That was always the house rule."

"Melanie Hogan…"

I laughed and gave her a squeeze as I went past her to where the cherries lay on the island, a pile of beautiful, bright red circles that made my mouth water.

"Talked to Jack today."

"Well isn't that nice. He's such a nice young man. That would be nice for you to find a nice man like that."

"I think Bryce would have something to say about that." I continued pitting cherries. "Did I tell you Violet asked if I was gay?"

Nana stopped what she was doing and looked at me, her eyes wide as saucers. "She did not!"

"Yes sir, she did. I don't think she'll be heading in that direction with me again, though. I think I scared her."

She chuckled knowingly and went back to her task at hand. "I'm sure you did."

We made small talk for the next fifteen minutes, until Violet slamming the door behind her interrupted us. Her footsteps were heavy as she went to her room and came back out a few moments later.

"Where'd you have to go?" I asked bluntly.

"I had some errands to run."

"So I heard. What errands would you have to run when you just got into town today?"

"What? Am I under house arrest here?"

"Nope. Just curious." I popped a cherry in my mouth savoring the sweet yet tart taste on my tongue. I stared at her waiting for her answer.

"It's my daughter's birthday. I can't tell you where I was. You'll find out soon enough."

"Oh." If there were a rock in the kitchen I would have crawled under it. Okay, so maybe I was being a little harsh with her. I'd try to ease up a little. Try to. Nana didn't say a word, but let our interaction play out on its own. She was a brilliant lady.

Finally, she spoke. "Did you change clothes, Violet? I thought you had on a black one-piece jumpsuit earlier."

"Yes, I thought I would clean up a little for the birthday dinner," she purred. She looked at me, down at my jeans, and said, "I hope I'm not overdressed."

"Nope." I smiled coolly. "You look just so—well, so you."

"Thank you, darling." She winked at me and reached for a martini glass.

She obviously didn't know how to read sarcasm. But Nana could. She sent me a look that could send me shaking in my boots if I still had them on. Instead, they sat on the rug near the door.

The doorbell rang and I jumped off the stool I had just sat down on. "I'll get it!" I said, eager to get out of the room to cool off. And thrilled Claire and Sydney were there to ease the constantly building tension before it snapped in two. It felt like the musical score to a horror film where the music got louder and louder and you just knew something bad was going to happen.

I swung the door open and enthusiastically ushered them in. Claire and Sydney to the rescue! Or at least Claire. Sydney was off to scout the house for Callie the cat.

"What'd you do today after you left the salon, Mel?" Claire asked as she took off her jacket and laid it over the back of a chair.

"Drank myself into oblivion."

"No, you did not."

"No, I did not," I admitted, finding immense satisfaction in Violet's reaction she tried to hide. She really wasn't too talented an actress. "I watched a movie and—"

"Which one?" Claire asked.

"Under the Tuscan Sun. My yearning to go to Italy has returned. But if you and lover boy keep it up, I'm gonna end up going alone."

"Melanie!" Claire said, shushing me, frantically looking around for Sydney.

I looked at her in disbelief. "You can't honestly believe she doesn't know something."

"She knows I have a male friend, but that's it."

"A male friend?" My eyebrows raised, my lips curling with amusement. "Claire, she may be young, but she's not stupid. The way you two look at each other, anyone within a ten-mile radius would know you're not just friends." Claire stared at me, speechless. "Trust me, honey, if she's been in the same room with the two of you, the cat's out of the bag."

Claire looked like she was going to be sick. "I can't see him anymore," she whispered.

I glanced at Violet who'd gone into the kitchen to help herself to another martini. Great, she's going to be sloshed before we even sit down at the table. I focused back on Claire. "What are you so afraid of?"

"I don't want her to think I'm betraying her father."

"Honey," I said as gently as I could and reached over to take her long slender brown fingers in my much smaller white hand, "her father has been dead for four years. He died a hero fighting for our country. Don't you think she has a right to honor that fact and be able to move on? If she doesn't see her mother is moving on, she's going to think she can't either."

"I don't want her to forget him. Hell, I don't want to forget him. And I'm afraid of that."

Claire quickly wiped a stray tear from her cheek with the palm of her hand when she saw Syd scamper through the room chasing Callie the cat.

"Come on," I said, walking into the kitchen, "this is a party, not a funeral."

Nana stood stirring something on the stove and Violet was finishing making her drink.

"So what else did you do today?" Claire asked.

"Got me some Vitamin D. I went for a walk in the woods by my house but didn't stay out long. Saw some tracks out there and got a little creeped out so I turned and went home."

A loud crash, followed by shattering glass elicited a small scream from Claire and a sharp intake of breath from me. Sydney came running into the room, her eyes wide. I looked at the shards of glass scattered on the floor, glass that had just a moment ago been fully intact in Violet's hand.

"Well, looks like someone's had a little too much to drink." I looked at Violet. "I assume you're familiar with a broom?"

Chapter 7

THE MORNING AFTER MY birthday dinner, I lay stretched out in bed, arms behind my head, looking at the sun lightening the morning sky through my skylight. I replayed the evening in my mind. Somehow, Violet had gotten me to agree to let her stay with me for a few days. Part of me hoped that if I agreed to let her stay, she would get what she wanted and decide to leave. And then life could get back to usual.

I got up and showered, dressed, had my usual toast and coffee, trying to be as quiet as possible so I didn't wake Sleeping Beauty. Last evening turned out better than I had anticipated, especially given the rocky start, but there was no flying utensils or bloodshed. That's something to be proud of, I guess. But that didn't mean I wanted any interaction with her this morning. Morning was my quiet time. My meditation and coffee-drinking tranquil time. Tranquil and Violet didn't belong in the same universe, much less in the same room. The morning progressed according to plan, so I was in good spirits when I left for work.

Not quite five miles from home, I remembered I'd forgotten my shears on my dresser. I had taken them home to give Nana a trim after dinner, which we never got around to. I pulled up in front of the house and opened the door as quietly as I could and tiptoed up to my room.

"Violet!" I said, my voice scaring me. My face burned. "What are you doing in my room?" I hadn't even been gone ten minutes. She had to have been awake and waiting for me to leave. She stood frozen in front of my dresser, hand on my hairbrush. Her other hand flew to her chest, but her face remained frozen in a look of horror.

"I—I—I was—"

"Never come in my room again. Do you understand? My room is off limits."

"I was just trying to get to know my daughter a little bit." Her full lips protruded into a pout, but I didn't buy it. "I wanted to see what kinds of things you surround yourself with. And I wanted to borrow your brush."

"You need to leave. Now!" I leveled my eyes on her.

"Melanie I'm sorry. It won't happen again. Please let me stay."

"I meant you need to leave my room. Now. You can take the brush. I've got plenty at work." She nodded and started toward the stairs. "And Violet?" She stopped and turned toward me. "If I ever see you've been in my room again you will no longer be welcome here. Am I clear?" I felt more like the parent than the child here.

"Yes," she uttered.

The feeling of my privacy being violated and my personal space invaded permeated the rest of my day.

"Melanie," Claire responded when I told her what happened, "maybe she's genuinely trying to make things right. Have you thought of that? Maybe you should give her the benefit of the doubt. Then if she blows it, you'll feel justified in your behavior. But don't you want to at least try?"

"I agree with Claire," Rubie piped up. We'd added her to the short list of people who knew my mother wasn't dead, but that she just abandoned her child. She was quickly becoming one of our circle, as high school as that sounded. "You don't want to be the reason you may never have a relationship with your mother, do you? Be the bigger person."

"You two are of no help whatsoever," I muttered. "You make good points, but you're no help." I wallowed in self-pity for a few minutes. "Fine. I'll try. As much as I can anyway. And the two of you can help me out."

"How?" they asked in unison.

"Tell us what you need from us," Claire added.

"Come over for hot chocolate tonight. Violet is there and we can have a girls night. No boys," I smiled at Claire. "Just for an hour or so."

"Deal!" Rubie answered for both of them.

"Syd too."

"She's staying with my folks this week. Spring break."

"Seven o'clock?" I asked.

"It's a plan."

When I got home Violet was watching some reality show on TV. Real Housewives of some county or state. I wouldn't know which since I can't stand any of those shows. As far as I was concerned they were akin to professional wrestling – nothing but drama and theatrics. I didn't like either of those things.

I was hoping dinner was ready, or even started would have been good, but no. Instead, she sat with a half empty martini at her side.

"Where'd you get the makings for the martini?"

"Hello to you, too, darling." She cast me a casual look over her shoulder. "I went through your cupboards and found some things to put one together. I hope it was okay to go through your cupboards? I had to eat, you know." I didn't miss the subtle sarcasm.

"One? How many have you had? And don't tell me just one." I couldn't recall having any gin in the house and certainly not dry vermouth. Olives maybe.

"One. Maybe two." She waved her hand through the air as if tossing aside an impending objection. "Don't worry so much, darling. I need to teach you how to lighten up a little. To live."

"Swell."

"What was that? I can't understand when you mumble."

"Nothing important." At least, it wasn't a lie.

"What's for dinner?"

"I don't know yet. I have a couple of friends coming over for hot cocoa tonight, so maybe you shouldn't have any more of those." I pointed to her glass. The last thing I wanted was for her to be drunk and make a fool of herself. And me. It was going to be interesting the way it was. And if I wasn't mistaken, her speech was slurred ever so slightly already. I haven't had enough conversation with her yet to know for sure.

"Hot cocoa?" she asked clearly amused. Don't you think you're a little old to be inviting people over for hot cocoa? Children have hot cocoa. Adults have adult beverages."

"Don't you think you're a little too old to be sitting around watching trashy TV and over indulging on your adult beverages?" I wanted to kick myself after the words were out. So much for keeping the promise to my grandmother that I would do my best to not instigate an argument and be the bigger person. Disappointment loomed at my lack of willpower, which seemed to flail at best. I flipped on the light switch to find a burned-out bulb.

"Oh, I forgot to tell you. The light bulb is out," she said with a quick glance over her shoulder.

"Obviously." Irritation rippled through me. I went to the linen closet where I kept the light bulbs and came back to climb up on a chair to replace the burned out one. "There are lamps in the room you know. Unless you like it in the dark."

"Dark doesn't bother me. It sets the mood."

"And what mood is that?"

"Nothing." She got up and began making another martini.

"Don't you think you've had enough?"

"For goodness sakes, darling," she drawled. "Don't be an old fuddy-duddy. I'm the mother, not you, remember?"

"Actually, there's not a single mother in the room." I crossed the living room and began closing the curtains and blinds. "You shouldn't have the curtains open when it's dark outside. It's too easy for people to see in."

"Who on earth is going to see in from way out here?" She stood at the counter and looked at me like I was crazy. "You live in the middle of nowheresville for Pete's sake."

"You're the one who asked to stay with—"

Suddenly a loud crack thundered through the air, glass shattered beside me, and I heard a whistling noise speed past me. I yelped and hit the floor in one swift move.

Chapter 8

"WHAT WAS THAT?" I asked, my voice barely a whisper, my breath heavy, and yet I was afraid to breathe. I looked over at Violet whose eyes and mouth formed giant circles as she stood frozen in place. "Get down!" I hissed. She crouched down, martini glass in hand. God forbid she should part with that. We kept our eyes focused on each other until a few moments had passed. Hearing nothing more, I crawled over to the end table and reached my arm up to grab my phone. "Violet, did you see anything out of the ordinary today?"

"I don't know what's ordinary around here, so how would I know if it's out of the ordinary?" Even her whisper sounded smoky and sultry.

I rolled my eyes and sighed. "Good point. Let me rephrase that. Did you see anyone outside on the grounds today? Or did any cars pull in the drive?"

"Just you and yours."

"Violet! Sometimes talking to you is like talking with a child!"

"Well?" she whined. "You asked if I saw anyone here or if any cars pulled in the drive."

"Yes, I did." I shook my head slowly feeling a pang of pity for this woman who decided she wanted to be a mother when she was struggling with being a human being. I bear-crawled across the floor. I needed to see what hit that window before I called 9-1-1. I didn't need them coming out here to find out it was a giant bird. I remembered hearing about an eagle that had latched onto a snowmobile helmet as the man was driving his snowmobile. And while I hoped it wasn't an animal that hit my window, as that would break my heart, I think at this point I'd take my heart being broken rather than nearly stopped from beating. Permanently. And what was that whistle? That was in the house, so unless an animal came through that window, I was looking at something much more frightening. I knew it wasn't an animal, but I held onto hope anyway. No such luck.

Claire, Cole, and Rubie nearly beat the police out to my house, and the police came with screaming lights and sirens. I called Claire *after* 9-1-1 and they turned into the driveway right after I let the officers into my house. Poor response time by the emergency personnel or exceptional time for Claire and gang. Good thing Cole was a police officer and he's the one who drove, otherwise they surely would have gotten a speeding ticket.

"Ma'am, can you tell me what happened?"

"I was closing the curtains and the bullet blazed right by me."

"I need you to start at the beginning."

"That is the beginning." By this time Claire and Rubie were standing one on each side of me, Claire had a protective arm around me. Cole was by the shattered window talking to one of the other officers.

"Were you here alone?"

"No, my mother is here." The words surprised me as soon as they were out. But even then, if I had said Violet he would have asked who Violet is and I would have had a whole lot more explaining to do, as I assumed they were going to look into every possibility. Saying she was my mother just seemed easier all the way around.

"Was she hit? Where is she?"

I looked around but couldn't see her.

"I'll go find her," Rubie offered.

"It's not a big house so it shouldn't be too hard," I said.

Claire wouldn't leave my side. I suspected not so much because she thought I needed protection but because she wanted to know the details and wanted answers.

"Take me back a couple of hours. What was the sequence of events?"

"A couple of hours ago I was at work. I got home about 6:00. My mother was watching television, I flipped on the light switch, discovered the bulb was burned out, I replaced the bulb, turned on the light and began closing curtains." I saw him looking at the martini makings on the counter. *Don't judge me, buddy.* "My mother was making herself a martini." It irritated me I felt the need to explain.

Rubie bounced into the room without Violet and shrugged her shoulders. "Says she's too shaken up to come down."

"Come down?" I asked.

"She's in your room."

Snooping, no doubt. I chastised myself for being so cruel. She probably was shaken up. This was pretty scary stuff for a prima donna. All sarcasm aside.

55

"We'll need to talk with her," the officer said. "Would you mind if one of the guys goes up there?"

"Yes, actually I do." I saw him look at me. "Look, I'm not hiding anything and I'm not trying to be difficult, but my bedroom is my private space. I'd like to keep it that way. I will go get her and bring her down." I left Claire standing there with him and went up to my loft where my bedroom was. Violet was standing at the window staring off into the darkness, arms wrapped around her waist. "Are you okay?"

"That's a strange thing to ask at a time like this. Of course, I'm not okay. I nearly got killed."

"Dramatic much? You were in the kitchen making your drink. I was the one standing at the window when the shot came through. I'm thinking I was probably more in the line of danger than you were."

"If I would have been closing those curtains like you told me I should have done, I would have been killed." She narrowed her eyes as she looked at me. "Was that your intention?"

I rolled my eyes and rubbed my temples, feeling one of my migraines coming on. "An officer needs to talk to you."

"Can't it wait? I'm really not in any shape to talk to him right now."

"No, Violet, it can't wait. I hate to break this to you, but this wasn't about you. Not everything in the world is about you. Come downstairs now."

"What if it *was* meant for me?"

Concern wormed its way under my skin. My eyes narrowed as I turned to face her. "Is there something you're not telling me? Because now would be the time to speak up."

"Of course not," she snapped. Gone was the frightened kitten and in its place rose a dragon. The transformation just about gave me whiplash.

"Then come on." I was ready to descend the stairs and turned to be sure she was following. She remained at the window almost trance-like. "Now." I stood and watched until she turned away from the window and began walking toward me, albeit slowly, and I was sure she was coming downstairs.

When we got back to the living room I saw Claire standing by Cole, his hand holding hers, as they listened to what the officer was saying. Her frown let me know it was something I probably wouldn't want to hear. Which only made me want to hear it all the more. I left Violet with the officer who said he wanted to talk to her and went to get in on the conversation by the window.

"Somebody want to fill me in?"

"Ma'am—"

"For the record," Cole interrupted, "I wouldn't call her ma'am. She doesn't like it so much."

"True story," I agreed. When Cole was the one to investigate the sinister events at the salon last summer he insisted on calling me ma'am motivated by nothing other than being a southern gentleman. After correcting him for the umpteenth time, he finally came to terms with the fact that southern charm had its time and place. "Now what were you going to tell me? And call me Melanie."

"Melanie," he said, "the guys are out canvassing your yard and can't find a single trace of someone being out there."

"But obviously, there was." I stared at him, but he remained silent, simply looking at me like he was wondering if he should continue. "So what are you thinking?"

"This doesn't appear to be an amateur."

"You mean it was a professional hit?"

"Well—yes, and no."

"If it was a professional hit, the guy was a bad shot. I was standing in a lit room when it was dark outside, in full view in front of a window. Easy target."

"That's the part that they're working through."

"Someone hired the wrong professional then I guess. Sure hope they didn't pay a lot for this one."

The officer looked at me strangely, apparently unaware of my cynical tendencies. For now. He nodded, excused himself and went over by his team. And here I thought black humor was a cop's forte. This one must have missed that part of his training.

Cole went outside to help the police and to see what he could find out. Claire and Rubie stayed by my side. My phone rang and when I turned to pick it up I saw the officer that was talking with Violet was now on his radio and she was nowhere to be seen. I decided to just let her hide out in my room for a while. Right now wasn't the time to be territorial. Besides, dealing with her drama right now wasn't an appealing thought. By the time I answered my phone I was too late, and it rolled into voicemail.

Claire, Rubie, and I went and sat on the couch, and again, one stayed on each side of me. You'd think they thought I was fragile or something. Except Claire knew better. And Rubie would if she stuck around long enough.

"Claire, I was thinking—"

"I was too. Thinking that this has got to stop. Someone's messin' with my friend and I don't like it."

"Seriously. Listen. What if this is somehow tied to William?" William was someone I dated briefly. *Very* briefly. If one could even call it dating. He was proof that my taste in men stank to high heaven and I should probably stay single forever.

"That's impossible." She looked at me, her brows furrowed, and an unusual frown.

"You know that for sure?"

"Yes, I do. We both do."

"What if there's someone else on his payroll?"

"He and his partner in crime are incapable of doing anything on the same side of the bars as we are. Remember?"

"How do we know they don't have someone doing their dirty work for them on the outside?"

"We don't. Not for sure anyway. But what would be his reason?"

"I don't know. Revenge?" I sighed. "Finding some way to finish what he wasn't able to? Maybe I'm just grasping."

"I agree. You're grasping. You have to admit that would be quite a stretch."

"What if—" I let my sentence fall into silence.

"What if what?" Rubie asked getting in on the conversation.

"Just what if there was a third person—or fourth or fifth, for that matter—involved that we don't know about? Maybe he was lying low, letting enough time pass by until he thought I would forget and let my guard down."

"I guess it's possible." We fell into thoughtful silence.

Cole came in and stood by Claire's side. I had to admit they made the most striking couple and made a grim situation a little brighter. She with her skin the color of milk chocolate, her wild hair contained by brightly colored hair scarves, that endearing gap between her front teeth and the softest brown eyes I'd ever seen; and he with his tall, lean yet muscular build, his arms looking like they would split the arm seams of his t-shirt, his short flat-top haircut, and a smile with teeth so dazzling white they were almost blinding. I watched and half listened as Claire replayed my thoughts to him.

"Mel, we looked down every avenue, and talked to them both before their...demise, and we never got even a hint that there was anyone else involved," he said. "We could check again, I suppose."

"Well, someone obviously doesn't like me too much. And it would almost be easier to grasp if it's not yet another psycho."

I was going to get to the bottom of this once and for all. Claire was right. This had to stop.

Chapter 9

VIOLET AND I STAYED at my grandmother's that night since we obviously couldn't stay in my house with the window shot out. Not to mention there was a team of officers there most of the night processing the scene, so I knew whoever it was wouldn't return with everyone there.

I got up early and left for work, all too happy to be at the salon, away from Violet, and in my element where I felt the most secure and at home other than at my house, prior to this little incident, and at Nana's, without the Violet piece of it intruding into the beautiful ordinariness. Right now the salon was my only slice of normal I had. And it felt glorious.

Space and a quiet place to process and work things through were exactly what I needed before the girls came in. I sat in the office sketching out a diagram of where I was exactly in the house, where Violet was, and where the bullet came through. I reversed my thoughts back to the time it all went down trying to remember every detail no matter how minor it may appear to be. Something was not adding up. But what was it? My elbow on the desk, chin resting in my hand, I tapped the eraser of the pencil on the desk with my other hand, the repetitive sound and movement helping me process as I studied the diagram. What was I missing?

Before I knew it, the bell on the front door jingled, signaling one of the three had arrived. I soon heard which one it was. I knew it wasn't Gina because we never gave her a key.

"Melanie?" Claire called before her long longs carried her across the salon and around the corner to the office. "Mornin', gorgeous."

"Careful. I don't want Cole to get jealous of me. He wears a gun." I realized the grim humor as soon as the words left my mouth. I grimaced and Claire smiled.

"Yeah, that was a little off-color after last night. How's Violet? Did she recover okay by the time you got to your grandmother's?"

"She'll be fine. I think she was just a little shaken up. Okay, a lot shaken up," I said. "What'd Cole say, anything?"

"Active investigation. He can't talk about it."

"Not even to you?"

"Not even to me," she reiterated. "That's not a bad thing, though, because I can't promise I wouldn't tell you."

"But it's not even his case. He's city police and this is the county. Or 'nowheresville' as Violet called it."

"But he's assisting since he was involved in the attacks last summer."

"I have a right to know."

"And they'll tell you what they think you need to know, Mel. You need to trust them."

"I don't trust anybody right now."

"I'm crushed," she teased lightly.

I was looking at her but thinking about something entirely different. "I'm missing something, Claire. For the life of me, I can't think of what it is."

"Maybe you're looking too hard. It's when you're not thinking about it that it will come to you."

I stared at her, yet not seeing her at all. Finally, I pulled my attention back to her. "Yeah, you might have a point."

"Are you going to stay at your grandmother's again tonight?"

"I don't know," I sighed and put my head down on the desk, face on my clasped hands. "I don't want to put her in danger if someone is out to get me. Or even Violet for that matter."

"Oh, someone is out to get you. I think we've determined that much. Why is another matter altogether."

"Hello?" Rubie called in her chipper voice.

"And let the party begin," I said standing up. Claire smiled, we high-fived across the desk and went out to greet the busy day.

Claire came over to my grandmother's for dinner that evening at Nana's insistence. Rubie had plans with her boyfriend so she couldn't make it. And secretly, I was glad. I just want it to be Claire tonight. Cole was busy helping the detective with my case, filling him in on what he knew from last summer and going through the evidence from last night's shooting.

I had changed into my typical gray sweat pants and sweatshirt, helping my grandmother with dinner while Violet sat on her lazy behind in the living room watching another episode of Real Housewives. Again, I didn't know from which state or county. I didn't care. Nana and

I made small talk mostly, stopping when Violet came in the kitchen to mix a drink.

"I'm sure there's something you could do to help with dinner if you really wanted to," I offered, not sure if I wanted her to or not. I preferred having time alone with my grandmother.

"Thank you darling, but I just had my nails done today."

"Looks like you broke one already," I said, pointing to her pointer finger, the only short nail in the handful of bright red polish.

"Oh no!" she wailed. I stared at her in wonder. Did this woman have a legitimate concern that wasn't about her? If so, I've yet to see it.

I contained my amusement as best I could. "It's not the end of the world. Just go get it fixed tomorrow."

"I most certainly cannot wait until tomorrow. Mother, can I please borrow your car again?"

"Now?" Nana asked, eyebrows raised in surprise. "But we'll be eating soon."

"It shouldn't take too long. Thank you."

I looked at Nana, expecting her to say something. When I saw she wasn't speaking up, I did. "I didn't hear her tell you it was okay to take her car."

"Darling, really," she said clearly exasperated and rolled her eyes. "Then I will take yours."

"Uh...no, you won't."

"Well, then, just carry on with what you're doing and don't worry about me." She blew me a kiss, grabbed the car keys off the key hook near the door and was gone.

"You know you don't have to let her walk all over you like that, right?"

"I choose my battles. This wasn't one worth fighting. Besides," she grinned and winked at me, "it's much more peaceful here with just you and me."

That was my Nana. "Are you okay, Nana? I mean, other than the obvious."

"Why do you ask?"

"You're out of sorts. Is it because of Violet?"

She looked me square in the eye. "No, dear, it's not Violet this time."

I felt my chest tighten. "What is it then? Are you feeling okay?"

"Melanie Hogan, someone tried to shoot you last night. How do you think I feel? And has it even occurred to you that you could have been killed?"

I felt unusual tears hot behind my eyelids. I blinked to clear them away. "Yes, as a matter of fact it has," I whispered. "But you know how I am, Nana." I looked at her, the concern in her eyes dulling the usual sparkle. "I don't want to focus on what almost happened. I need to figure out how to make sure it doesn't happen again."

"This was very serious."

I put my hands on her arms and looked into her eyes. "I know it was, Nana. I'll be careful. I promise. I just don't want it to be a shadow over my head here. This is my place to feel safe. Here, with you."

She patted my hand and gave me a hug. "Well, then, let's be sure you stay safe so we can have many more times together here, huh?"

The doorbell rang. I wiped my hands on the towel that lay beside my cutting board, crossed over to the door, swung it open wide. "So much for peaceful," I called over my shoulder to my grandmother. "Claire's here." I grinned and enveloped my dear friend in a tight hug. "You know I'm kidding."

"Yes, I do. You're just a laugh a minute." She hugged me back and walked past me to the kitchen to give Nana a hug. She peeked in the living room. "Where's Violet?"

"She broke a nail and you'd think she got hit by a car, for crying out loud. She just had to get it fixed, dahling," I drawled.

Claire laughed. "Hey! You do a fine impersonation of her."

"Girls, be nice," Nana said, her grin peeking through in direct conflict with her tone.

"She started it," Claire said.

"Wow! You're quick to throw me under the bus, Claire. I thought you had my back."

"Not at the expense of getting Nana mad at me."

She looked so darn cute with her hair wild and willy-nilly without a scarf to tame the craziness. And, she, too, had on sweats which was an extremely rare occasion for her. "I see you dressed up. Was that just for me? I feel honored."

"Of course." She made a face at me. "I hit the gym right after work and showered there before I came over here.

"Well, it's a good thing you showered. Come on," I threw the kitchen towel at her, "you can help cut these—these—whatever these things are."

"They're called parsnips." Claire nudged me aside and took over. "Even I know what they are."

"You would. Aren't they a root? Nana, why are we eating roots?"

"Because they're good for you."

By the time we finished getting dinner ready, Violet's headlights turned into the driveway, illuminating the darkened dining room. She came in slightly out of breath.

I looked at her nails. "I thought you went to get your nail fixed."

"They were closing and couldn't get me in. That's very poor business. They should stand behind their work," she complained.

"It's not their fault you broke a nail at closing time."

"Whatever." She sounded more like Sydney than a grown woman.

"Where'd you get them done at? Remind me not to go there." I reached up into the cabinet and took down four water glasses.

"Maybe you could fix it for me."

"Nope. Not tonight."

"And why not?"

"You can come into the salon tomorrow and I'll fix it for you then. I won't even charge you. Gina the nail tech could fix it, but you'd have to pay her."

I looked over to where she had been just a moment ago to find she had left the room. "Guess that won't be happening," I muttered.

We had just finished up dinner, Violet conveniently retreating from the kitchen table. In fact, from the entire kitchen area to go Lord only knows where, while the rest of us cleared the table and cleaned up. I, for one, wasn't a bit surprised. I was surprised, however, that it didn't bother me this time.

The cleanup done, we were just sitting down at the table to play a game of Texas Dice when Claire's cell phone rang.

"Lover boy?" I teased. "Doesn't he know girl's night boundaries?"

Claire wasn't on the phone for more than a few seconds before her face contorted in a look of horror, her usual milk chocolate complexion looking pasty. She took the phone in the other room, and I had to hold myself back from following her to listen in on the conversation. After what seemed like hours, she came back to the kitchen and sat down, looking directly at me, her big brown eyes pools of mystery.

"What is it?" I asked, afraid to hear the answer.

"Someone heard a gunshot out by your house. Strange thing is the call came from a house across the lake earlier today. Cole said they found a body about half hour ago. Melanie," she paused and put her hand on my arm, "it was in the woods right by your house."

Chapter 10

ROSE WATCHED THROUGH THE window as Melanie and Claire left in Melanie's car to meet the police and Cole at her house. Violet came into the room.

"What's all the ruckus about, mother? And where is my daughter?"

"There's been a terrible thing happened out by her house. Violet, I don't think the two of you should stay out there for a while."

"What do you mean? What happened?" Violet leaned against the counter and studied her broken nail.

"There was a shooting."

Violet's hand flew to her mouth, her eyes wide open. "Is Melanie okay?"

"Of course, she is. She was here."

Violet exhaled loudly. "Well, that's a relief. But what's the problem then?"

"Violet, a person was shot. Killed," Rose explained as if Violet wasn't grasping the reality of it all.

"I heard you. But do you or Melanie know who this— this—dead person is?"

"Melanie and Claire went over there now."

"Speaking of which, how well does Melanie know this Claire girl anyway? Can she trust her?"

"She's the closest thing to a sister she's ever had." Rose smiled. "Those girls are joined at the hip."

"They're not girls. They're women." Violet paused for a moment. "Melanie's not going to forgive me, is she?"

"For goodness sakes, Violet," Rose exclaimed. "Give her some time. You've only been back for a few days."

"Well, if you ask me, she's not even meeting me half way here. She's an iceberg that hasn't even begun to thaw."

"Nor should you expect her to." Rose's voice changed from patient to one of warning not to criticize the girl she'd raised and come to love as her own. "You are the parent—"

"She's made it perfectly clear I'm not her mother, and she will not let me be her mother, either."

"Yet. Give her some time. You can't expect damage done over decades to be undone over a couple of days."

"Whose side are you on?"

"The side of reason and logic. And if push comes to shove, Melanie's."

"You are my mother. You're supposed to be there for me."

"And you're Melanie's mother. You were supposed to be there for her."

"Ouch," Violet muttered under her breath. "I see where I stand. Melanie doesn't even want me here. Don't you get it? She'd like nothing more than if I just disappeared."

Rose sighed, weary with Violet's continued selfishness. She'd hoped she would have eventually outgrown it, but it didn't look like that had happened, or even would happen. Anytime soon, anyway. "Be patient, Violet. Give it some time."

"Actually..." her voice trailed off and she looked away from Rose, her behavior telling Rose a whole lot that wasn't said.

"No." Rose shook her head slowly, then more adamantly. "No, no you are not." Her eyes were wide with concern, and she felt an invisible protective shield going around, Melanie.

"Not what?" Violet asked all too innocently, holding up her hand and studying the back of it.

"Leaving."

"Mother, I have a job, you know. I can't just up and leave it for no good reason."

"So just like that, you have to go back to work? Things aren't working out the way you wanted them to, when you wanted them to, so you hit the road again?"

"It's not like that and you know it."

"No, I don't know it. You've gotten very good at leaving, Violet. And what do you have to show for it?"

"I have a successful career, and—"

"And what? What exactly do you have?" Rose interrupted. "And how successful is this career? Whenever you've bothered to check in with us you talk about some big movie you're trying out for. Some of them you've claimed to have landed the leading role. But do you know what's strange? I've never seen a single one of them come out in theaters."

"When's the last time you were even at a movie in a theater, mother? Probably never."

"Violet, you have had a wandering, restless spirit for as far back as I can remember. And that was fine when it was only you that you had to worry about. But when you have family—well, when you have a family, it requires sacrifice."

"What would you know about sacrifice?" Violet raised her voice. "When were you and daddy ever there for me?"

Rose felt heaviness in her chest. "I'm sorry you feel that way, honey."

"Don't 'honey' me. Besides, that's exactly how I feel. Why do you think I left?"

Sadness engulfed Rose and she turned toward the kitchen sink. "When were you thinking of leaving?"

"In the morning."

Rose felt like a sword pierced her heart. "When are you going to tell Melanie?"

"Tonight if she gets home before I go to bed."

"And if she doesn't?"

"I'll write her a letter."

"I see." A tear escaped her, a lump formed in her throat. She wasn't so much sad for herself, but seeing Melanie's heart get broken yet again by the woman who should have protected her from hurt ripped her heart wide open. Maybe she should just be grateful there hadn't been enough time to bond before Violet up and left again. It reminded her of the old band-aid theory—it was less painful if you ripped it off quick. She just hoped Melanie would feel the same way. And then something occurred to her. "Violet—do you even have a flight booked? You can't just call the—"

"Yes," she said, cutting off Rose mid-sentence.

"When—how—"

"I called about an hour ago and told them there's been a death so it's an emergency. Now that there really has been one I guess I wasn't lying. About that part anyway."

"Violet!"

"Oh, mother, stop it. I could make the sun rise and set and you'd still fault me for it." She left the kitchen, leaving Rose alone with her grief. A moment later she was back. "You can take me to the airport tomorrow, right?"

"No." Her answer was slow. Deliberate.

Violet was already walking away again and then stopped cold, turning slowly toward Rose. "No?"

"That's right."

"Well, how am I supposed to get to the airport then?" she asked, sounding appalled that she'd been told 'no.'

"You'll have to figure that out for yourself."

"What—is this your way of punishing me? I don't do what you want so you make me pay?"

Rose stayed facing away from Violet and focused instead on the cars passing by off in the distance. I'm not making you pay, Violet," she sighed a sad sound. "But I will not help you leave Melanie. Not this time. Not anymore."

"Fine," Violet spat. "I'll call a cab."

"You do that."

Rose braced herself for the slamming of a door she knew was sure to come and didn't flinch when it did. Instead, she hung a hand towel that lay on the counter, one that she'd cross-stitched a long time ago, the pattern of a farm house surrounded by trees and flowers, below it the words 'Home Sweet Home.' Yes, indeed, this was her home sweet home. The home that held warmth, love, and laughter from a little girl who'd grown into such an amazing woman, and one she had the privilege of raising and sharing life with. She padded to her room, closed the door ever so gently behind her, sat in her reading chair in the corner nook and opened her Bible. There was power in prayer. And right now a whole lot of people needed prayer. Among them, Violet.

Not more than fifteen minutes after she'd gone to her room, she heard Violet's bedroom door open, followed soon after by the familiar creak of the old oak front door as it opened and closed. Violet, sneaking out as if she were fifteen years old again. Rose hadn't been able to keep her home then and she couldn't now. "Keep her safe, Lord," she whispered.

Chapter 11

IT WAS AFTER MIDNIGHT by the time I got back to my grandmother's house. I'd decided to stay there for a few days to give her peace of mind, knowing she would worry herself sick if I stayed at my house. My window, temporarily boarded up, wasn't due to be permanently fixed until that following day anyway. I planned to go to my house long enough to let the people in that would fix my window and to get some clothes and toiletries to take to my grandmother's. Also, it probably wouldn't hurt to spend a few days under the same roof as Violet to give a fair shot (pardon the pun) of working through some issues. If I wasn't going to work as hard at trying to make things work with her as I had been at avoiding facing and dealing with those issues, there wasn't even a chance. And a slim chance was better than none, I supposed. Besides, someone was out to kill one of us. With both of us under the same roof, it would be harder for the killer to accomplish his mission since there was safety in numbers.

I sneaked quietly into the house, trying hard to silence the creak of the door so it wouldn't wake anyone.

Nana, bless her, had left the light on above the sink for me as she always does when I stay there and always had as far back as I can remember. Often she would either wake up when I got home from a night out or wait up for me, and we'd sit at the kitchen table over tea and talk about my night. I could tell her anything. And I usually did.

Tonight, though, I wasn't up for conversation. I needed time to process in my head what had all happened, what it meant, and who could be behind it. Not to mention I needed to get some sleep if I was going to be worth anything at all at work the next day.

Thankfully, I made it to my room and quietly closed the door. I put my ear up to the wall to see if I could hear any movement in Violet's room. Grateful there was no sound and confident she was sleeping, I moved around a little more easily, slipping out of my clothes, and wiping my face with a facial cleansing cloth instead of in the bathroom sink. The only thing I needed to try and figure out was how I was going to brush my teeth. I definitely needed a sink for that. And not brushing them wasn't even an option. I had always been a little fanatical about oral hygiene, to where I brushed so ferociously when I was younger that I brushed enamel right off. Each time ice cold liquids or ice cream hit certain spots it reminded me of that all over again.

Since the kitchen sink was further from the bedrooms, I crept my way stealthily there. I had just about finished when Nana's voice startled me, and a spray of toothpaste landed on the window in front of the kitchen sink. I heard Nana's chuckle, but it was a sound that was heavy tonight, not joyous as it usually was. Something was wrong, and I had a good suspicion what it was.

"Violet?" I asked quietly, studying her eyes for what I could find there.

"She's gone."

My heart started fluttering wildly. "What do you mean by gone?"

She came to me and took one of my hands in her own. "She got a call for a job."

"Bull—you know what." I was angry, and at that point, I didn't care if the entire world knew it. Surprisingly, the anger faded quickly and I felt peace fall over me, brief as it was. "You and I are enough. We don't need her." As soon as the words were out, I knew I was being selfish. I hadn't even thought about how she might feel. Whether or not I liked it, Violet was her daughter.

I finished rinsing the toothpaste out of my mouth, swiped the kitchen towel over my lips and set my toothbrush down. Turning toward her, I looked deep into her eyes then hugged her. "I'm sorry, Nana. Are you—"

"I'm okay, dear." She pulled back and sat down at the table, motioning me to join her. Reluctantly, I did. More than ever I just wanted to go to my room, close the door, and shut out the entire world. If only for the night. "I tried to get her to stay for a few more days at least—I worry—I had hoped—"

"I know, I know. But Nana, I think you were hoping for a joyous reunion more than either Violet or I was. You had such high hopes for a reconnection between us, and I'm so very sorry I couldn't do it. A force greater than myself was preventing me from letting down that barrier. And now I'm glad I did."

"You are my sunshine. You know that?" She smiled sadly.

"And you mine. Now get to bed," I ordered and reached over to give her a hug. "You wouldn't mind if I stayed here a few days, would you?"

"Mind? I'd be disappointed if you didn't."

"Thought so." I leaned over to give her another hug and smiled over her shoulder before I pulled away. "I'm going to turn in. I'm exhausted."

"Aren't you going to tell me what happened at your house?"

"Would you mind if we talk about it tomorrow? I'm dying to get to bed. My fuel tank is on empty."

"You're not going to work tomorrow, are you?"

"Yes, I am. I have people counting on me. Truth be told, I need them more than they need me right now." I stooped to give her a peck on the cheek and went to my room, closing the door with an exaggerated gentleness before I lay down on my bed and wept. For a reason I couldn't explain, the house felt so incredibly empty. And hard as I tried, I couldn't figure out why. It wasn't as if there had been any connection between Violet and me. And yet, somewhere deep within me, I now realized I harbored the hope of one. And that hope had just walked out the door. Again.

Chapter 12

AS USUAL, GETTING TO the salon the next morning raised my spirits. The moment I stepped out of my grandmother's house into the cold spring morning air and the sunshine, it was like a breath of fresh air for my soul. I didn't sleep worth beans, and yet felt some strange relief this morning. In a sad way, I felt happy, odd as it was. My life was a little less of a mess without her in it. With someone trying to kill me, I didn't need her to worry about too. And if it was Violet they were after, well, now that she was gone, maybe the threat would be too. But I knew that wasn't the case. Call it women's intuition. Regardless, no Violet meant no false hope that accompanied her visit and nothing to distract me from figuring out what was happening around here.

"The next time I tell you I'm bored remind me of Violet who can't sit still for a minute without being bored. Then slap me. Hard!" I told Claire.

"You have a healthy sense of curiosity and of wanting to problem solve. There's nothing wrong with that," she told me. "You just need to reign yourself in from going out and looking for it when it does a fine job coming to you all on its own."

"True that!" I exclaimed and rolled my eyes. "So Rubie, it's a good thing you couldn't come over last night, huh?"

"Now I wish I would have. I'm feeling a little out of the loop."

"It's not a loop you would have wanted to be in," I remarked dryly. "You either, Connie. Consider yourselves lucky."

"Is Violet going to stay at your grandma's or is she going to brave it at your house?" Rubie asked.

I looked at Claire just as she sucked in her breath. Wishing she'd warned Rubie, no doubt. "I don't know where she's staying. All I know is I'm staying at my grandmother's. For a couple of days anyway."

"What about your—"

"She left." I abruptly stopped her from completing the obvious questions. It was a conversation I didn't feel like having again right now. I'd already filled Claire in earlier and that was enough talking about Violet for the rest of the year. "Has anyone heard from Gina?"

"Doesn't take a rocket scientist to figure that one out," Rubie mumbled. "Geez!"

"Figure what out?"

"That the subject is off limits. I got whiplash from your fast subject change."

"No, seriously. Has anyone heard from Gina?"

"She has a client here waiting," Connie said.

"Oh, yeah, sorry," Claire said from across the room as she leaned over Mrs. Swenson at the shampoo bowl. "She called and said she wasn't feeling well so she wouldn't be in. But I assumed she called and rescheduled her clients. Guess not."

Gina's appointment stood to leave. I went to meet her. "I would reschedule you, but I don't know Gina's schedule. I'm so sorry."

"You have nothing to be sorry for," she quipped. "You didn't do anything." And out she went.

I watched as the door closed behind her. My client who had just sat down in my chair swiveled around and said, "Guess it's safe to say she wasn't too happy. I hope Gina wasn't counting on her to return."

"Well, I don't know about you girls," Rubie added, "but something is seriously wrong with that chick. She's wound tighter than tight and about as friendly as a rattlesnake. And let me tell you, that's not a good combination."

We all laughed despite ourselves. Claire even laughed, and she's the last one who would ever think of laughing when someone was poking fun at another. But Rubie—well, she just had a way with words, and a whole lotta sass, that could send even Mother Teresa into a fit of laughter.

"Has anyone heard from Jack?" Rubie asked. "Is he still planning on coming in today?"

"Oh darn!" I stopped in mid cut. "I forgot to call him and tell him about anything that has been going on. He won't be a happy camper."

"Just think of it this way," Rubie said, "you saved him a heart attack and whole lot of needless worry. So the way I see it, Bryce should call to thank you."

"Are you gonna call and fill him in before he gets here?"

"No," I sighed. "I'll wait. There's nothing he can do about it anyway."

"My point exactly," Rubie added.

"If he's planning on staying he'll just have to stay at my grandmother's." I thought about it for a minute more and had another idea. "Hey, Claire, Sydney's not home, right? Maybe he could stay at your house."

"Heck yeah! That'd be fine with me. It's not like Cole has anything to worry about."

"Girlfriend," Rubie injected, and shook her head, "he could be straight as an arrow and Cole still wouldn't have anything to worry about. The two of you make love hard to live up to."

"We're just very lucky to have found each other when we did."

"Yeah, once you got past being wigged out about Sydney knowing. And a whole lotta guys had their heart broken and their hopes shredded the day you met Cole." I grinned at her. "And yet, the flowers still keep comin'."

"No sir, they do not," Claire laughed.

"Oh, but they do! Maybe not as frequently, but they do. What about the black roses you got last week? Creepy, but flowers nonetheless."

The rest of the ladies agreed with me, and I gave Claire a winning, I-told-you-so look.

"The card was creepier than the black roses." Claire visibly shuddered.

"What'd it say?" asked Mrs. Swenson.

"Some weird stuff about the petals being soft as black velvet and she'd look good wearing them," I said.

"Oh dear!" she gasped, her hand going to her chest. "That's disturbing." She turned her head to look at Rubie. "You married?"

"Not yet. Boyfriend, though."

"A boyfriend she keeps secret," I said.

"Well, don't say yes unless he treats you good," she huffed. "Otherwise, you'll end up with one of those cuckoo men that sent Claire the black roses."

"Yes, ma'am." Rubie gave her a mock salute.

"I'm not sure Rubie would tolerate anyone not treating her good. I've got a feeling she can hold her own," her client added.

"She already knows you, Rubie," I chuckled. "And that's why we love you."

"Awww, shucks." She tilted her head down and feigned embarrassment. "You girls are just too much."

The banter continued for the rest of the day, Rubie keeping us in stitches. Finally at 5:30 Jack came through the door.

"Dang! Someone's been doing a whole lot of chemical something in here today." He wrinkled his nose.

"I can't smell anything," Claire said, sniffing the air.

"Me either," Rubie and I chimed in unison, and Connie laughed.

"That's because you've all burned your nose hairs and can't smell."

"There could be worse things. At least, we can go in a public restroom and not worry about it," Rubie said so matter-of-fact Jack looked dumbfounded.

"She has a point, Jack," I laughed and gave him a giant hug. "How's my friend and how much do you love me?"

"Depends. What'd you do?" He hugged me back.

"It's what she didn't do."

I threw Claire a dirty look. "Tattle-tale."

"I'm just breaking the ice a little before you tell him."

"Tell me what?" he asked, clearly impatient.

"Let's hit Grizzley's, shall we? This could take a while."

"Rubie, do you need to check in with Shane first?" I teased.

She wrinkled her nose and stuck out her tongue at me. "No!"

"I'll do my thing over here while you ladies finish up. And then," he said, pointing at me, "you're going to tell me what you apparently should have told me before now."

"Who appointed you my father?" The look he shot me shut me up but a chuckle bubbled just beneath the surface. It was fun to get him riled up.

The last of us had just walked out, and we all waited while Claire got her key at the ready to lock up. Her phone rang, so I grabbed her key and locked the door while she took the call.

Door locked, I turned around to see Claire, once again, looking pasty in the streetlights that lit up the parking lot behind her. *Now what?* This look hasn't served me well the past few days.

"What is it?"

"You're not going to like this," she warned, her voice barely a whisper.

My heart began beating wildly. "I'll need to know what it is to know whether or not I'll like it."

"They found the gun a ways away from the body, and..."

Her voice faded as my attention was whisked to the squad car that pulled up to the curb. Cole got out of the passenger's side and another officer from the driver's side. The officer walked around the car and up on the sidewalk in front of me. I looked at the silver-plated name tag pinned to his uniform. Officer Carter.

"Melanie Hogan, you're wanted at the police station for questioning in the murder of Jane Doe."

My heart began beating at a dangerously fast pace and I started seeing tiny little black dots floating in the air in front of me. I forced myself to take a deep breath.

"Jane Doe?" Claire asked. "Who's that?"

"The victim didn't have any identification on her," Cole said. "They're still working on that. It appears there haven't been any reports of missing persons either."

"Did you see the body, Cole?" I heard Claire ask. It sounded like her voice was coming from somewhere off in the distance. Like I was having an out-of-body experience. I could only hope I was, and that this wasn't really happening. But the stark reality was it *was* happening.

"Not up close. Not close enough to know if I recognize her or not from any past run-ins with the law," I heard him answer her.

"Officer Carter," I said when I found my voice again, "what do you have on me that you're bringing me in?"

"Claire?" Jack said, the tension in his voice thick. "What body? Somebody tell me what in Sam hill is going on."

"We found a gun near the body," Officer Carter said, taking my elbow in his hand. "It's a 9 mm automatic, Ms. Hogan."

"And?" I asked, hot discomfort spreading throughout my body.

"It's registered to you."

Chapter 13

"FOR GOD'S SAKE, SOMEBODY fill me in right now, please." Jack's voice was as tight as an over-tightened guitar string.

"That's impossible," I whispered. "My gun is in my nightstand drawer."

"Apparently not anymore," Cole said as he stood by Claire.

"For God's sake!" Jack boomed, an unusual outburst that made me jump. He was typically so controlled. "Somebody tell me what's going on!"

"That will have to wait, sir," Officer Carter said, barely casting him a glance. "Come on, Ms. Hogan. I would like to ask your permission to bag your hands so we can test for gunshot residue at the station."

"Of course. You'll find there's no evidence, because I didn't do it."

"Says every person ever arrested," he said under his breath.

"I'm not every person," I said, meeting his eyes, daring him to say something, *anything*, else.

Jack, Claire, and Rubie watched, helpless, as Officer Carter did his job bagging my hands. Once completed, he led me to the patrol vehicle, hand on my elbow. I got in the back door he so generously opened for me, feeling like the criminal I wasn't. I looked at Claire helplessly as he closed the door behind me. "Such a gentleman," I retorted.

"Ma'am—" he said when he got in the driver's seat.

"What is it with you people calling me ma'am?" I asked, voice taut with irritation. "And just so you know," I said as I forced myself not to gag in the smelly, dirty plastic back seat of the patrol car, "someone's framing me and if you don't find out who it is, I will. Preferably on this side of the jail bars," I added, mumbling. "And what's with the no cuffs? Not that I'm complaining," I added quickly.

"At this point, you're just wanted for questioning."

"Wanted for questioning? You mean I have a choice?"

"Yes."

"Coulda fooled me. I'm not being arrested?"

"We found spent shell casings by the body of the unidentified victim, and they are the same type that belongs to the gun found in the near vicinity of the body, that gun being registered to you."

"Am I being arrested?" I asked again.

"The gun alone doesn't give us probable cause to arrest, ma'am—Ms. Hogan. But we need you to at the station for questioning nonetheless."

I looked and saw Rubie saying something. "Could you roll my window down, please? My friend is saying something." He hesitated a fraction too long. "Since I'm not being arrested and all," I retorted. The window rolled down halfway and I looked at Rubie.

"Want me to get you a lawyer?" She called out to me.

"No. I've done nothing wrong."

"We'll meet you at the police station, kiddo," Jack said.

I turned my head to look at him, feeling guilty for something I didn't even do. "Actually, could you and Rubie go to my grandmother's and explain what's going on? I don't want her to hear it somewhere or see anything on the news. But be sure to tell her I'm okay and will be there as soon as I'm done at the station."

"You got it," he said.

"Claire?"

"Yeah?" She was right beside me, her head peering in the open car window.

"Someone is setting me up and I'm going to find out who it is."

"Cole and I will help you. In the meantime, keep your chin up. Cole and I will meet you at the station."

"What would I ever do without you?"

"You'll never have to find out."

She blew me a kiss as Officer Carter closed the window and we sped away.

Chapter 14

THE POLICE STATION WAS bustling with activity, reminding me it was a Friday evening. It was easy to see how all the top cop show writers get their inspiration for story lines. All one had to do was visit a precinct and spend mere moments observing and one could have enough to fill an entire season's episodes. It was as if all the town crazies come out of the woodwork. And it was still early. I looked around, disappointed not to find Richard Castle and Kate Beckett. I would be entertained by all of the commotion if nothing else. I could sense eyes looking at me and could only imagine what people were thinking—a 40-year-old woman, all of five foot two, jeans and high heels, hands in bags.

But Officer Carter had other plans for me that didn't include watching the reality show I was in the middle of. He whisked me to a back room where they began swabbing my hands for GSR, of which I knew they would find none. And yet, knowing that, I was still more than a little wigged out. I was being questioned in a murder for crying out loud. What was next? Was I going to crack and confess to a murder I didn't commit? Were they going to bully me into a confession so they could close their case and call it a win? That's what happened on TV shows. They had to get those ideas from somewhere. My jaw set firm, and my eyes narrowed. Let 'em try. Bring it on, boys.

Testing on my hands completed, someone led me to an interview room and left me alone for what seemed like hours. There was a one-way mirror that lined a good part of one wall and was obvious to anyone who had half a brain. I wondered who, and how many, were on the other side studying my every move down to each breath. Was I breathing fast? Were my eyes darting around the room for an escape? Were my hands and legs shaking? Was I restless and fidgeting or tapping my fingers? Now I knew what it must feel like to the zoo animals, not having privacy enough to even pee without all the gawkers watching. I'm not sure I would feel the same about going to the zoo ever again. I had to show these guys I'm not their suspect.

It seemed like I'd been sitting there, still as I possibly could, trying to put on the appearance of being entirely unaffected, forever. As casually as I could muster, I glanced at my watch. Could it really only have been twenty minutes? That didn't seem possible. Finally, someone came into the room and sat down in the chair opposite me, on the other side of the table.

"I've been told not to call you ma'am," he began. "So hello, Ms. Hogan. My name is Levi." He smiled and extended a hand.

"Can we just get this over with please?" I asked with all the politeness I could muster, making a point of not reaching for his extended hand. I wasn't feeling quite that friendly. And if I had to guess, he wasn't either. It was all a trick to get me to trust him so I'd open up. I would open up, all right, but not because I trusted him. Only because I had nothing to hide. "Are my friends here?"

"Who are your friends?"

"Claire and Cole. Officer Cole Mahoney."

"I can go check for you if you'd like me to."

"Should they be in here with me?"

"If you'd like them to. You're not under arrest."

"I'm good. But I reserve the right to change my mind." I barely recognized my own voice. I sounded like a petulant child.

"Of course."

His genuine friendly tone irritated me. It would be easier if he were an arrogant jerk so I could focus on how unfair the whole thing was and how I was being mistreated. That theory was flying out the window quickly.

"Do you mind if I record this interview?"

"Nope."

"Nope you don't mind or nope, I can't?"

"I don't mind if you tape the interview." I crossed my arms in front of me, crossed one leg over the other and sat back in the chair with a little bit of attitude. Okay, maybe a whole lot of attitude.

"First of all, you're aware you tested negative for gunshot residue."

"Of course. I expected nothing else."

"Do you admit you own a firearm?"

"Yes. That would be the reason the gun found was registered to me." I winced as I realized how that sounded.

"I just wanted to be sure you're the one who registered the gun and that someone didn't fraudulently register it in your name."

"No, sir. I admit to owning a gun."

"'Sir isn't necessary," he smiled warmly. "You can call me detective Wescott. Or Levi is fine, too. 'Sir' is just a little too formal. How long have you had it? Your gun."

"About six months."

"Why did you decide to get one, if you don't mind my asking."

"I don't mind at all. For self-protection."

"Is there a reason you feel the need to protect yourself? I mean other than the obvious in today's world."

"I believe you already know the answer to that." Busted. I knew Cole had filled the police in on my attack last summer.

"Yes, but I thought the people responsible for your misfortune are locked up."

He had a point. Maybe his question was innocent after all. "It left me feeling a little...vulnerable, I guess you could say. Living alone out in the country has its benefits, but I found out it's not always the safest."

"Anyone else live in your house with you?"

"Nope."

"Not married?"

"Divorced."

"Any reason your ex would want to harm you or have any reason to be in your house?"

"I would hope he wouldn't want to harm me. I didn't do anything to him. It was the other way around." Again, I winced. I sounded like a bitter ex-wife, of which I'm sure they hear from all the time. "He left me, not the other way around," I tried to explain. "And, no, he wouldn't have any reason to be in my house." I watched as he jotted something down. "You don't watch NCIS, do you?" I blurted. He looked at me with a trace of amusement and I felt my cheeks get warm. "My friend Rubie loves that show and said there's a guy in that show who always thinks the wife or ex-wife is the killer."

"Tony Dinozo."

My heart sank a teensy bit. "I don't know his name. I don't watch it. So you do then? Because just so we're clear, this isn't a television show. But since you're looking at every connection to my ex, if anything happens to him while I'm a suspect here, I didn't do it." His chest heaved slightly. The smug son-of-a-gun. Anger sparked but I quenched it fast. The last thing I needed was for the detective to think I'm a hot-head.

"Does he still have a key?"

"He didn't live there with me very long. I changed the locks after our divorce."

"Does anyone else have access to your house?"

"Only my best friends Claire and Jack. And Rubie has been there a time or two."

"Who's Jack?"

"A very dear friend and one I would trust with my life."

"Has Jack been alone in your house lately?"

"No."

"Ms. Hogan, where was your gun?"

"I keep it in my nightstand drawer. Or I did, anyway."

"Do you ever take it out with you when you go anywhere?"

"I haven't, no."

"When's the last time you saw it?"

"About a week ago."

"In your nightstand?"

"Yes."

"Who knows you have a gun?"

"Claire, Jack, my grandmother...and Rubie."

There was a knock on the door and he excused himself like the gentleman he was trying to be. I wondered just how hard of an effort it was and when he was going to reveal the bad-cop side. He spoke with someone at the door in hushed tones and came back in the room.

"Your friends want you to know they're here."

"Thank you."

"Would you like a bottle of water?"

"If you want my prints you can get them anywhere at the salon, from my house, or even on this table since my hands have been touching it."

"And you said you watch little TV. Sounds like you watch too much." He smiled, and I felt my cheeks turn pink. "Will we find your prints on the gun?"

"Of course, you will. I just told you I had it out about a week ago."

"You said you saw it a week ago. What did you have it out for? Was it because of safety concerns?"

"Well, I didn't open my nightstand drawer just to admire it, Detective Wescott. And, no, it wasn't for safety concerns. I like to stay familiar with it. It's safer that way, wouldn't you agree? Nothing worse than a woman with a gun who doesn't know how to handle one."

He chuckled. "Don't think I'll touch that one." I smiled despite myself and the severity of the situation. "Has anyone else had access to your gun?"

"No, not that I can think of."

"Melanie," he surprised me by using my first name and met my eyes intently. "It's important you think about that very hard and not dismiss even the smallest possibility. I'm not out to get you like you probably think I am. I'm hoping to clear you and eliminate you as a suspect."

"No one else has been alone in my house."

"What about your mother? The day someone shot out your window, you told the officer you came home from work and your mother was making a drink, sitting in the dark because she hadn't changed the light bulb that had burned out."

"She didn't know I had a gun."

"You didn't tell her?"

"No. Violet—my mother—and I aren't exactly close. I don't tell her anything." I matched his stare for a moment. "Is there anything else, Detective, or am I free to go?"

"Just one more thing. Where were you yesterday between three o'clock and ten o'clock p.m.?"

"At work until five-thirty and then at my grandmother's."

"Can anyone vouch for that?"

"Claire, Rubie and Connie while I was at the salon. My grandmother and Violet while I was at her house."

"Violet?"

"My mother."

"And what about the time between leaving the salon and going to your grandmother's?"

I looked at him, my heart suddenly pounding. "I was alone."

Chapter 15

WE'LL BE IN TOUCH. BE sure you don't leave town. Detective Wescott's words echoed in my head.

And then my words. I was alone. The three words that made me a suspect. The facts had not changed between my extreme confidence from a couple of hours ago to now, but I was feeling a whole lot less confident. I needed to figure out who was setting me up and why. The first thing to do was to call together a meeting of the minds with Claire and Jack. As well as Rubie, too. Rubie! She knew where I kept my gun! And she was up in my room to get Violet after the window shoot-out!

When I pulled into my grandmother's driveway I spotted Jack's car. Sweet man, staying until I got here. Claire asked me to stay at her house but I'd told her since Jack was occupying her sofa, I would stay with my grandmother. I knew she would be worried sick. Suddenly I felt homeless, and like my life was a series of wondering where I was going to lay my head for the night. And it was a feeling I didn't like one bit. It rocked my comfortable, consistent little world I'd worked so hard to create for myself.

I unlocked the door and let myself in, trying my hardest not to wake anyone who would already be sleeping. As it turned out, I didn't have to worry about it. Nana was sitting at the kitchen table with a cup of tea, and Jack was sitting in the darkened living room on the phone. I assumed he was talking to Bryce.

Nana stood immediately and enveloped me in a hug. "My sweet, sweet girl," she cooed. "What on earth…"

I held her tight and pulled back, planting a kiss on her cheek. "It's okay, Nana."

"How dare they do that to you?"

"They're only doing their job," I said, surprising myself that I was actually sticking up for the police. And yet, I knew they were doing exactly what they had to do. "I just need to find out who got my gun, how they got it, and why. Why go through all that trouble to frame me?"

Jack hung up from his call, came into the kitchen, and sat down with us at the kitchen table that held so many midnight conversations between Nana and me. "That was Bryce."

"Figured as much," I said.

"He said to tell you he's thinking of you, and he knows you didn't do it."

"Tell him thanks for the vote of confidence. I'm impressed." His left eye narrowed and his head tilted. "What?" I said, a wee bit defensive. "I'm being serious this time. Coming from Bryce, that's pretty huge." He sat back in the chair, and crossed his legs, one ankle resting on the other knee, showing off his Kenneth Cole tassel loafers. "You have more shoes than I have underwear."

"Everybody needs a vice. Mine's shoes." He winked at me and gave me a tired smile. "Tell you what, when they figure out you're innocent we'll go buy you some more underwear, okay?" I chuckled and shook my head. "We all know you're innocent, Melanie. Nothing is going to change that."

"Well, let's hope the police believe that too. And that the evidence doesn't convince them otherwise. Did you talk to Claire? When we left each other at the police station it sounded like she thought you were staying with her."

"I called her. I didn't want to leave your grandmother alone to worry about you."

"So he stayed here and worried with me, the sweet darling boy," Nana said, patting his hand. "Sweetheart," she looked at me, "you must be exhausted after what you've been through. Why don't you go to bed and we'll talk in the morning."

"Good idea. Two late nights in a row. I can tell I'm not as young as I used to be."

"None of us are," Jack quipped lightheartedly. "And in case you forgot, you're forty now."

"And you're right on my heels, buddy, so watch it." I tried my best to be threatening but I was simply too tired to be anything at all. "Where are you staying tonight? Please tell me you're not going home."

"I'm going to stay on the couch. Your grandmother has it all made up for me."

I looked at Nana, her eyes looking so tired in the pale light that peeked through the window. The skin at the corners of her eyes crinkled and looked almost translucent. Suddenly I wondered if she was feeling okay. She'd been through so much.

"Come on, Nana. I'm going to tuck you in tonight. You need to get some rest. And don't you be worrying about me. I'm fine now and I'm still going to be fine in the morning." I stood and put a hand on her arm. Stray wiry tendrils of hair had worked their way free from her braid, and I brushed them away from her face. "Come on you precious woman."

Nana in bed, I checked on Jack to see if he had turned in yet. As tired as I was, I was too wound up to go to sleep. I wanted a glass of warm milk and a little night time chat with Jack. Luck was on my side. He was standing at the window, staring off into the blackness. He had on jeans, a button up shirt that was untucked, and he'd slipped out of his shoes and stood in bare feet. Poor guy was so out of sorts he wasn't even himself. He never has his shirt untucked much less go barefoot.

I began making my milk. "Want some?"

"Thought you'd never ask."

I finished heating our milk the old-fashioned way, on the stove, poured it into white ceramic mugs, and we went to sit in the living room. We left the lights off and the curtain on the picture window open, the yard light cutting through the room, illuminating one side of Jack's face.

"So tell me your side of things," he began. "I heard it from Claire, but I want to hear it straight from the horse's mouth."

"Violet was staying at my house, and when I came home from work one evening I went to close the curtains, which she had left open because she was sitting in the dark all because she didn't want to take the time to change the light bulb that had gone out. When I was reaching to close the curtains someone shot through the window, just missing me. They said it looked like a professional hit, which makes no sense. If he was a professional he wouldn't have missed me. I was standing in front of a completely uncovered window with the room lit up like a Christmas tree and it was dark outside."

"He easily would have seen you."

"Exactly. Clear as day. Then they found a body in the woods close to my house last night. And you know the rest." Despite how exhausted I was, as I talked, my anxiety kept building, escalating, like a stone rolling downhill gaining speed, going faster, faster, faster. I took a couple of slow deep breaths. "I didn't do it, Jack. You know me better than that."

"Of course, you didn't." Jack moved beside me and put a protective arm around me and kissed the top of my head. "Geez, kid, you get yourself in the worst messes."

"I didn't do anything! That's the point! Whatever time the shooting was, I'm sure I'll have an alibi for. I've hardly been alone for two seconds. I just need to find out who did it."

"Where's Violet, anyway?"

"My grandmother didn't tell you?" I rested my head on his shoulder. "She did what she does best. She left again.

"Where did she go?" he asked.

"She can't stay in place anywhere for too long. And adding to that, she got pretty freaked out with everything that's happened. She's a prima donna who hasn't had to experience anything like that. It's out of her class." Yes, I know I sounded snide, but under the circumstances, who could blame me. I stewed in my self-pity for a few minutes.

"Talk to me," he began. "What are you thinking?"

"I'm thinking the chances of this being someone else in my stalker friend's employ isn't unlikely. It's not too hard to give instructions from where he's at. It happens all the time. Even if he's not calling the shots, maybe someone is paying him honor by getting back at me." I paused to look at Jack and tried to gauge what he was thinking. "Last summer I thought Cain was maybe to blame, though it wasn't likely. Once again, I guess it's possible, but not likely. There's no motive. He wants nothing more than to have me out of his life, not back in it."

"Maybe he wanted you out of his life at first and has suffered from regrets."

"So he tried to kill me off? That's hardly a way to get me back in his life."

"Maybe it's the if-I-can't-have-you-no-one-can-have-you type of deal."

"Nah," I shook my head. "He's a cold heartless jerk, but he's not crazy. There's a possibility that it's…Nah, I guess not."

"Who?"

"Jack…Rubie knew where my gun was and had access to my room. Only for a brief time, but all the same…" I watched as Jack chewed on that, mulling it over. "I mean, Rubie's super talkative, bubbly, sweet…but she doesn't talk about her life much. And her boyfriend, well, who's to say he's on the up and up?"

"I don't think it's Rubie. But all the same, I'll keep my ears open for anything that doesn't sound right."

"And what about the other bozo who was terrorizing me last summer. Buford. And his partner in crime, Maria. But, I mean, the police warned him not to come near me and issued him a ticket for harassment. And she wants nothing to do with me, so…"

"Murder?" He shook his head. "I don't think so. I have to be honest with you, Melanie, none of them sound like viable options."

He was quiet, the light reflecting on the lenses of his glasses. "How do we know it's not one of the officers?"

"I thought that same thing, but for what reason? It's not like they have an ax to grind with me. Not that I know of, anyway. But then I don't know of anyone who has an ax to grind with me." I took a sip of my hot milk and lay my head back against the back of the double recliner chair I was curled up in and covered my legs with the purple afghan Nana crocheted years ago. "Someone obviously does."

"Have you thought about mother dearest?"

"As little as I have to," I grumbled. "But she was in the house with me when the person shot through the window."

"And you think the two are related? The shot through your window and the dead body?"

"It's too much of a coincidence not to be. Two gunshots in the middle of the country, just yards apart from each other, and little more than a couple of days in between."

"Well, you have been a magnet for trouble."

We tossed ideas back and forth until it was well after one o'clock in the morning and I could tell he was having a hard time keeping his eyes open. Finally, he yawned and stretched his arms above his head.

"What, am I boring you that much?"

"No, it's just that late. And I'm getting old."

"Don't say that. Since I'm the same age, you just called me old."

"Can it not be about you all the time? Just this once. Besides, we're not the same age. Yet."

I laughed quietly. I loved this man to the moon. "Let's call it a night," I stood to give him a hug. "Need me to tuck you in?" I teased.

"No, I have my big-boy pants on."

I laughed, despite the seriousness of the matters at hand. "See ya in the morning." I looked at my watch. "Well, technically, I guess it is morning. See you in a few hours."

When I left for work the next morning both Nana and Jack were still sleeping. I was quiet as a cat stalking its prey as I showered, dressed, and locked the door behind me, not even taking the time to make coffee. This was a Caribou day if ever there was one.

I got to the salon, my Caribou cup in hand, and saw Claire's car parked in the lot. Next to her car was Cole's. My curiosity piqued.

"You guys stay here last night or what?" I asked, trying to sound jovial as I could for what little sleep I got and the black cloud that hung over my head threatening doom.

I looked at Claire, her sober face startling me, and my heart began racing. "Now what?"

"They made a positive ID on the body."

"And?"

"It's Gina."

Chapter 16

SOMETHING DIDN'T MAKE SENSE. "It's Gina?"

"Yes," Cole confirmed.

I dropped my bag on the chair in front of my station and turned to face them again. "Cole, what was the time of death?"

"Between three and six."

"Uh-uh."

"Uh-uh? Melanie, what are you thinking?" Claire asked as she rested her hand on Cole's back.

"You said Gina called in yesterday and she said she wasn't feeling well."

"Oh yeah, that's right!" she said.

"What was she doing in the woods all the way out by my house, especially when she was sick? She lives in the complete opposite direction." I began pacing the floor. "Besides that, she doesn't know where I live, so she wouldn't have known she was by my house at all." I stopped and looked at each of them as the reality settled around me. "Guys, this isn't about me at all." I slipped out of my black leather jacket and tossed it on the chair beside my shoulder bag. "Claire, can you ever remember us talking about my house when Gina's been around?"

Claire put some serious thought into that before answering. "Not that I remember. But, think about it, have we always paid that close attention to what we say? Or even when Gina is around? She's usually so elusive even when she's here, that—" she stopped in mid-sentence, her big brown eyes wide.

"What?"

"Last year, with everything that had been going on and with what went down, she probably heard us talking about it then."

"Uh-uh. Think about it, Claire." I began pacing again, as much as I could, anyway, in my high heeled black leather ankle boots. Elvis's "These Boots Were Made for Walkin'" inappropriately came to mind. Maybe I was losing my mind. "Gina was the victim, not the one doing the shooting. It wouldn't surprise me if the person who shot Gina is the same person who shot through my window." I stopped and looked from Claire to Cole and back to Claire again. "Okay, first scenario – the gunshot through my window was meant for me. What if Gina had been working for my stalker? What if they were working together? Gina blames me for his fate, as well as Buford and Maria, and was out for revenge?"

"That theory sounds legitimate if Gina wasn't dead. But it begs the question of who shot Gina? Who else is in on this?"

"Whatever became of Buford?" I asked Cole. "You asked him to stay away from me and filed charges, but you know as well as I do he wouldn't have gotten jail time for that."

"No, he got probation."

"So he's out there somewhere."

"I would assume so. But following someone and making an empty threat is a whole lot different than attempted murder."

"Besides," Claire added, "I thought they determined it looked like a professional hit. Did they find something else to make you think otherwise?"

"There's no way a professional would have missed me. If he was actually trying to kill me."

"The second?" Claire asked.

"Second what?" I asked.

"You just said you gave us the first scenario. What's the second?"

"If Violet was the target, how is she connected to Gina?"

"Assuming the two shootings are connected," Claire said.

"I'd bet money on it," I said. "So if Violet was the target of the shot through my window and then Gina gets murdered, how are Violet and Gina connected? That's what I need to figure out."

"How well do you ladies know Rubie?" Cole asked.

Claire and I both looked at him as if we hadn't heard what he said. "Rubie?" we both asked. Had that thought not crossed my mind only the day before, Cole's question would have been comical.

"Yes."

"I thought about that," I said, my stomach flipping over, making me want to throw up. "Rubie wasn't with any of us during either episode. And she knew where I kept my gun."

"But Rubie's the sweetest person I know," Claire said.

"Not the sweetest I know," Cole murmured and gave her a wink.

"Oh, pu-lease," I groaned and rolled my eyes. "Not now. Besides, I'm insulted."

"There are adjectives that best describe people, sweet just isn't the one that describes you," Claire said. "Loyal, honest, protective, determined..."

"I get it," I said with an eye roll.

"Has either of you thought about the fact that all of this happened after Rubie came into the picture? And has anyone met her boyfriend?"

"I've thought about that as well. He's been in once or twice, but saying we know him is a stretch," I said. "In fact, he and Rubie could pass for siblings if I didn't know better." As soon as the words were out I couldn't shake the feeling that I was missing something there.

"Do you know for a fact that they aren't?" Cole asked.

"There were no open displays of affection if that's what you mean. But that doesn't necessarily mean anything. Not everyone is comfortable with that." But even as I said the words, I was still uncomfortable with where my mind was going with it.

"He doesn't have a motive," Claire said.

"Yeah," I said, hesitating a minute, then shaking my head again slowly. "Rubie and her boyfriend probably aren't involved." The question was, was I trying to convince Cole of that or myself?

"I'm of the belief that anybody is capable of anything if the stakes are high enough."

"You're also a police officer, and you guys probably get pretty cynical seeing everything you do."

"Like you're not?" Claire asked with amusement.

I walked over to the coffee maker to measure in the grounds, inhaling deeply of the fresh, dark roast grounds.

"Speak of the devil," Cole said.

I turned to see Rubie walking toward the front door, the bounce in her blonde curls matching the usual bounce in her step. My stomach tied in a knot as I watched her. She came through the door, stomped some lingering snow off of her shoes on the rug, looked up and stopped short. "What?"

"Huh?" Claire and I asked.

"What are y'all lookin' at me for?" Her cheeks were pink from the cool morning air, her blue eyes sparkling. "What'd I do?"

"Nothing that we know of. Unless you want to fess up to something," I said, teasing. Or at least, I thought I was teasing. Did I really believe Rubie was capable of what happened or had Cole simply watered the seed of doubt in my head after I'd already planted it?

"We have some news." Claire looked at her, the seriousness in her brown eyes making her look even more innocent than she was.

The trace that was left of Rubie's smile faded to a near frown. I watched for any sign of something other than surprise. "Uh-oh." She stopped dead. She swallowed. Her eyes darted from me to Claire.

"Wanna tell her Mel?"

"No, you go ahead."

"I don't give a hoot who tells me, but someone spit it out!" She said, sounding near panic. I continued to watch her closely as Claire continued talking.

"They've ID'd the body found my Melanie's house," Claire said. "Rubie...it's Gina."

"Gina?" How one short word could change two octaves, the last part a high-pitched screech, was beyond my understanding. "But how? Wait, don't answer that. We already know how. But why? Who?"

"That, indeed, is the question," I said. I saw Cole watching her closely, studying her reaction.

"That's still a mystery," he said.

"We were all trying to work through it when you walked in the door."

"I feel like I'm supposed to say something here, like, It was Colonel Mustard, with the revolver, in the library."

"That was always my favorite game as a kid," I said. I forced myself to look away from Rubie.

"Was?" Claire asked and snorted. "Go figure. Not just when you were a kid. You still make me and Jack play it with you."

"What can I say? I'm a hopeless detective. Or should I say a hopeful detective?"

"How about you work on solving crimes that don't involve you? In fact, I have an idea," she said, putting a finger up in the air, "just keep yourself out of the equation altogether."

"And therein lies the problem, my friend, I don't find it, it finds me."

"Well, find better hiding spots."

"I'm going out there after work."

"Out where?" Claire asked.

"Where they found Gina."

"In the woods?" Rubie asked.

Her reaction was interesting to say the least. Horrified? But why? Because of going in the woods after dark or because of what I might find? "Yup. I need to see if I can find anything out of the ordinary."

"What could you possibly find that the police haven't already found?" Rubie asked.

"Claire," I said, ignoring Rubie's question, "I know those woods like the back of my hand. I was just out there the day prior and saw boot footprints."

"Why didn't you say anything before this about that?" Cole spoke up reminding me he was in the room.

"Because I forgot about it with everything that's been happening."

"That's something pretty significant to forget."

"Excuse me," I threw at him with more than a little sarcasm. "It's not like anything else has been happening. Besides, I thought I mentioned it to Claire that same day. Didn't I?" I looked at Claire.

"Look, Melanie, I'm sorry. It's just that—well, that piece of information could be critical to the investigation."

"Well, I'm telling you now. And I'm also telling you I'm going out to those woods to where Gina was found."

"You're not going alone," Claire said adamantly. "I'm going with you."

"No, you're not." Cole's voice was firm.

"Cole, I'm not letting her go out there by herself. It's not safe."

"Which means it's not safe for you either." His eyes pleaded with her. They stared at each other in silence for a moment, neither making a move to give in. "Fine. You're obviously going to go no matter what I say, so I'll go too."

"You will?" she asked. She sounded surprised, which in turn surprised me. Did she honestly think he would let her do something dangerous without him? Even I knew better than that.

"Yes. Melanie doesn't have a gun anymore, remember?"

"I'll bring mine," Claire offered.

"How about I bring mine and we call it good." As he looked at Claire, he reminded me of a little boy hoping to get his way. Yup, he was a lost cause in this love thing. He turned his attention to Rubie. "Why don't you come with, too?" He was up to something. I could feel it.

The rest of the day there remained a niggling suspicion in the back of my mind that I was missing something big. Hard as I tried to focus on what I was doing, I was sure by the end of the day I would have cut someone's hair short when they only wanted a trim or colored their hair black when they wanted highlights. Somehow, I got through the day without creating any casualties. And throughout the day, the three of us looked at Gina's manicure table, instruments laid out as if she were going to come in and begin working any moment. I finally cleared the top of the table off, putting all of her things in a drawer. An empty reminder was less troublesome than everything in place, staring us in the face, taunting me with what loomed over my head. Suspicion.

Chapter 17

TWO OF GINA'S CLIENTS came in that day. We simply told them she no longer worked there, offering no further explanation. Both clients were now considered suspects in my book. Giving the appearance of not knowing she was out was a good cover. I watched as each of them left, including paying attention to what car they drove off in.

Jack came by about one o'clock, which was later than I expected him. I thought he would have been on the road back home no later than mid-morning. When he said he stayed with my grandmother for a while to keep her mind off of the events that had unfolded, and even played Texas Dice with her, my heart warmed. All the good men were married or gay. And both were off limits for me. Go figure.

As soon as we closed up the shop that evening, I went to my grandmother's house to retrieve proper hiking attire. Claire and Rubie each went to their respective homes to do the same. We were going to meet at my house, Cole included, at 6:30. Nana wasn't thrilled with the idea, to say the least, but reluctantly gave her blessing when she knew Cole would be there. I wasn't sure if I should feel thankful I had her blessing or slighted that it was only because there would be a man there. I had proved time and time again that I could handle myself just fine without a man around. Maybe I was making more of it than there was to be made and it was simply a generational thing. Whatever it was, I didn't have time to ponder it any further. I had someplace   I   had   to   be.

I drove my little black Nissan 370Z, my present to myself when my ex-husband, Cain, left me. It was a minor comfort, but any little thing helped. I turned in the drive to find Cole's car already there, saw the kitchen light on so I knew Claire was with him. It didn't surprise me they came out together. Not only was it practical, but Cole wasn't about to risk Claire heading out into the woods without him.

I walked through the kitchen door, instantly consumed with bittersweet nostalgia. The window was completely fixed, and the glass cleaned up.

"Did you ask them to do that?" I asked Cole, pointing to the spotless floor beneath the window.

"They were happy to do it."

"What a guy." I half-smiled. I may give him a hard time sometimes, but he's been so good to Claire, and for that I was grateful. She deserved the best, and from what I could tell so far, even despite my reluctance to see it and determination to see otherwise, she found it in Cole. I wondered how much of my desire to see the worst in him was sheer resentment for him taking so much of her time. "Have you heard from Rubie?" I asked Claire.

"No. But she'll be here. It's not quite six-thirty yet."

"Did either of you..." I let my voice trail off.

"Did we what?" Claire asked.

"When Rubie found out the body was Gina's, did she seem genuinely surprised to you?"

"Did you notice something?" Cole asked, an eyebrow raised.

I shuddered. "No. I can't believe I'm even questioning her."

"We can't be too careful here," he said.

"Being careful and suspecting a friend of murder are two completely different things. And you," I said, glaring at him, "planted that stupid idea in my head."

He held up his hands in defense. "There're just too many things that started after she came into the picture. Besides, don't forget she had complete access to your gun." He paused. "And I don't believe for a minute that I'm the one that planted that idea in your head."

"I don't care what you believe," I mumbled, knowing I was busted. "But for the record, she freaked out when I told her I had a gun."

"Yeah?" he challenged. "What a great way to make you think she's innocent."

"Stop it you two!" Claire glared at Cole, then at me. "This is getting us absolutely nowhere."

I shrugged and bit my tongue before I said anything more. Besides, while we waited, there was something I needed to see. For proof if nothing else. As if the police telling me wasn't proof enough. I crept up the stairs to my bedroom in the loft, walked slowly to my nightstand, put my hand on the wrought iron handle and left it there for a moment. I noticed the beating of my heart, strong and racing, as I finally pulled the drawer open and found it void of my gun. My stomach felt heavy and my legs weak. I don't know what I really expected to see, my gun miraculously appear so I could bring it in and say, Here, see? You guys had it all wrong. My gun was right where I left it!

I closed the drawer, sat on the edge of my bed, and looked around at the room that had brought me so much comfort over the past few years. I desperately wanted that back again. And there was only one way I could make that happen. Newfound determination rose and I half expected to hear the angels and choirs sing. Instead, I heard the door open downstairs and Rubie's voice. My cue that it was time to head out and figure out what in the heck was going on.

We trudged outside, each with a flashlight in hand, to begin our investigation. Cole had told me the police hadn't come up with any leads, and I couldn't help but wonder how hard they were actually trying since they had their suspect in me. Sure, Detective Wescott said I wasn't a suspect, but a person of interest. They can call it whatever they want, but I knew they're suspecting me. And now that the body has been identified as Gina, they would look at me even closer. In fact, I was fully expecting a visit from them at the salon today, asking me to come in for further questioning. Or worse. I had to figure out who was behind this before I was behind bars and unable to find the actual shooter.

"Something doesn't make sense," Rubie said, her voice carrying easily between us as we were only slightly spread out, each surveying a different piece of land with our flashlights. I watched her from the corner of my eye to see exactly how familiar she was with the area. "If they're looking at Melanie as the killer because it was her gun," she said, "how do they expect that she would have shot in her own window, at herself?"

"They aren't sure the two incidents are even related," Cole answered.

"I'm sure they are," I answered. "In fact, I'm convinced they of it."

"How so?" he asked. "The bullet that came through your window isn't a match to the one that killed Gina."

"And you call yourself a police officer," I scoffed. "What are the odds that two shootings so close together are going to happen in the middle of nowhere?"

"Odds and gut feelings don't make it fact."

"I realize that. But what if Gina was the one who shot through my window?"

"But why?" Rubie asked.

"I don't know that yet. But what if she's the one who shot through my window—"

"That would go against their belief that it was a professional hit," Cole interrupted.

"You know as well as I do it wasn't a professional hit. But even semi-professional, how well did any of us know Gina? Really know her. For all any of us know, she could be a sniper."

"I sure didn't know her," Claire said.

"Me either. But I haven't been there very long," Rubie said.

"In the time you've been there, you've gotten to know her every bit as well as Claire and me. She's always been extremely private."

"And downright rude sometimes," Rubie said.

"I'm not so sure I'd call her rude, just...well, just reserved." Claire, always the optimist.

"I'm goin' with rude." Rubie was determined to hold her ground. "Have you ever listened to the way she talked to some of her clients?"

"Which makes me wonder if one of them got a little fed up."

"Just because someone gets fed up doesn't make them a killer. If that were the case, we'd all be in prison," Rubie said.

"Well, all I know is that's exactly where I'm going to be if I don't find something to exonerate me and find it fast."

We walked a while, flashlights scanning the area in all directions, illuminating twigs, dried shrubs and patches of snow. We were each searching for something we didn't know we were searching for. Just something, anything, that didn't belong.

"Ever shot a gun, Rubie?" I asked.

"Heck no!" she said. But she said it a tad too quick. Or did I imagine that? Darn you, Cole!

"Melanie, where were the footprints you said you saw?" he asked.

"Melted, I assume."

He chuckled briefly. "I would assume that as well, Sherlock Holmes. But where were they? As in the location."

"Along the path Rubie is walking."

"I haven't seen a thing," she said. "And believe me, I've been looking."

Rubies words vanished into the darkness as I spotted something that made me stop dead in my tracks. I couldn't believe my eyes. I didn't know what to do, and it put me in a dilemma that could go either way. But as my luck had been going, it wouldn't be for my benefit to speak up. And yet, if I didn't, but instead conceal what I was looking at, and someone found out, I would be charged with tampering with evidence. And that was something I couldn't afford right now given the mess I was already in. I stood frozen in place trying to decide what to do as the others walked on.

"Melanie?" Claire asked. I looked up, the beam from my flashlight going to her face which was watching me closely. "What's wrong?"

"Something's definitely wrong alright," I whispered. Do I tell her and hope she doesn't tell Cole? Or do I keep it to myself? Oh, the agony of trying to decide if I should trust my dearest friend in the world with my fate right now when her love life entered the equation. My heart was pounding as I tried to determine the action that would determine my fate. She began walking toward me, Cole and Rubie turning toward me as well. My grandmother's words that she had spoken numerous times as I was growing up, Honesty is always the best policy, finally won out.

"I found something," I said, realizing too late that Cole had heard me too. Me and my big mouth.

Cole was by my side in the blink of an eye. "What is it?"

I groaned in aggravation. "A white glove."

"Does it look familiar?"

"I'd say so, yes," I said. My voice sounded raspy, the blood pulsed in my ears. "It's mine."

Chapter 18

COLE REACHED FOR THE glove while pulling a plastic bag from his pocket with his other hand. I wondered how many plastic bags he brought with him. Obviously, he'd come expecting to find something.

"Cole, you can't take that," Claire whispered.

"Babe, I have to." He looked from Claire to me, holding out his hand.

"No, you don't," I said. "You should, but you can't."

"Why not?" He kept his hand out, obviously hoping I would come to my senses and change my mind.

"Because short of tackling me, which I would advise against, I'm not giving it to you."

"Melanie..."

I snatched the bag from Cole's hand, put the glove in the bag, and tucked it in my pocket, zipping it for good measure. I looked at Cole. "Don't look at me like I just killed something." As soon as the words left my lips, I realized the poor taste. "Well, that was just awkward," I mumbled, feeling my cheeks get hot.

"Cole," Claire said and came to stand by me, "you can't take the glove. It will get Melanie into more trouble than she's already in."

"Claire, I'm a police officer."

"Hey, Mr. Obvious, you're a police officer who saw none of this," I said.

"Only I did," he challenged me. "You're withholding evidence in a murder investigation. I won't be an accomplice."

"Well, since I didn't find the glove but actually pulled it from my pocket and dropped it..."

"You dropped it on the tree branch?"

I could tell by his rare sarcasm that he knew he wouldn't win. "Yes, as a matter of fact, that's exactly what happened. "I pulled it out of my pocket, it got caught in my zipper, and flung into the air and thank goodness got caught on a tree branch. Otherwise, it would have gotten dirty."

"Your pockets don't have zippers."

"By golly, they don't," I said, my eyes wide as if he'd just discovered something huge.

"Give me the glove, Melanie."

"No."

"Claire, honey," he said, "can I please have a moment alone with Melanie?"

"You don't need to go anywhere, Claire," I said, my gaze holding Cole's cold eyes."

"Babe?" He said. I could tell he was trying hard to keep his cool.

Claire sighed. "I should knock your heads together, is what I should do," she grumbled and turned to walk away, snatching Rubie's arm on her way, pulling her along.

"Melanie, you're being selfish," he said when Claire was out of earshot.

"I'm being selfish?" I asked incredulously. "My butt is on the line for a murder I didn't commit, and you're—"

"You're putting my job on the line trying to save your butt."

"Sorry to break the news to you cop boy, but it's not your butt that's on the line."

"I can help, but not if I'm fired."

"No one has to know."

"I will know," he argued.

"I'm not giving you the glove, Cole. End of story."

"Well, I can't promise you I won't do my job and—"

"Are you here as an officer or a friend?"

"You're making it really hard to be a friend right now. Besides, it's not that black and white, Melanie. There isn't always a line that separates the two."

I glanced in the shadows at Claire standing by Rubie several feet away, their flashlights the only light to see them by. I looked at Cole, narrowed my eyes. "You better put my friend before your job. I will do whatever I have to do to protect her." I looked towards Claire again.

"I'm not the one she needs to be protected from."

"What exactly are you saying, Cole? Spit it out."

He sighed an exasperated sound and tilted his head back. "Look, Melanie—"

"Two days. That's all I'm asking."

"I can't promise you that."

Our eyes met, each willing the other to give in. "Cole?"

"No promises, Mel. Sorry."

"You're being a jerk."

"I once heard that who you are under pressure reveals your true character."

I jumped at Rubie's voice directly behind me. She looked away, sucking air in between her teeth when she saw my glare.

"Ooohhh," she said quietly, "I shouldn't have said that."

"Yeah, probably not," Cole said, his eyes still trained on me. "I think anyone in Melanie's position would be more than just a little tense and irritable. Her future is being decided by someone who's obviously trying to set her up."

I watched him with a question in my eye. A question I was desperate to know the answer to. The answer that would give me the time I asked him for. But I didn't see what I was hoping for. My stomach plummeted as though I was on a roller-coaster than just dropped from the highest peak.

"They're going through a lot of trouble to do it," I finally said as I forced my stare away from Cole. "But who and why?"

"Mel, you're out here walking all the time. You could easily have lost your glove one of those times, right?"

I felt myself recoil at the mention of the glove. The stupid glove was causing an irreparable rift between my best friend's boyfriend and myself. A rift that would eventually permeate the relationship between me and Claire. I'm glad I hadn't had time to eat before coming out here. I felt like I was going to vomit.

"It's possible, but not probable. The last time I was out here, the same day I saw the boot prints, I had them on. I'm positive I wore them back to the house and didn't drop one."

"Drop one like you did today?" Cole asked.

I could feel the tension in his voice. "Yeah, that's what I meant."

"Don't say anything more. At least in front of me," Cole warned.

"You wouldn't turn her in, would you, Cole?" Claire's voice sounded hurt.

"It's just best if I don't know some things," he said, avoiding answering her question. "If I don't know the answer I don't have to pretend otherwise. Or get caught in a tight situation if I'm put on the spot."

"Just give me two days, Cole. Please." He studied my face, my eyes pleading with him. "If after two days I don't come up with anything, then I'll give it to you. Fair?"

"By then the chain of evidence is tainted. In fact, it already is." He shook his head slowly. "No promises," he mumbled, just loud enough for me to hear. "Besides, give what to me? I'm sure I don't know what you're talking about." He shook his head, looked down, then off in the inky black distance.

I let my breath out, which I hadn't even realized I was holding. "A girl can hope." I began walking again and looked at him over my shoulder.

As we headed back to the house, Rubie remained silent. Couldn't blame her. She probably didn't trust herself to talk for fear she'd say the wrong thing again. I sidled up next to her and put my arm around her, bumping her with my hip.

"We good?" I asked.

"You tell me." Her usual jovial self was subdued.

I nudged her with my shoulder. "Hey, I'm good. Are you?"

I felt her look at me. "I'm good."

"Then we are." I felt her body relax and her step got a little lighter. "Hey, don't take me so serious, okay? I can be—"

"You're awesome, Melanie. It's me and my big mouth that—"

"Are beautiful," I interrupted her. "Nothing but beautiful." I squeezed her shoulder before letting my arm drop, patting my pocket for assurance the glove hadn't fallen through a hole in my pocket. Last time I checked there wasn't a hole, but with the way things have been happening, I couldn't be too careful. Satisfied when I felt the small lump, I crossed my arms across my chest and shivered.

"Criminy, it's freezing out here!" Rubie said.

I silently cursed Cole for growing my suspicion about Rubie, at the same time wondering if there was something to it.

The promise of marshmallows swimming in hot chocolate with whipped cream waited for us at my house. Along with a round table meeting of the minds. First, though, I had to call Nana to be sure she knew I was okay so she could get some sleep without worrying.

Cole lit a fire in the fireplace to take the chill out of the air. Not that it was so cold, but the dampness soaked through our clothing. Add to that the lake air and it was definitely a night for a fire.

Rubie and I made the hot chocolate and soon we were all sitting in the living room, Rubie and I each hugging a throw pillow, and Claire and Cole cuddled on the end of the sofa. I felt a pang of admiration, and perhaps even a sliver of envy. I stretched my legs out in front of me, resting my feet on the gnarly oak coffee table in front of me and my head against the back of the chair.

"Ok," I began, "my first question is, have either of you girls seen anything or anyone suspicious among Gina's clientele? Heard anything odd?"

"Nothing that would make me suspect murder." Claire shook her head. "But she didn't talk much to them either unless she knew them well. And even then, she was kind of detached from them."

"Well, we know one thing for certain, it wasn't a professional hit. A professional hit wouldn't have missed me when I was in plain view."

"I'm not so sure," Cole mused. "Because a professional could have missed on purpose, narrowly missing what people would automatically think was the mark. Maybe he wasn't trying to hit you at all, but the opposite. He missed on purpose to scare you."

"Hmmm." I have to admit I hadn't thought of that. "And that was my stalker's M.O. when he was terrorizing me, Claire, and Jack. Which makes me wonder if that's the avenue I should look down." I was relieved some of the tension between Cole and me had vanished. At least for now. The threat of him going forward about the glove still hung around my neck like a noose.

"We've already discussed that. It's not possible."

"I know we already talked about it. I was there. But sarcasm aside, do we know for absolute certain they weren't working with anyone else?"

"No."

"How do you know that, Cole?"

"Know what?" he asked.

"That there was no one else involved."

"Because all leads ran cold. We exhausted every option and questioned them both endlessly."

"So because they didn't give up a name or identity of someone else you just automatically think it's the truth? Like you can trust either of them? Maybe it's someone who's close to them and this is their way of getting me back."

"By hiring a hit man?" Rubie added to the conversation. "What I want to know is why the police didn't find the glove."

"Good question, Rubie. Do you have any idea how they would have missed it, Cole? We were out there at night and found it."

"Maybe the killer—or whoever it is trying to frame Melanie—came back and planted it there after the police left," Rubie suggested. "In fact, maybe it was the police."

"In the officers' defense, the glove—" he cleared his throat and looked at me, "that I don't know yet whether I saw or not, was a white glove and there was a layer of snow on the ground."

"I'll give them that," I said. "But why haven't they been out there since then to look for clues instead of sitting back assuming they have their suspect? I have to wonder how hard they're really trying."

"Oh my gosh!" Claire exclaimed, eyes wide brown saucers. All heads turned to her. "I just thought of something! About what Rubie said."

"We're dying to hear," I said. "Pardon the pun."

"Do you think someone from the police force is in on this? Cole, are there any crooked cops you know of?"

"If we knew they were crooked, they wouldn't be a cop, babe. Besides, we're the good guys."

"Uh...not always," I said as if he had just said the dumbest thing in the world. And at the moment, I was thinking it was. "Just because you are one of the good guys, doesn't mean all of them are. Jack and I already wondered if it was the police."

"You ladies have watched too much crime TV."

"On the contrary," Claire said. "I hardly watch any at all. All I'm saying is it would have been all too easy for the evidence to be planted there by someone in the line of duty while investigating the crime scene."

I exhaled long and slow. "Yeah, I have to admit that certainly adds a new twist to things. Cole, how well do you know the officers? And what about the deputies from the sheriff's department? And has Detective Wescott been investigating out at the scene?"

"I don't know all of them, of course, and those I know I don't know well. But if you're looking at Wescott, I would be extremely confident in saying you're way off the mark."

"How can you be so sure? If he has something to hide, he's sure not going to let you know about it."

"Because he's definitely one of the good guys. He's true blue through and through."

"True blue as in he'd defend those in blue no matter what?"

"Absolutely not. Not if they're in the wrong." His unwavering confidence in Wescott convinced me. For now, anyway.

"So, Melanie, what's the connection between the person who shot at you and Gina's death?" Rubie asked.

"I don't know yet." And the fact I couldn't think of a single thing to tie them together was not setting well with me. I was running short on time. "Anyone want more hot cocoa?"

"I'll get it," Claire offered.

"Got any peppermint schnapps?" Rubie asked.

"No. Even if I did I wouldn't give it to you yet anyway. I need sober minds helping me stay out of prison, not compromised ones helping me get there." I looked at her and smiled warmly despite the bit of panic that began rolling in my stomach. My phone rang and I looked at the incoming number, not recognizing it. I let it go to voice mail.

"Aren't you going to get that?"

"No. It's not Jack or Nana, so it can't be too important. Not more important than what we're doing anyway. And that's trying to keep my butt out of jail."

"What was the number?" Rubie asked as if she would know the number of someone calling me I didn't even recognize the number for.

"218-235-5555," I answered, reading it from my missed call screen.

"That's an extension from the precinct," Cole said with a frown. "You'd better check if the caller left a message. Better prepared than surprised at this point."

I took a deep breath and tapped the button to listen to the voicemail the caller left as Claire hovered over me. I felt my pulse quicken as I listened to the voice on the recording. When it was done I ended the call and looked at all eyes on me. "That was Detective Wescott. He would like me to call him as soon as possible."

Chapter 19

I FINISHED MY CALL to the Detective and hung up, putting my phone face down on the end table. I didn't want to see it light up again with another incoming call. My time to figure this mess out was closing in on me all too fast.

"What did he want?" Claire and Rubie asked at the same time as if reading a script.

"Wants me to come in for more questioning."

"Tonight?" Claire asked, concern evident.

"Yeah. But I told him I'd be in first thing in the morning."

"She won't get in trouble for that, will she Cole?"

"No. She's not being arrested at this point."

"And I need to be sure it stays that way," I said.

"What about work?" Rubie asked. "Want us to reschedule your appointments?"

"It's Sunday, genius." I smiled at her, not quite feeling it. I had to admit, I was nervous. It seemed like the evidence and things that made me look guilty were just one step ahead of me and gaining ground fast. For every step I took, the evidence against me seemed to take two.

"Detective Wescott works on Sunday's?" Claire asked Cole.

"The first few days of a homicide investigation are critical. Besides, he doesn't have a life outside of work except for his kid." He looked at me and said, "That's going to work to your advantage right now. He'll want to solve this case as quickly as possible. The more time that goes by, the chance of finding the actual killer diminishes."

My heart fluttered and I wondered if it was going to fly right out of my chest. "Well, let's just hope he's not looking for answers so quickly he misses something big. I don't want to go down for something because a crucial piece of evidence got overlooked."

"Like the glove?" He asked, shaking his head slowly.

"What glove?" I asked.

"You can trust Wescott, Melanie." Cole insisted. "He's good people."

"Right now, buddy, I don't know who I can trust other than the people sitting in this room with me right here, right now. In fact, one of you I don't exactly trust right now, either," I said, my eyes boring into him."

"Exactly what does that mean?" Rubie asked.

"You can trust Jack and your grandmother," Claire jumped in. I suspected she was trying to divert Rubie's attention.

"Yeah. Jack and Nana, too," I said. "So let's toss out some more ideas and help solve this thing."

"Good idea. The clock is ticking," Cole said.

My stomach lurched in distress. The time I had was completely in Cole's hands. "No pressure," I mumbled. My nerves were frayed. Being in the hot seat had never been my forte. I preferred to stay behind the scenes, not front and center and in the spotlight.

Cole and I volleyed possibilities back and forth for a while before I realized Claire and Rubie had been awfully quiet. I glanced from one to the other and saw why. Rubie had fallen asleep curled in the corner of the chair, a curly strand of silky blonde hair hanging loosely over her face, and Claire's eyes had closed, her head resting on Cole's shoulder. He gently stood, laying Claire's head on a throw pillow and covered her with a blanket, while I reached for another blanket to cover Rubie.

"Now I know what Jesus must have felt like when he went to pray the night before he was betrayed and the disciples who were to keep watch kept falling asleep."

"Sorry to burst your bubble, but you're not in the same league as Jesus." I appreciated his attempt at humor, welcoming anything that diminished the growing tightness in my gut.

"I'll remember that Officer Mahoney." The gravity of the situation consumed me again. "Cole, what do you think is going to happen?"

"What I think isn't important, here, Melanie. What's important is that we find the killer so you can get back to what you do best."

"Which is what? Attracting trouble?"

"Being counselor and therapist to all of those women—and men—who visit your stylist chair."

"Yeah," I half-smiled, looking at my cup to avoid what I was afraid of seeing in his eyes. Pity. "We're kind of similar to bartenders in that way. People sit down and feel the need to spill their world to us."

"And you like it. Admit it."

I chuckled quietly. "Yeah. As long as I'm not the one that's doing the spilling." We were quiet, deep in thought for a few moments. "I know I give you a hard time sometimes—"

"Sometimes?"

"Don't push it," I warned. When I looked up at him and met his eyes, I couldn't even pretend to be angry. After all, he hadn't said anything about the glove yet. My voice softened. "Thank you for being here. Helping me through this. And for being there for Claire. I'm just pretty protective of her."

"Ya think?" He made a sound that sounded like a snort. "You don't have to protect her from me, Melanie. You're better off using your energy—"

"I'll always be protective of her, Cole. That's not gonna change." I let my head fall back on the chair and looked up toward the ceiling, absently staring at an obviously lost and confused fly, dazed and disoriented. I felt his pain. "Other than the suggestions that have already been thrown in the ring, I can't think of anyone else who would go through this trouble to frame me. And why they'd want to."

"Melanie, there's something none of us have even thought about. Or maybe you have but haven't mentioned it. But there's one name we haven't thrown in the ring yet."

"Who's that?"

"Your mother was here when the shooting through your window happened, right?"

"Yeah." My eyebrows rose quizzically. "But she was here all day and in the kitchen making a drink when it happened."

"So you said. But what if it was meant to scare her and had nothing to do with you at all? We've already determined the person most likely missed you on purpose. So what if it was about her?"

"I've already thought of that. The part about it being about Violet and not me."

"And?"

"I think it's a good possibility."

"Fifty-fifty chance anyway."

"Good one, genius," I said and shook my head. "I just don't know how that connects to Gina's murder."

"I don't know that yet."

I thought about what he was saying. The truth of the matter was, I had thought about her having access to my room. If she was snooping, it was possible she could have found my gun. But what purpose would she have had in taking it, much less using it? And granted, she wasn't much of a mother to speak of, but even she wouldn't set me up like this. As for whom the shot was intended, me or Violet, well...I would love nothing more than for this to not be about me. And since Violet was gone now, she wouldn't be in danger anymore.

"Maybe that's why she really left," Cole said as if he were reading my mind.

"Uh-uh." That part I was sure of. "Violet has always had the wanderlust bug and can't stay in the same place for too long before she gets restless. She was pouting because she wasn't getting her way here and I wouldn't let her manipulate me."

"You know that for a fact?"

"Yes." I was certain. "Besides, she had a job come up."

"What does she do?"

"Actress."

"Hmmm. I've never seen her in anything and I watch a lot of movies."

"I haven't either. They're obviously small screen B movies."

"Yeah, maybe."

But I could tell he wasn't convinced and was thinking something he didn't want to share. I could almost see the wheels churning in his head. But when it came to Violet, I didn't want him to share it. I was done giving up even one more moment of my time thinking about her. Especially now when I needed to use my time for thinking of more important things. Like how I was going to get myself out of this mess.

"What time are you meeting with Detective Wescott tomorrow?"

"Nine."

"Are you going to give him the glove?"

"You mean the glove I didn't find?" I gave him a tired smile. I felt like my tank was empty and I was running on fumes. "Are you going to say something if I don't?"

"That's a question I'd rather not answer, to be honest. Not tonight."

"What do you think will happen if I do?"

"It could go either way."

"Are you going to say something?" I asked him again.

"You asking me not to is—" he sighed and shook his head. "I can't say what I'm going to do. I don't know yet. I need time to process."

"Why don't you do exactly that? Take time to process. Like two days."

"Melanie—"

"I know, I know," I said, too tired to be irritated, too wired to be calm. My emotions were in direct conflict and were waging a war inside of me. "Not giving me an answer one way or another is a cop-out. Just sayin'."

"Probably is," he said. "But if I do the wrong thing Claire would never forgive me. I just need to figure out if it's worth putting my job on the line for."

"If it's worth putting your job on the line for?"

"Yes, it. I don't mean Claire, She's worth it, hands down. Compromising my values and the oath I took isn't."

"You're really sweet on her, huh?" I shook my head slowly.

"I've never met anyone like her in my life. That's why I'm telling you, I'm the last person you need to protect her from."

"Famous last words." I narrowed my eyes at him, trying my hardest to appear tough, too tired to put forth the energy. "Don't ever hurt her, Mahoney, or I'll make sure you're through."

"You probably don't want to make jokes like that at a time like this," he said.

"Now you're telling me what to do?"

"Just sayin'."

"You're not recording this are you?"

"No. It'd be your word against mine."

"And mine holds so much weight these days."

Chapter 20

ALL OF US ENDED up staying at my house for the night and I had to admit, despite everything going on, and not going to bed until two o'clock in the morning, sleeping in my own bed, knowing I was safe, I slept better than I had in weeks. I left the house at 8:30, but before I left I woke up Cole to let him know so he could let Claire and Rubie know when they woke up. I quietly let myself out, locking the door behind me.

The air was crisp and fresh this morning, the frost sparkling on the ground like millions of diamonds scattered on its surface. I inhaled deeply and filled my lungs with the freshness that one could only find in the country, outside of the polluted city limits. There truly was something magical about being away from the hustle and bustle of daily living and being one with nature. I was just looking forward to the day it was just one, me, with nature again, with no other unwelcomed visitors.

In my hurry and preoccupation of getting out to the woods last evening, I had forgotten to put my car in the garage. I dug out my ice scraper from under the driver's seat, scraped the light layer of frost from my windows, then scraped Cole's and Rubie's as well. It felt good to be doing something so ordinary, so common, when things felt anything but ordinary and common.

I had on my typical and common jeans and black high-heeled boots, a common plaid shirt, and my common black leather jacket. Everything as frustratingly common as I could make it, hoping to trick my mind into believing it was just another ordinary day. Simply starting my day by taking a shower in my own shower felt like paradise.

Windows scraped, I took my travel cup filled with my coconut chai tea from the roof of my car where I had set it just a few short moments ago that in some ways felt like hours ago. My sense of time had been all shaken up and turned upside down over the course of the last few days.

As I drove into town, I kept my radio off and enjoyed the drive in nothing but sheer silence, just me and my tea and the road. And the thoughts that tumbled through my head as quickly as I tried to out-drive them. Moisture hung in the air as a hazy layer of fog, making everything appear like a dream or a scene from a movie. One with a happy ending would be nice. As I came up to the Mississippi river, the fog was so heavy I had to turn on my headlights and fog lamps to see anything at all, and as soon as I passed the river, the fog dissipated to nearly none. There was still ice along the edges where the river didn't flow very fast, and in a matter of a week or so, that, too, would be gone. Would I be around to see it? I had to wonder, the way things were going.

It was nine fifteen when I pulled into the police department parking lot. The coffee I had stopped to fill my travel mug with on my way, the one that had only moments before held the last of my chai tea, was worth being fifteen minutes late. The last thing I needed was caffeine to ramp up any negative energy, but keeping calm hadn't been at the forefront of my mind when I filled up. Hopefully being revved up on caffeine would help clear any brain fog.

I grasped my cup from the cup holder and sat still for just a moment, taking a few deep, calming breaths before opening my door to the unknown. What could Detective Wescott possibly ask me about that I would have any useful information? Would it be an interview, as he claimed, or an ambush? Was I being set up? I touched my hand lightly against my pocket where I'd hidden the bagged glove, yet undecided whether I was going to give it to him or not. I would see how the interview went and test it out. Finally, I forced myself out of the car and walked on legs that felt like Jell-O to the front doors of the police station.

Detective Wescott was half leaning and half sitting at a desk talking to another detective, his head tilted back slightly as he found something amusing. Sure glad he's finding something so funny right now because I sure didn't. The moment he saw me his amusement came to an abrupt halt. In its place was a look of something resembling pity. Or was it kindness and I'd simply forgotten what kindness looked like coming from a stranger. I knew one thing for certain, if this continued, he would no longer be a stranger, but all too familiar. A kind of familiar I could do without. And handsome as he may be, I was more than happy to keep him a stranger.

"Detective?" I extended my hand.

"Ms. Hogan, thank you for coming in." He shook my hand and gestured for me to follow him, this time in his office instead of an interview room. Maybe Sunday was the day to come in if you were being questioned in a homicide. At least the level of comfort elevated to a personal office instead of an impersonal and cold interrogation room. "Have a seat," he offered, indicating one of the two chairs that sat opposite his side of the desk. To my surprise, he picked up a notebook, mini tape recorder, and pen, and sat in the other chair rather than behind his desk.

"Yours?" I said.

"Excuse me?"

"The picture of the boy on your desk. Is he yours?"

His eyes warmed as he looked at the photo I was inquiring about. "Yes, he's mine. Do you mind if I record this?" All business again.

"Depends on what you're going to be asking me and recording." He stopped himself from pressing the record button, the motion started before even waiting for my response. "I'm kidding. Just a shot at humor—a stab at—" I stuttered, my face suddenly burning hot. "Forget it," I mumbled. "No, I don't mind if you record it." I sucked in a deep breath, exhaled slowly, and looked up as he was reaching for the tape recorder, and just in time to see an amused half smile.

"So we've identified the body that was found out by your house. Her name is Gina Sorrell."

"I heard."

"You did?" He looked momentarily surprised. "Oh, I suppose you did. Officer Mahoney?"

"Yes, sir."

"That's unnecessary," he smiled.

"What is?" We'd just barely started and already I did something wrong. This was clearly not going well.

"The whole sir thing. If you keep that up I'll have to call you ma'am."

"Detective." I felt relief, despite how brief and small, it was still relief. And I welcomed it.

"Tell me about your relationship with Gina."

"We didn't have a relationship. She rented space from Claire and me for her manicure business."

"How well did you know her?"

"Not well at all."

He frowned and looked confused. "How long had she been there?"

"About a year. Give or take."

"And you didn't know her very well? I know where I get my hair cut the gals are always having a grand time laughing, talking…"

"We do, too. The rest of us, that is. Gina was never one to join in."

"Did she pay her rent on time? Or did she do or say anything that would have made you—"

"Want to kill her?" I asked, to the point, an edge to my tone that surprised even me. "No, Detective. She didn't."

"I was actually going to ask you if she did or said anything that would have led you to believe someone was upset with her or that she was in trouble."

Again, I felt my cheeks flush. "Sorry," I mumbled, looking down briefly to brush an invisible piece of something from my jeans. I crossed one leg over the other, exhibiting a sense of confidence I didn't feel. "Uh, no. Claire and I thought of that, too, and were trying to remember her clients, if we heard something that would trigger concern. But none of us could come up with anything."

"What about the other staff? Anyone have any grudges?"

"No."

"Feel free to take a few minutes to think about it."

"I don't have to. No one on my staff is a murderer." Were they?

"I'm sure you don't think they are. If you knew they were, you wouldn't keep them there, now, would you? Do you have background checks done on your people?"

"My people?" I said. "You make it sound like I'm a mob boss. There are no my people, Detective. I have contract employees. Nothing more, nothing less."

"Do you do background checks on them?"

He was great at ignoring my sarcasm, thank goodness. The last thing I needed was to give him a reason to go out of his way to find me guilty.

"No. I don't do backgrounds. As long as they pay...well, perhaps I should."

"How did Gina pay you?"

"Cash." I'd never given that a second thought until now. "Always, as a matter of fact. And nothing other than cash from the first month's rent."

"Do you find that odd?"

"I didn't. But, yes, now I do. In fact, she worked part-time at best and didn't have another job that I knew about. Makes me wonder how she made enough to live on."

He asked a few more questions, most of which I couldn't answer since they were relative to Gina's life, until he closed his notepad and clicked off the tape recorder. Apparently I wasn't much help after all. At least he wasn't cuffing me. Guess I could thank my lucky stars for that much.

As soon as I stood to leave, he reminded me once more not to leave town.

"I won't," I said. "In fact, I'll be going back home to my house now that the window is fixed."

"Do you think that's a good idea?"

"Why wouldn't it be?"

"For safety reasons, maybe you shouldn't stay there yet."

"Detective, I'm flattered." I said with a touch of cynicism. "If you're worried about my safety you must have even the smallest hunch that I'm innocent, as much as you would like to believe otherwise."

"As a police officer, it's my duty to help prevent crime and disorder. Even if that means protecting the very people who create it."

Jerk. I stood to leave, grateful I was still a free woman. At least for right now. As I walked out of the dank precinct into the brisk air, I slid my hands in my pockets. Huh...I had completely forgotten about the glove. It was a secret I decided to carry with me for a just a little bit longer.

Chapter 21

WHEN I GOT BACK to my house, Rubie's car was still there but Cole's was gone. That Claire would have left Rubie there alone surprised me. And if Rubie wasn't involved, would she stay there alone given the circumstances? Maybe Rubie was due the benefit of the doubt, and she was simply being a trooper given she was clearly out of her element. But could I afford to give her, or anyone, the benefit of the doubt?

I slammed my car door shut and glanced down at my watch. Almost eleven o'clock already. I had been gone for over two hours. Claire and Rubie were both sitting at the kitchen table deep in conversation over a cup of coffee. Conversation that stopped immediately when I entered the room.

"Wow! Could you guys be any more obvious?"

"What do you mean?" Claire asked, her innocence exaggerated.

I dropped my chin and looked at her, straight-faced. "Really? You're seriously going to play that way?" My pulse ticked up a notch. I prayed Claire hadn't told her she'd been mentioned as a suspect.

"We weren't saying anything bad, Melanie. Honest." Rubie said. "We were just talking about the year you've had."

I poured a cup of coffee and plopped my butt down in a chair at the table with them. "It hasn't been boring, that's for sure."

"Bet you're wishing for boring again, huh?" Claire asked, her brown eyes oozing with gentleness.

"As long as it's on this side of the jail bars. Rubie, could you run up to my room and grab my hair brush?" Claire cocked her head to the side and squinted at me.

"Sure," Rubie said and left the kitchen.

"What's that about?" Claire whispered.

"I'm surprised Cole left you alone here if he's suspecting her." I jerked my head toward the stairs.

"Trust me, he didn't want to. I made him. And then he didn't without making a big deal about the fact that if anything happens while he's gone there will be hell to pay. I'm telling you, Mel, it was embarrassing."

"Better to be embarrassed than—"

"You can't tell me you think she's guilty," Claire said in a harsh whisper.

"I don't want to think that, no. And I don't think I do. But—"

Rubie breezed back into the kitchen, laying my hairbrush on the table in front of me. "Here ya go."

"Thanks." I started running the brush through my hair to make my request look legit.

"Let's go do something fun today to keep your mind off of all this—this stuff." Claire raised her arm and circled it around the room.

"I don't think I can, Claire. I really need to—"

"Melanie," she interrupted, "there's nothing else you can do right now. In fact, it's best that you don't do anything for the time being. Anything that relates to your case, that is."

"That's not true. That I can't do anything right now. I can pray for a miracle."

"You can pray while we're doing something fun. Something that'll provide a healthy outlet for all the fear and anxiety."

"Fear? What fear? I have no fear. I'm fearless!" My voice vibrated with exaggerated, false bravado.

"We get it. And your nose is growing, Pinocchio."

"Let's go shopping!" Rubie said with enthusiasm that I met with contempt.

"I really hate shopping."

"Seriously? How can anyone hate shopping? That's the craziest thing I've ever heard."

"Suggesting shopping to Mel is the craziest thing I've ever heard," Claire said.

"How can anyone hate shopping?" Rubie repeated.

"Easy," I said.

"I got it!" Claire said, slapping her hand down on the table. She stood and nearly tipped over her coffee cup. "Put on your hiking shoes, girls. We're going geocaching!"

"Huh?"

I laughed. "Rubie, you've clearly never heard of geocaching. Girl, it's time you learn."

"What is it?"

"Grab a pair of my tennis shoes. You're about to find out."

"Tennis shoes?" The way her face scrunched up you'd think I had just told her we were going to go snake hunting. "Tell me this has nothing to do with bugs. Please?" she pleaded.

"Can't tell you that." I smiled at her and went to fetch her a pair of my sneakers.

"What about Claire? She'll never fit into your tiny shoes."

"I keep a pair here just for this reason," Claire answered. "I just can't believe how easily you agreed. I was quickly preparing my argument."

"Claire, you're kinda girly, if this had to do with bugs, you wouldn't do it, right?"

I laughed and tossed the sneakers at her. "Stop being a little girl and get a move on."

Dressed for the fun, we piled into Rubie's car since mine only sits two.

"Since I don't know what we're doing, you can drive, Mel." Rubie threw me her keys.

"I'll navigate," Claire said and high-fived me before getting in.

Rubie folded herself into the back seat. Claire took her iPhone out and began the process.

"Okay, Claire, tell me where I'm driving."

"I still have absolutely no idea what we're doing. Someone fill me in."

I looked at Rubie in the rearview mirror. She was perched on the edge of the seat, holding on for dear life as I sped out of the driveway.

"Geocaching is where you use your phone to navigate to specific GPS coordinates and find a geocache hidden there."

"And I ask again, what's a geocache? Am I just supposed to know what that is?"

"They're hidden containers found by using the coordinates looked up on your iPhone."

"What's in 'em?"

"Anything and everything."

"Do you keep 'em when you find 'em?"

"Nope."

"Then what's the point? And what do you mean by anything and everything?"

I glanced at her to see her waiting with bated breath for my answer.

"People can put anything in them at all, but they always contain a log book or sheet for the player to log their find. It's a free treasure hunt. And who can pass up a treasure hunt, especially when it's free?"

"That remains to be seen." The skepticism in her voice was unmistakable.

"Just wait. You'll be hooked," I said. How could she not? At least, I hoped she would be. How could *anyone* not be, for that matter?

"So do you take what you find?"

"No. I told you, you don't get to keep your find. Now no more questions. Just enjoy the learning experience and watch the pros." I grinned at her in the mirror. I had already almost forgotten about my woes. Almost. "Claire, where are we going?" I glanced over at her to see her studying her iPhone. Seconds later she was leading me to the treasure.

We arrived at the site of the geocache, Rubie still confused about what we were doing. Heck, she wasn't just confused, but utterly lost about why we were doing this at all.

"Think of it as shopping, Rubie," I offered, trying to help her enjoy the experience. "But instead of shopping for new things, you're shopping for other people's treasures."

"Why would I want someone else's treasures? I'd rather just go buy my own."

"Quit being a party-pooper."

"We're trying to help Melanie get her mind off of her—situation," Claire said. "Play along and pretend you're enjoying it." She reached in the back seat, patted Rubie's knee and gave her a wink.

Seeing Claire's kindness towards Rubie made me think about Violet, for some Godforsaken reason. Why, I had no idea, since kind and Violet don't belong anywhere near each other. Perhaps there was no logical explanation, my mind just had a will of its own, so to speak. It was determined to linger there. We were on our way to the second location when something became crystal clear. How could I not have seen this before? I pulled the car over and turned in my seat to face Claire.

"Why are you stopping?" she asked. "This isn't the location."

"You won't believe what I just thought of." I felt breathless from my revelation.

"Do tell," Rubie begged. "Maybe it will be something I can understand instead of this geode catching stuff."

"Geocaching," I absently corrected her, glancing in the backseat and then back at Claire. "I knew I was missing something but couldn't figure out what it was. I've been doing mental gymnastics trying every which way I could to figure out what I was missing." Claire was silent, her eyes pleading with me to hurry and spit it out. "Do you remember when I came into the salon after dropping off Violet at the hotel?"

"Of course."

Rubie was sitting on the edge of the back seat, leaning forward to catch every word I was saying. In fact, she was leaning in so close I could almost feel her breath.

"Okay, now this may be a long shot, but hear me out. When you were asking me about Violet, Gina made some vague mention of my mother. I've never told her Violet was my mother. In fact, you and Jack were the only people who knew that. Rubie didn't even know. Gina's comment about my mother being in from California seemed odd, but now it's making sense. When Gina started working at the salon and filled out her contract, her prior address, where she moved here from, said California."

"California's an enormous state."

"I get that. But her being from California, and somehow knowing Violet was my mother, and that she's from California—guys, I think they knew each other!"

"But how?" Rubie asked. "They clearly don't run in the same circles. Violet's a movie star and Gina's a nail tech at a little salon in a small town."

"She's hardly a movie star," I argued. "I've never seen her in a single movie. Or even a commercial for that matter. She's a movie star wanna be." I looked at one, then the other, seeing that they still weren't following me. "If she's not a movie star, then where's she getting all of her money? Something tells me she's into something, and it's not on the up and up. Not only that, but Gina can't possibly make enough from working at A Cut Above part time to live on. She's getting money from somewhere else."

"But what does that have to do with Gina's death?"

"Those two were involved in something, and somewhere in the past, they were involved in it together. I'd bet money on that."

Claire's eyes about bugged out of her head. She gasped and grabbed my arm, practically cutting off my circulation and I winced. "That's it! Mel, maybe that's exactly it! They were involved in something that involved a lot of money. Cole says money and drugs are at the root of most crime they deal with. Was Violet involved with drugs?"

"Like I would know anything about her. But I know someone who might."

"You're grandmother?" Rubie asked.

"Yup."

"If she owes money," Claire said, "those guys can be ruthless in trying to collect. They'll stop at nothing."

"Maybe it was some kind of sick love triangle," Rubie suggested. "Maybe they were involved with the same man."

"Or the same John," I said.

"You don't think your mother was a prostitute?" Rubie asked, her jaw hanging open.

"I would hope not. But I don't know that for sure." I shuddered at the thought of it.

"If it was some sort of love-gone-wrong thing, it doesn't seem like Gina and Violet would attract the same type of man. First off because Violet is so much older than Gina, and second, they just seem like they run in completely different circles," Claire said.

"Well, opposites attract," I said and looked at Claire, smiling. "Look at us." We were all silent for a moment, concocting different scenarios in our heads. Finally, I said, "That shot through my window? Ladies, that was meant to scare Violet. Not me. They were professionals, all right. Professional money collectors. I bet they were collecting on a drug debt." I took a minute to digest the revelation, trying to piece things together into a scenario that would make sense when I presented it to Detective Wescott. "This little treasure hunt was more successful than I'd ever hoped when we set out. We found the mother lode."

Chapter 22

I STARTED THE CAR and headed back to the house. I had to change, get Claire back to her house, then head over to my grandmother's house. I had some questions I needed to ask her about Violet. Maybe it would help me put some more of the puzzle pieces together. I needed something solid before I met with Detective Wescott.

Rubie gathered her things and headed out to do the shopping she'd wanted to do in the first place. I felt a sharp pang of guilt as I watched her bounce out the door thrilled to be on her way to something that would make her a whole lot happier than the happiness we had attempted, unsuccessfully, to force on her. I think it was safe to say she wouldn't be geocaching with us anymore. But I had to give her an A for effort and sportsmanship. I gave myself an F for trusting her.

Claire called Cole to run our theory by him while I jogged upstairs to take a shower, turning up the water as hot as I could stand it. The steam saturated and opened every pore. When my fingers began to prune, I toweled off and dressed in a pair of faded Levi's, shredded at the knees, a pair of black boots and a white sweater, the sleeves hanging halfway down my hands, only my fingers showing. I dried my hair, pulled it back into a loose braid, a few naturally wavy strands falling free around my face and against my neck. By the time I emerged from the loft and into the living room, Claire was sitting on a chair in the corner, knees tucked up and hugging a pillow.

"What'd Cole think?"

"He's impressed you thought of it and put it all together."

"He has no faith in me whatsoever," I said as I crossed to the refrigerator and took out two bottles of water, tossing one to her. "Good catch. You should find an agent."

"Ha ha. Hilarious. Cole thinks you should talk to Detective Wescott about your idea."

"I need to talk with my grandmother first. There're a couple of things I need to know. If she even knows the answers."

"He also wanted to know if you gave Wescott the glove. I told him that knowing you—"

"I didn't." I said quietly and looked away, not wanting to see what was in her eyes.

"What?" I jumped at the strength and pitch of her voice.

"You heard me right." I looked back at her, willing her to understand. "I couldn't. Not yet."

"Melanie…I thought—"

"I just need a little more time." I brought my thumb and forefinger together, separated by a wisp of air. "And Wescott admitted—sort of—that he believes in my innocence."

"He said that?"

I shrugged. "Well, not really. But one can always hope. I need to get together some proof so he knows I'm innocent."

She sighed. "I get it."

I breathed a sigh of relief. "Thank you."

"For what?"

"For always being there. For always supporting me even when you think I'm making a mistake."

"You made a tremendous breakthrough today. Now if you can find any validity to it, you'll have won the war."

"The battle. The war will be harder to win, I'm afraid."

"So I have to ask—what made you think of it? The whole drug thing?" Claire's voice sounded amazed and exhausted at the same time.

"When I was explaining to Rubie about geocaching, telling her about the GPS process and finding the geocache—well, it made me think of the whole geo part of the word meaning geography, which made me think of California, and then finding the cache, which made me think—well, it's just how my mind works. Each thought plays off the other, sometimes making absolutely no sense to anyone but me."

"Well, let's hope it pans out."

"Yeah, like gold. Hope is what I'm riding on these days."

I dropped Claire off at her house where she'd left her car the evening before when Cole drove her out to my house. From there I headed over to Nana's house, having called on my way to let her know I'd be there. I hoped that if she knew I was coming, we could cook dinner together. Those were the times we had our best conversations.

I let myself in and was thrilled when I smelled something chocolaty wafting from the kitchen.

"Nana!" I called out. She came around the corner, her periwinkle eyes twinkling, her cheeks rosy and plumped from smiling.

"Hello, dear." She wrapped me in a hug.

"Is that smell what I think it is?"

"If you think it's brownies, gooey in the center, then, yes, it is."

I pulled back and groaned my delight as I envisioned placing a fresh hot brownie on my tongue.

I watched for a moment as she went back to preparing dinner. When I knew where and how to help, I stepped up to the counter and we fell into our routine. One we had down pat by now, each knowing what needed to be done. I've been a continual work in progress with this cooking stuff, but, at least, I was making progress. Nana had been beyond patient as she taught me how to cook, something that didn't come easily for me. But once I caught on, it was like someone uploaded an instruction manual into my brain and things clicked. Thank goodness she hadn't given up on me before that happened.

Nana was making her homemade noodles and I was grating Parmesan cheese while the red sauce was simmering on the stove.

"Did Violet have any addictive personality traits?" I asked as casually as I could muster.

"That wasn't my area of expertise, but I would say that's certainly a possibility."

Nana had been a registered nurse before she retired several years ago. "How old was she when you first started seeing the signs?"

"About sixteen, I would say."

"What kind of addictions? If you had to guess, I mean."

"I don't know, dear. Why?"

"Just curious."

"She didn't share much when she was a child. She always hid deep inside of herself somewhere. She was her own worst enemy and always seemed to fight demons."

"Do you think she was taking drugs?"

"I would hope not. But I think she probably was. Can't say as I'd be surprised if I heard she was."

"Do you think it's possible she might still be?"

"Hmmm. I don't think so. I think she drinks a lot, though."

"I got that same feeling." I grated my Parmesan in silence for a moment. "What about other addictions?"

"She used to bet on horses, I know."

My curiosity piqued and I felt my heart race a bit. "Oh? When was that?"

She looked over at me. "Where is all of this coming from?"

"Curious."

"Melanie Hogan, I know you better than that. You're going somewhere with this."

I set the cheese grater down and wiped my hands on a towel. "I have a hunch," I admitted. "But at this time, that's all it is. When did she bet on horses?"

"About ten years ago, I believe. A couple a times a gentleman called asking if she was here. I told him no, she didn't live here, and he asked me if I would tell her when I see her that Lenny called."

"What makes you think that was related to betting on horses?"

"I could hear the racket in the background. And he didn't sound like a nice man."

I smiled. That totally sounded like something my Nana would say. I wondered exactly how a nice man sounded and how a man who wasn't nice might sound in comparison. But I chose not to ask and change the conversation over to something more positive and pleasant.

"In fact," Nana said, abruptly changing that plan, "the same man called again just the other day while your mother was here. I'll remember that voice till my last dying day."

Chapter 23

THE INVESTIGATION JUST GAINED yardage. My breath caught in my throat and I forced myself to take a few deep breaths before speaking. I didn't want to alarm her, but I needed more information.

Five deep breaths later, finally under control, I asked, "Did you give her the message? Violet."

"When I remembered, yes. But it was a day or so later."

Breathe, Melanie, breathe. "Do you remember exactly when you told her?"

"Why all the questions, dear? You didn't answer me when I asked that earlier. What are you up to?"

My mind raced faster and faster, gaining momentum. I could tell by the silence that Nana stopped what she was doing, and I could feel her looking at me. I decided the best thing to do was to just come clean and be honest with where I was going with this. I picked up the cheese grater again, toying with it, then lay it back down. I leaned against the counter, the edge resting right at my waist. I picked up the hand towel and wiped my hands again before twisting the towel around and into a ball.

"The dead woman found by my house, her name was Gina. And Gina was the manicurist at my salon. To make a long story short, I think Gina and Violet knew each other from California."

"How could that be?" She waited patiently for me to let her in on what I knew.

"Gina wasn't exactly an open or, shall we say friendly, girl. She was odd, to say the least. But she paid her rent on time every month, in cash—"

"That's odd, isn't it? Who pays cash for something like that anymore these days?"

"Exactly. That's all part of her secretiveness. Anyway, Gina made some remark about Violet being my mother and was curious if she was going to stop by the salon to meet everyone. No one knew Violet was my mother except Claire and Jack. Not even Rubie until after that."

"I'm not so sure I like where this is going." I watched as an unusual frown formed. "Continue."

"Well, you and I have talked before how we've never seen Violet in any movies, even though she claims to have landed all these big roles—or at least been in the running for them. Either she has the worst luck in the world and misses out on every single part, or she's full of baloney. My guess would be—"

"—she's full of baloney," Nana finished for me. "So where does the part about Gina and Violet—"

"I'm getting to that. Violet seemed to have very expensive taste and high-end clothing and cosmetics for not being a successful movie star as she claimed to be. Add to that the fact that the police think the person who shot through my window was a professional. Which, by the way, explains *why* he missed me rather than *how* he could have missed me. He missed me intentionally.

Because I don't think I was his target at all. I think it was Violet."

"What in the world has that girl gotten herself into?"

Her voice was barely more than a whisper. Worry lines furrowed her brows. Despite everything Violet had done to her, I had to remember that she was still Nana's daughter. I wondered if I should have just kept all the details to myself until I had solid proof rather than worry her based on mere suspicion. Though I had to admit my suspicions were getting stronger as there became more of a solid foundation for them to build upon. I was convinced I had just crossed the line from lukewarm to warm. At the very least to warm. "If Gina and Violet were in the drug trafficking business, that explains the shot through my window and Gina's murder. I would bet this Lenny guy is to blame."

I saw Nana swallow, her eyes reflecting the fear that housed itself in her. I made a point of backing off from discussing it any further and attempted to distract Nana by filling her in on Claire and Cole, telling her about Rubie and how she was the perfect complement to mine and Claire's friendship, how even Jack seemed to like her. And for Jack to like someone he hardly knows speaks volumes. The only part I left out was Cole's suspicion of Rubie. And mine, as much as I strived to believe otherwise. Until the last five minutes, that is. My suspicion had just taken a whole new turn.

"Just be careful, dear," she'd warned me gently.

"Of what?"

"I just don't want you to find out she's hiding something like this Gina girl."

My stomach flip-flopped. Nana had her doubts, too? "Gina and Rubie couldn't be more opposite." Could they? "Besides, you know me, Nana. I've lived my entire life within the confines of careful. And look where it's gotten me."

"Smack dab in the middle of everything that's not careful. Or safe."

"I'll be fine." I walked around the center island in the kitchen and gave her a hug. "Don't worry so much." But I'd be lying if her concern about Rubie didn't have me worrying again. Should I take it as a sign that first Cole, now Nana, raised the question about Rubie?

"Someday when you have a child I'll remember to tell you that."

I pulled my attention back to her. "Huh?"

"Telling me not to worry. I'll remind you of that when you have children of your own."

"You're going to be waiting an awfully long time for that. Unless Claire decides she wants to give me Syd."

"Sounds like you might wait an awfully long time." She chuckled. "Come on, let's eat."

We carried the fixings to the table and sat down in our usual chairs and said grace. I unfolded my cloth napkin, which she insisted on using for every meal, not just special occasions, and placed it on my lap. I picked up the noodles and began scooping some on her plate and then my own.

"Do you s'pose that's why she was on her computer all the time? If she wasn't watching those silly TV shows with her martinis, she was on her computer with her martinis."

"I don't know, Nana, but I'm going to find out." I swirled my fork, gathering up some spaghetti noodles. "I'm not sure you ever really told me," I said, "but when did you tell Violet about the call from Lenny?"

"Hmm, let me think." I watched as she mentally replayed the past few days. "Well, now that I think about it, it was the day she said she was leaving here."

Aha! My heart skipped a beat. I had officially crossed the line from warm to hot.

Chapter 24

I STAYED THE NIGHT at my grandmother's house again. By the time we finished eating and I helped her with a few things that needed to be done around the house, it was late and I wasn't ready to go back to my house in the dark on my first night back there. Especially knowing the shooter was still out there somewhere and whether I was the intended target. Next time he may choose not to miss and I'd rather not find that out. Besides that, after running everything past Nana about the Violet and Gina theory, I know it was a comfort to her I stay with her.

I got up in the morning before she did, a rare occurrence to be sure, and started the coffee maker. Coffee brewing, making the comforting sounds as it percolated, I tied my robe tight around me and went outside in my slippers to pick up the paper from the drive. I pulled the paper from the cold frosted plastic wrapper, poured a cup of coffee and sat at the kitchen table, eagerly opening the pages to see if it said anything about Gina. As far as I knew, she didn't have any family, so there probably wouldn't be an obituary unless the funeral home took it upon themselves to write one. And if that was the case, there wouldn't be anything yet, because the body was still being held at the coroner's office after the autopsy and hadn't been released yet. I flipped through the pages, expertly and thoroughly scanning each to see if there was any mention of the shooting at all. Finding nothing, disappointment settled in my gut. I was counting on the media telling me more about the crime I was a person of interest in since I obviously didn't have any first-hand knowledge of how it went down. Although I was getting closer.

I folded the paper back in its original shape, making it look like I hadn't even touched it. No need letting on to my grandmother how eager I was to rifle through it. I slipped out of my robe, tossing it onto my bed as I passed my room and went to take a shower before my grandmother got up. Half an hour later I went back to the kitchen for another cup of coffee and found Nana making breakfast.

"Good morning, Mary Sunshine," she said without turning around.

I smiled at her pet name for me. When I was little I used to tell her, *My name is not Mary, Nana, it's Melanie.* And she would softly laugh.

"Either your hearing is far too good or I'm far too loud. How did you know I was here?"

"I could feel you." She turned, came over to me and gave me a brief hug, going back to her business of making breakfast at the counter.

"You sure slept late this morning. It's 7:30 already."

"I've been awake for a while."

"Oh, I see," I grinned. "Waiting for breakfast in bed were you?"

"Praying for breakfast in bed." She swatted my behind as I walked by her. "What time do you have to be to work?"

"Same as always. My first appointment is at 9:00 but I have some paperwork to do earlier if I can."

"Well, sit your skinny butt down in that chair and eat something first. No one leaves my house hungry."

"Ain't that the truth." She slid a plate in front of me and I took a bite of eggs, followed by a sip of coffee. "I'm going to call Detective Wescott today. I want to see if he has time to meet with me so I can test out my theory on him."

"Careful so you don't incriminate yourself."

Her statement caught me off guard and I wondered if she somehow knew about the glove that remained hidden in my jacket pocket. "I can't incriminate myself, because I've done nothing wrong." *Except withhold evidence in a homicide investigation.* The thought was wrought with guilt.

After eating half of my eggs, a piece of toast with her fabulous homemade strawberry jam, and half a cup of coffee, I put on my jacket and headed for the door, giving her a quick hug and peck on the cheek.

"See ya later," I called over my shoulder.

"Tonight?"

I heard the hope in her voice, stopped, and smiled at her.

"You'd have me living here if you could."

"And what's wrong with that?"

I shook my head then blew her a kiss. "Absolutely nothing. But I have a home."

"But—"

"I'll call and let you know. Love you!" I called as I shut the door behind me.

The morning was absolutely beautiful. The days were getting longer, and that in itself was marvelous. Added daylight, warmer temps...life was good. Well, it would be again soon. I was going to make sure of it.

I pulled up to the salon and saw Cole's car parked beside Claire's again. I felt a sinking feeling in the pit of my stomach as I got a feeling of deje'vu. Lately, seeing their cars together in front of the salon hadn't been a positive thing and carried with it bad news.

I opened the door to the two of them standing there hugging, Claire's unmistakable laugh easing my tension a little.

"What's going on?" I asked, not really wanting the answer. My stomach was a tense ball of mess. Had he come to give me a heads up he went forward and 'fessed up about the glove?

"Nothing, why?" Cole answered too quickly.

"Because lately when you're around it's to give me bad news."

"Ouch! That's harsh."

"So nothing's new? You don't have anything to tell me about the investigation?"

"No. I'm just here seeing my lovely girlfriend." He studied me, his eyes bearing down on mine. "Anything you want to tell me about the investigation?"

"If I see you moving a cot in the back room I'm putting my foot down," I said, ignoring his question. "Don't you have crime to fight out on the street, Officer Mahoney?"

"I figure if I follow you around I've got it covered."

I made a face at him and stuck out my tongue, feeling every bit the five-year-old that I probably looked like. No wonder Sydney and I got along so well.

"Claire's told me you've come up with quite the theory about connecting some of the stuff going on."

"Yup. Since she's already told you, I won't tell you again."

"Detective Wescott is going to think you're trying to take his job."

"If he would do it, I wouldn't have to," I said. "Speaking of the fine detective, I'm going to see if I can meet with him today. I want to let him in on what I've figured out for him."

"Go easy on the guy. A man's job is his identity."

I stared at him speechless. "You're kidding, right? Go easy on him? I'm the one they're trying to pin a murder on." I started walking to the office and stopped to look at him. "Besides, that was a sexist thing to say. Just sayin'." I let him think I was serious just for the fun of it. Cole was the least sexist man I think I'd ever known. Except maybe Jack. "So guess what Nana told me?" I stopped and turned to look at Claire, continuing without waiting for her to answer. "She suspects Violet used to take drugs, we all know she drinks too much, and she said Violet used to have a thing about betting on horses. How much you wanna make a bet she still is?"

"That was a terrible play on words," Cole said.

"Wasn't intentional. But it was good if I have to say so myself." I shrugged and turned to go back to the office. "What do you guys think?" I called over my shoulder.

"It that's the case, where does Gina factor in?" Claire asked.

"I don't know that part yet. But I will. Soon."

As soon as I dumped my things on an empty chair in the office and sat down at the desk I called Detective Wescott. I had to know when he could work me in so I could figure out how to reschedule a client or two, or if

Claire, Connie, or Rubie could squeeze one of mine in for me. I was in for a surprise, though, when he answered on the first ring, said he was in the area on an entirely different matter (something I was trying to decide if I believed or if he was secretly watching my every move trying to trap me in some way), and offered to drop by the salon. Either way, it worked better for me so I didn't have to mess with my schedule—or anyone else's.

I was just finishing up the paperwork when I heard the door open and Claire's laugh. Cole must be leaving. I stood, put my arms above my head and stretched long, bending to each side. I had to get some sleep tonight. My eyes were closed, and I was enjoying the feeling of every muscle being stretched to capacity, when a deep voice interrupted my moment.

"Ms. Hogan."

A small scream escaped my lips as my eyes flew open. Detective Wescott stood in the doorway, an amused grin plastered on his face. "A heads up woulda been nice, Claire," I called to the front of the salon.

"No sleep last night?"

"I slept fine, thank you." I brought myself back to center. I motioned to the chair across from the desk. "Go ahead and move my things onto the floor and have a seat." He began reaching in the inside pocket of his leather jacket and I instinctively put my hand up and he immediately stopped mid-reach. "No. No recording, please. Off the record, as they say."

"I was actually getting a cough drop."

That stupid amused smile again, ever so slight. I'm glad he thought this was so funny, because this could be a nugget of information that could save my hide and keep me on the outside of those restrictive bars. Besides, orange isn't my color unless it was exactly the right shade. And whichever shade prison jumpsuits were wasn't the right shade. I sat down and took the briefest moment to put all my thoughts in order and began.

When I finished spilling every detail of the ball of yarn I'd carefully untangled, I watched closely as he seemed to study me. A little too closely, actually, and I felt myself squirm. *He thinks I'm plum crazy.* I was furiously wishing I could reverse time and make this conversation to not have happened. Maybe I was having a dream and I would wake up in my bed, none of this having happened at all.

"I'm impressed."

Huh? "Impressed about what? That I could come up with something? That I'm capable of—"

"It's a darn good theory and gives me a lot of information I didn't have."

"It-it is?" I could have kicked myself for stammering like a little girl who had just gotten her daddy's approval. Not that he was near old enough to be my father, but all the same. Coming from the one who was in charge of digging up information on a case that could determine my entire future, I was beyond relieved that he didn't think I was crazy.

"Yes, it is," he confirmed. "And online betting is alive and well in California. There're five racetracks that I know of in the state. And those are just the ones I know about, so there are probably a lot more. They have off-track betting, too, so she wouldn't necessarily have to be at a track to bet. Makes it just that much easier for her. My guess is if she spent a lot of time with her computer, as your grandmother suggested, the whole thing makes even more sense."

"I gotta be honest, I think the person who shot through my window and the one who shot Gina are the same person."

"I differ with you on that one."

"How so?"

"The person who shot Gina was an amateur."

That conclusion changed again, I guess. "Well, it certainly wasn't me then, detective." I was grateful to see a trace of a smile. No matter how small of a success it was. He stood to leave. "Umm...wait. Detective?"

"There's more?"

"Well—kind of." I paused wanting to be sure I was doing the right thing. Conscience won. I walked over to where my jacket hung on the coat rack and reached in the pocket pulling out a plastic bag. "I did some investigating of my own in the woods and found this."

He turned it over in his hand and shrugged. "A white glove?"

"Uh-huh. It was near where the body—Gina—was found, and I picked it up."

"Do you know whose it is?"

I felt a lump in my throat and swallowed. "I do."

He waited. "Well, whose is it?"

"It's kind of mine."

I could see the wheels churning in his brain and half expected to see smoke coming from his ears. "Kind of yours? Either it is or it isn't. Which is it?" His head turned slightly to the side.

"Yes."

"Yes, what, Melanie? It's yours or it isn't yours?"

"It's mine." I could feel heat rising up my neck and face and averted my gaze from his for a split moment before making myself look at him again. I filled him in on the glove mystery. "I'm kind of hoping you could use your investigative prowess to find someone else's DNA on it."

He frowned. "I certainly hope so, Ms. Hogan. For your sake and mine." He started for the door, stopping before he went around the corner and turned back toward me. "I realize you have someone waiting on you and you have to work right now, but keep in mind I'm going to have to speak with you further. Especially now. And Melanie?"

"I know," I sighed, "don't leave town."

Chapter 25

WHEN I FINALLY REGAINED my composure, I went out in the salon where all the girls were busy. Connie and her client were engaged in a serious conversation about which was better, Jenny Craig or Weight Watchers, Claire was listening intently as her client was telling her something of obvious importance, straining to hear above the white noise of the blow dryer, and Rubie was the one doing the talking in her duo. My client, Mrs. Anderson, was pretending to read a magazine.

I walked over to her and extended my hand, reaching for hers, taking it warmly in mine as she offered it to me. "I'm so sorry to keep you waiting, Mrs. Anderson. I hope it wasn't too much of an imposition."

She struggled to her feet, smoothing her shirt over her plump belly and leaned near my ear. "Honey, if you tell me who that gorgeous man was that came out from your office, I'll forgive you for keeping me waiting. Woooeee!" She exclaimed, dramatically fanning her face.

I laughed at her and felt a surge of gratitude for this crazy place that kept me from going crazy. Ironic how that works.

Mrs. Anderson was busy talking my ear off as I colored and cut her hair. I kept seeing Claire out of the corner of my eye as she tried to catch my attention, of which I was doing everything I could to avoid right now. I needed to keep things as normal as I could today, and if I looked at her I would see the concern in her eyes. I couldn't deal with that at the moment. I could, but I didn't want to. Rubie, on the other hand, was bubbling with excitement over something she was telling her client, talking more than servicing. Every time she talked, she stopped working. At this rate, she'd be working on the same client at closing. I chuckled, shook my head. Her client didn't seem to mind one iota and was clearly amused and smitten with her chatty, cute stylist.

It was twelve-thirty when we all three could take a breather. Claire offered to go next door to the grocery's deli to get us something for lunch and I brewed a fresh pot of coffee. A light spring snow was falling outside, covering the mud-covered snow banks, making everything look fresh and clean.

"So who was Mr. Hot Stuff that came out of your office this morning?" Rubie asked.

Claire obviously hadn't said anything to her. "Detective Wescott."

"Mmm-hmm," she grinned.

"I don't see it."

"Open your eyes!" she screeched. "How in the world can you not see it when you look at him?"

"All I see when I look at him is someone who's trying to pin a murder on me."

"I hate to say it, Mel, but if he wanted to pin it on you, I think he would have by now. If you ask me, he's giving you special treatment by doing everything he can to prove your innocence."

"I'm glad you're so sure," I said. "Cause I'm not."

"Pathetic, that's what you are, Melanie Hogan," she teased.

"Probably. I'm gonna go call Jack before Claire gets back with lunch."

"Tell him hi," she called behind me.

I picked up my cell phone just as it played the tune letting me know a call was coming in. "Hello?" I answered without looking at the display, assuming either Jack beat me to the call or Claire was calling with a question.

"Hello, darling."

My blood froze and I couldn't find my voice until I croaked, "Violet."

"Of course. You sound surprised. Don't you check caller ID before you answer?"

"Even if I had, it shouldn't surprise you I don't keep your number in my phone."

"What's with the attitude, darling?" Her voice hinted at irritation.

"What's with the attitude?" I gasped. She had some nerve. "I've got important things to do and people I want to talk to. You don't fit in either category."

"What on earth has gotten into you?"

"I'd tell you, but you don't stay around long enough for me to speak a complete sentence."

"Darling, don't you think you're being a little harsh?"

"Stop with the darling, Violet," I said, mimicking her drawl on darling. "What do you want, and why are you calling?"

"To speak to my daughter." Her voice was chilly. I shivered.

"She's not here."

"If this is how it's going to be—"

"You brought it all on yourself, mother dearest. Hey, Violet? I have a question for you. What movies have you been in?"

"Too many to count. I'd never be able to name them all."

She was bluffing. I could feel it. "One or two would do."

"Is this a test? What exactly do you really want to know, Melanie?"

"Been doing any betting lately Violet? Horses maybe? Or drugs?" The words were out before I even realized I spoke them.

"I don't know what's gotten into you, Melanie, but I will not sit here and take it. I called to see how you're doing and this is what I get? Well, I for one, don't have to listen to it."

"Why would you feel the need to call and see how I'm doing when you've never cared before?"

"Because you're my daughter." She sighed impatiently.

"That fact has never drawn you to call before."

"Oh for goodness sakes, Melanie. Don't be so dramatic. I've called you before."

"But never once to see how I'm doing. Only to let me know how you're doing. And to tell me how you're so successful and up for the next big part to movies that never seem to make it to the screen. Why would you call suddenly to check how I'm doing?"

"This was clearly a mistake," she said, voice icy cold. "Good-bye, Melanie. The next time I call maybe you'll be more civil."

"Actually, it wasn't a mistake at all. You just helped without even knowing it. I just have one more question."

"What would that be?"

"Do you know Gina Sorrell?"

"Who?"

"Gina Sorrell," I repeated, knowing full well that she heard me the first time. "I know you know her, Violet, so don't act like—"

"Of course, I knew her," she said, sounding almost bored. "I have to go, darling. My agent is calling." The next thing I knew, the line was dead. I guess it's true when they say that silence speaks louder than words.

Instead of calling Jack, I had another call to make first.

"Wescott," he answered, gruff, abrupt.

"Detective? Is this a bad time?"

"Ms. Hogan—no, not at all." His voice sounded weary. "I just wasn't expecting you to call. What's up? More evidence you decided to turn over?"

"Not evidence. Information. What time are you there until?"

"What time can you be here?"

"Six-thirty?"

"Well, I guess I'm here until at least six-thirty then."

Chapter 26

RUBIE AND CLAIRE WERE still working when I put my jacket on, grabbed my shoulder bag and headed for the door.

"You guys sure you don't mind closing up without me?"

"I don't know. What do ya think, Rubie? Should we let her off easy?"

"She's been a pretty good girl. I guess we could," Rubie said.

"She has not been good," Claire said. "Unless someone is with her twenty-four-seven she gets herself into some kind of trouble."

"That's true. Also, she's been keeping us out of the loop about what's going on," Rubie said.

I chuckled and shook my head. "You guys know as much as I do."

"Yeah, but you get to spend time with that attractive detective."

Leave it to Rubie to bring that into the mix.

"The same detective who's investigating me for murder. That is so not attractive." I slung my bag over my shoulder and headed out, calling over my shoulder, "I'll call you guys later."

"You better!" They called back.

The precinct was considerably quieter this evening than when I was here Friday evening. Made for a more peaceful wait but didn't provide as much free entertainment. I was looking at the wanted posters on the wall, thankful mine wasn't one of them, when I heard the deep, all too familiar voice behind me. I jumped, my hand flew to my chest, and I turned to look at him.

"A little warning would have been nice."

"No need to be so jumpy. You're in the safest place you could possibly be."

I watched a man shuffle across the floor in handcuffs arguing with someone beside him that wasn't there at all. The officer leading him looked to be all colors of bored. "Says you," I mumbled.

"Come on back to my office."

We were walking between desks and cubicles when someone stopped him. "Detective, you got just a minute?"

"Melanie, why don't you go wait in my office and I'll be right there. You remember where it's at?"

"Of course. It's only been three days," I said dryly. "I'm here more than I'm home."

Once in his office, I sat in the same chair and studied his certificates and photos that hung on the wall, many of them lopsided. This was definitely a man's office. The chaos would drive me crazy. I looked at the stacks of papers on his desk. How could he keep them straight and know where anything was? I hoped any paperwork claiming my innocence didn't get lost in those piles.

Within minutes he walked in, a frown fixed in place.

"Bad news?" I asked.

"Could be."

"About my case?"

"You could say that." He paused and looked at me as if he were deciding whether to deliver the could-be bad news. "The glove you found near the crime scene tested positive for GSR."

My heart began beating faster and harder. "You tested it for other DNA too, though, right?"

"Whatever we find, we have nothing to match it to."

"But you found someone's other than mine?"

"What news did you have for me?" He leaned back in his chair, folded his hands behind his head, and stretched his legs in front of him under the desk.

"Since the glove has been carried around in my pocket for days, it's not exactly reliable, is it? Wouldn't that be compromised or something like that?"

"Is that what you wanted to tell me?"

"No. I'm just asking." I knew I was grasping, but right now I wasn't above that.

"It's also called withholding evidence."

"Oh, yeah. I guess there's that." So much for helping my case. "Violet called and wanted to know how I was doing. She never calls me to see how I'm doing. Never has. Not once. She's called to tell me how she's doing, but not to see how I'm doing."

"And?"

I imagined he was thinking what a waste of time it was and what he could do after hours instead if this is what he stayed to hear. "The only reason she would ask me that is if she had a reason to believe I wouldn't be okay. Also," I added, "I asked if she knows Gina."

"Knows or knew?" He rocked back and forth in his chair, his hands still clasped behind his head, one ankle crossed over the other showing well-worn black combat boots.

"What?" I asked, confused.

"You asked if she knows Gina, or knew Gina?"

"I asked her if she knows Gina. I didn't want her to know that I know she's dead. That Gina's dead," I clarified, feeling immediately stupid. Obviously, it was Gina that was dead. "I just wanted to know if my suspicion of there being a connection between the two of them was correct. It was."

"How can you be sure?"

"Because she said she *knew* Gina. Violet obviously knew she was dead."

"That's why I asked if—"

"I know what you asked. And I answered." I smiled tentatively, hoping what I just delivered was the waited for package to get me off the hook.

"Good work. So I'm curious," he sat forward, rested his forearms on his desk, "why do you call your mother by her first name?"

"That has nothing to do with the case. In fact, it's a case all on its own." I heard the bitterness in my own voice.

"That bad?"

"Long story."

Chapter 27

AFTER RELAYING THE REST of my hunch about Gina and Violet, him quietly taking in and processing what I said, Detective Wescott asked if he could go to my grandmother's house to take some swabs for my mother's DNA and prints.

"Not unless you have to and you're telling me I don't have a say in the matter." He didn't say anything, just looked at me. "Please don't judge me. I'm not hiding anything. I just don't want her to be burdened with the intrusion of police work in her home. She doesn't need fingerprint dust or any other dust polluting her home from an investigation."

"You haven't told her you suspect your mother?"

"Yeah, that too." I sighed. "I kinda did, but I don't want her to have to worry about any of this unless something turns up and she needs to know more." That, and selfishly, I wanted it to stay clear of any kind of bad memories. The police being out there at all would make it feel tainted. More so, it was because of Violet and any criminal activity she might be involved in.

"Well, since she's been at your house I suppose we can go there. If that's not off limits, too, that is."

"If I say it is?"

"I'll pull rank and say we have to do it anyway."

"Hm." I pursed my lips, pretending to put great thought into it. After giving it ample time, I said, "I suppose it's decided then. Let's go." I stood and turned, obviously too fast, and tripped on the chair I'd just got up from. I felt a large, firm hand steady me just before I nose-dived and heard him chuckle.

"I meant to do that," I said. Had it been Claire, Rubie, Jack, or probably anyone else in the world, I would have laughed. But when it was in front of the person who was trying to prove my innocence, all I felt was humiliation.

"I'm sure you did." He held his hand out, motioning for me to go ahead of him. "At least, I know one thing for sure now."

"What's that?"

"That you're not perfect after all."

"Very funny." I tucked my chin down so he couldn't see the smile tugging at my lips.

I led the way and he followed in his police cruiser. What is it about knowing that a police officer is behind you that makes you extra cautious about speeds, turn signals, every law, no matter how insignificant. Heck, even jaywalking, if truth be told. And it still rattles me even when I know I'm following every law to the T.

What seemed like hours later, I was flooded with relief when I turned into my driveway. The light from the power pole illuminated the yard in a hazy glow. A light, fresh dusting of snow glistened. I love living out here and was longing for the day I could stay out here permanently again.

I parked my car in the garage and by the time I was to the front door, Detective Wescott was beside me. I glanced at him from the corner of my eye as I unlocked my door and chuckled. "You look like a doctor who's making a house call with your clipboard and bag."

"Think of it as an evidence doctor with a fraction of the pay a medical doctor gets."

"You're both above my pay grade, so no complaining accepted here."

"Doubt that one."

The first thing I noticed when I walked through the front door was the feeling and the smell of vacancy. My own house was beginning to look abandoned and it played with my emotions. I wanted the warmth and security I once had here, the comfort, my retreat from the rest of the world.

"Everything okay?"

I startled as I was brought back to reality, remembering someone was here with me, and that he had been watching me.

"Absolutely fine," I lied, feigning a smile. "I'll just hang back and let you do whatever it is you need to do."

"Where was your mother—Violet—most of the time?"

Impressive. I didn't see the sensitivity coming from him. "Pretty much all over, except my bedroom. Although," I added as an afterthought, "that's not exactly true. She was up there too. I caught her snooping around one day by my dresser when I came home unexpectedly. And then after the shooting through my window, she retreated there."

Detective Wescott's head snapped around to look at me. "Isn't that where you kept your gun?"

"Yes, but—"

"Show me where you kept it."

"One officer went up there to dust already."

I led the way up the stairs trying to remember if I'd left it in disarray the last time I'd left. My life had become such a series of events that I was having difficulty remembering what was done where and when. I held my breath and squinted my eyes when I got to the top of the stairs in anticipation of what I would find. A quick visual sweep of the room left me relieved I didn't look like a complete slob anyway. Until I reached the nightstand and looked down to see a pair of panties lying there in plain view. I did a quick shuffle with my feet to kick them under the bed, banging my shin on the bottom of the log bed frame.

"Crap!" I said, gritting my teeth.

"You don't have to hide those on my account." His voice held nothing but disinterest in my find as he focused on my nightstand and looked around the room.

Not only was my shin throbbing, but my cheeks felt red hot from sheer embarrassment. Why would I expect to hide anything from this man anyway when he was a trained detective?

"She was primarily by your dresser?"

"As far as I know. I wasn't with her every second. I have something she doesn't."

"Which is?"

"A job. A legal one, anyway."

I stood back as he set his bag on the nightstand, took out his tools and set about doing his work.

"I saw an episode of CSI once. How you do this and how they did aren't the same."

"Nope. We don't catch the killer in an hour's time either."

"Are you sure you can trust me alone in the house? Standing behind you?"

He paused and turned to look at me over the rim of his glasses he now had on. "Meaning?"

"Well, I'm a suspect in a homicide investigation."

"A person of interest," he corrected. "There is a difference."

"A simple play on words is all."

He went back to the task at hand and said, "I'm going to ask that while I'm investigating this case, please do not say something like that within earshot of me again."

"Yes, sir," I said, laced with a little attitude motivated by humiliation. I definitely wasn't scoring any points in proving my innocence here. "I was just—"

"You don't need to explain," he cut me off. This guy was infuriating! Rude, arrogant, and everything in between. Cole may think he's an outstanding detective, but as a person, I decided he was anything but outstanding. He finished what he was doing, packed his things back in his bag and turned to face me, taking off his glasses and putting them in his jacket pocket. "My apologies if I came off a little harsh."

"No apology necessary." The nicety was obligatory only.

"I'm doing my best here to prove your innocence, contrary to what you may think. And to do that, and make it stick, I need to play things completely by the book and leave absolutely no room for error or for critical judgment. I need you to work with me on this. You making those statements doesn't help your case at all. "

"I get it. And I even appreciate it," I mumbled. And this time, I meant it. Now wasn't the time for my cynicism and misplaced pride.

"By the way," he said, looking around at the knotty pine walls that, in my opinion, perfectly complemented my rustic log bedroom furniture, "you have a beautiful house."

"Thank you. It's my little slice of heaven and a retreat. Or it was, anyway," I added.

"Is this hickory?" He asked, pointing toward the hardwood floor.

"It is."

"Nice."

I walked him to the door and stopped, my hand on the door handle, and looked up at him. "Were you able to find anything up there?"

"I lifted a few prints, yes. And I swabbed for touch DNA so I can hopefully put together a DNA profile. I'll take it to the lab and see if we get a hit."

"Let me know?" I opened the door for him.

"Of course, I will. Where are you going to be staying tonight?"

"Here."

His eyes narrowed. "I don't think that's a good idea."

"I need to get some normalcy back to my life, Detective."

"There will be time for that after we catch the killer."

Hope sprang to the surface and threatened to bubble over. He just as good as said he doesn't believe I'm guilty. I could have grabbed him and hugged him. But that would just be awkward. "I'm safer inside than going out in the dark to my car, which is in the garage, and then driving somewhere."

"Get what you need and I'll wait for you."

"Yeah? You don't have somewhere you need to be?"

"Home to a beer and Seinfeld re-runs. But unless it's going to take you two hours to get a couple of things together, I'm willing to wait."

"Seinfeld? You mean you don't watch CSI?"

"I live it. Why would I want to watch it too? Besides, I leave that to you wanna-be detectives." He winked at me. "Now get going. I'll wait right here."

"Yes, sir." I gave him a mock salute and headed for the stairs, calling over my shoulder, "You don't have to stand by the door, you know. You can have a seat in the living room or on one of the kitchen barstools."

"Does the barstool come with a beer?"

"In the frig," I hollered down from the top step.

"Naw," he called back, "If I sit down I may not get back up."

Ten minutes later I came downstairs to see he'd changed his mind and he was comfortably sitting at the kitchen table tapping away on his iPhone.

"Ready."

His eyebrows raised, his eyes widened. "Already?"

"You told me to hurry."

"That, I did," one side of his mouth curved into a tired smile. "I just didn't expect you to listen."

Chapter 28

TUESDAY DAWNED BRIGHT AND sunny, and I was bursting with energy. Or maybe it was just my dazzling, sunny attitude. Unusual for me in the morning, since mornings are typically when I'm not energetic but at my most peaceful and quiet self.

I went out to get the newspaper to find the new snow melted overnight and the ground was bare save for the snow banks that would probably be left standing until at least the end of April. The air smelled fresh and clean, and it reminded me of a Downy or Febreze commercial. I closed my eyes and inhaled deeply. It was easy to see how they got the names for their scents. Clean Breeze. April Fresh. Meadows and Rain. When I opened my eyes and saw a patrol car roll by, sharply reminding me of my predicament, my happy bubble burst. I shook it off. I would not let anything distract me from a clear mind in which to get myself off the hook.

Nana had been thrilled when I showed up on her doorstep last night, and when she woke up to find me already dressed and drinking coffee, she was surprised.

"Up so early, dear?" She gave me a hug, her permanent smile in place. Or it used to be permanent anyway, before Violet cast a shadow on things. Maybe I was being unfair by making Violet the author of everything bad. After all, last summer she wasn't even around. It was me that was causing Nana to worry.

This was two days in a row that I had woken up before she did, and I had to wonder if the events of the past week, or heck, the past year, were taking their toll on her health. I would have to keep an eye on her. She was a strong and healthy woman, but even the strongest trees blow over in a strong enough wind.

"Nana, I have to run. I worked in a client early today. But I want to talk tonight."

"About what? Did something new happen?" Her smile turned into a frown, worry lines creasing between her eyebrows.

"No, nothing happened," I said quickly before she had time to fret any more. I want to talk about you."

"Me?"

I couldn't help but smile at how genuinely surprised she was. "Yes, you."

"What about me?"

"We'll talk tonight, okay?" I gave her a peck on the cheek, picked up my coffee cup, shoulder bag, and headed for the door. "I'll be by right after work."

"And I'll have dinner ready." Her fixed warm smile was back in place.

"Love you, Nana!" I called.

I wasn't at the salon for even five minutes before Mrs. Winsted was knocking for me to let her in. I opened the door, holding it for her until she made her way in with her gimp and cane.

"Good morning, Mrs. Winsted." I tried to sound as pleasant as I could for a customer that was more oft than not less than pleasant. I wished she'd find another stylist for all she complained about, but I guess if she kept coming back that meant I must be doing something right.

"Good morning, Melanie. Thank you for getting me in so early."

"Of course. Do you have something special going on today?" I asked close to her ear to accommodate her failing hearing. I sometimes wondered if it was all an act, because she could hear the darnedest things when one thought she wasn't within earshot.

"If you call a memorial service something special, I suppose." Her voice was a nasally whine. Most people would think she was coming down with a cold, but it's something that made miserable Mrs. Winsted miserable to listen to.

"Oh my, I'm so sorry," I said, truly sympathetic. I wouldn't wish that on anyone. I led her by her arm to my chair, got her settled in and began putting the cape over her shoulders.

"Not so tight this time or it will be my memorial service people will attend," she complained.

Here we go. "So are you wanting the usual done today?"

"Yes. But maybe you could do something so it will last a little longer. I'm not made of money, you know."

Why did I come in early for this? "I'll do what I can," I said as kindly as I could. I was desperately hoping Claire or Rubie would be in early to save the day and bring the brightness back to the day that I had when I woke up. "Family or friend?" I asked.

"Family or friend? What are you talking about?"

"The memorial you have today. Family member?"

"If you want to call it that. I'm the closest thing to family the poor thing had."

"Poor thing is right," I mumbled under my breath. I was half expecting God to strike me down for my nasty attitude toward this old woman. I just hope I won't be so grumpy and angry when I got old. I wanted to be exactly like my grandmother. Except she's not old. Not to me anyway.

"—Melanie?"

The sound of my name brought me reeling back to Mrs. Winsted's complaining voice.

"I'm sorry?"

"How could you not hear me for goodness sakes? Aren't you listening? I said be careful not to put too much spray on it this time."

"If you want it to hold longer, I'm going to have to use spray, Mrs. Winsted. You know that."

"Well, I guess that's fine," she harrumphed.

Part of me wanted to keep spraying until the bottle was completely empty, grab another and empty that one, too. And again, I wondered if God would strike me for having such a rotten attitude burning within me. Nana always used to tell me, *A parent disciplines a child for doing wrong, dear. And God is the ultimate parent.* One of the few times she actually used religious talk. Rather, it was her actions that made one know she and the big Guy upstairs were pretty tight. How could He not have her as one of His favorites?

"—what's wrong with you today, but I'm worried you won't do as I've asked. You're not even in the same room as me, and I'm trusting you with my hair."

"Nope, I'm in the same room as you, Mrs. Winsted. Trust me." I bit my tongue to silence any more bitterness from escaping. "I'm sorry to worry you, but you really needn't worry. Truly. Your hair will be fine," I said, attempting to comfort her.

"How can you stand to wear those high heels every day? And for goodness sakes, don't ladies wear dresses anymore? What is it with all these jeans they wear these days?"

That was the straw. I snapped. I forced myself to take slow and controlled deep breaths, put my arms down from completing the finishing touches on her hair, swiveled her chair so she was facing me and looked straight at her.

"Mrs. Winsted," I said as calmly as I could, "you seem unable to find a single good thing about my work—or me, for that matter. If you feel you'd be better serviced elsewhere, by someone more suited to what you're looking for, I won't stop you. I want you to be happy with what you're getting, and that's clearly not here with me."

I watched as her jaw dropped open leaving her mouth agape, her eyes confused. "Whatever are you talking about? You're the only one who does my hair just as I like it."

I could do nothing else but smile, a combination of what-do-I-do-with-that frustration and amazement that something kind actually came from her lips. *God? This is truly a test, isn't it?* It occurred to me I'd spoken more to God in the past forty-five minutes than I have in the past several years. Why stop now? "Mrs. Winsted, what is the name of your loved one. I'll pray for her."

"Why, it's Gina. She used to work here for Pete's sake."

Chapter 29

IT TOOK A MOMENT for the impact to fully hit and for Mabel Winsted's words to register. As soon as she'd left the salon, scarf in place to keep her hair from getting blown around in the wind that was picking up, (not that tornadic activity could move it by the time I got done with it) my mind began swirling in circles trying to fit together what I just heard.

The door opened and Claire breezed in, coming over to give me a hug.

"What's that for?"

"Cause I just saw Mrs. Winsted leaving. Not only did you come in early for her, but she left with the both of you still alive." Her eyes flew open, her hand to her mouth. "Oh my gosh! I'm so sorry. I just meant—"

I laughed at my sweet friend. "Stop it right now! I know what you meant. And believe me, it was touch and go for awhile there. I even told her if she feels she can get better service elsewhere than maybe she should go there."

"No sir! You did not!"

"Yes, I certainly did." I laughed. Claire looked like she was about to faint.

"And?"

"She gave me a compliment and asked why she would go somewhere else when I'm the only one who could do her hair just the way she liked it."

"No, sir!"

"Yes, sir!" I laughed again. If her eyes got any bigger, they were going to swallow up her entire face. "But—I need you to help me talk through something." I knew my Claire. While I process things in my head, in this case failing to do, Claire can talk through any situation and get the answer. "Mabel mentioned something, and I'm trying to figure out why it's setting so odd with me."

Claire sat in her stylist chair and I sat in mine, the one kitty-corner from hers. "What'd she say?"

"She had to get in early because she has a memorial service to go to today."

"And?"

"It's for Gina."

"Gina? As in our Gina?"

"I wouldn't call her our Gina, but Gina who used to work here, yes. But here's the odd thing—before I knew it was for Gina, I asked her if the memorial she's attending was for a family member or friend. She said it's more a family member because she was the closest thing to family Gina has ever had."

Claire scrunched up her nose. "Poor thing."

"Claire!" I exclaimed. "I would totally expect that to come from me but never from you. You never say an unkind word about anyone. Even if they deserve it."

"I'm sorry, Mel, but that woman is awful."

She looked at me with puppy-dog eyes, and I chuckled, still taken aback. "Know what's even more odd?"

"What?"

"She said she didn't tell us about the memorial service because she knew we didn't like Gina."

"Why in the world would she say something like that?" She went from sad to horrified in all of three seconds. If that.

"Think about it. The only way she would have ever gotten that idea was if Gina told her something."

"Do you think Gina really thought that? I feel awful."

Tears were forming behind those long dark lashes of hers.

"Honey, you can't help what other people think. You've never given her—or anyone, for that matter—reason to think you don't like them. This one's on Gina. Don't take it on yourself."

"But maybe that's why she was always so quiet and—well, standoffish."

"Or maybe she was quiet and standoffish because Gina was who she was. Don't make it about us."

"You probably have a point." She didn't sound completely convinced, but reluctantly trying to believe that.

"I thought Gina didn't have any friends or family in the area. Did she ever mention to you she did?"

"No, never." She sat back, crossing one long leg over the other. "But she really didn't mention anything in the way of personal information."

"And Mabel has obviously never come in at the same time that Gina was working. Which wouldn't be odd in and of itself, because Gina was here part-time at most.

But if they were like family, don't you think she would have made a point of coming in when Gina was here?"

"Yeah, you're right...maybe Gina was doing her nails at home?"

"Hmmm...hadn't thought of that. And get this. She asked about my mother."

"Violet?"

"Yes. But she said 'your mother'. Don't you think it's odd that Gina knew Violet is my mother, and now Mabel does too? When the only people who knew, from me, anyway, were you and Jack, and later Rubie?" I looked past Claire, into the space beyond her, not really seeing anything at all. "I just cannot figure out, for the life of me, how it's all connected. I know it is though. It has to be."

"So if Gina knew that, and if she knew Violet in California, it had to be from Violet herself."

"And Gina would have had to find it interesting enough to tell Mabel Winsted. But why?"

"And why would she even think Mrs. Winsted would care?"

"Exactly."

"Do you suppose—no, that's silly to even think that." She shook her head as if dismissing the idea.

"Do I suppose what?"

"Nothing. It was silly."

"Claire, at his point nothing is silly. Every idea we can come up with could be the one that solves this and finds Gina's killer, getting me off the hook for something I didn't do."

"Well, we've been looking at Gina's clients as suspects. Maybe we should look at your clients, not Gina's." We looked at each other, each trying to stitch together the frayed ends.

"Okay, maybe you're on to something. We know Mabel didn't kill Gina because, let's face it, she can't even get from her car into the salon without help. There's no way she would have made it down to where the shooting was. But I wonder if she knows who did? I still think it was Lenny, though."

Rubie came bursting through the door in a bubble of energy typical of Rubie. That girl was a breath of fresh air. "Whatcha all talkin' about?"

"You," I said. When I saw her smile disappear, I quickly added, "I'm kidding! We were talking about Violet and Gina."

"And Mabel Winsted," Claire added.

"What does she have to do with Gina and Violet? And what does Violet have to do with Gina?"

It occurred to me we hadn't included Rubie in on the latest revelation about the connection between Violet and Gina, so I started at the beginning, Claire filling in whenever I left anything out.

Rubie whistled when we were all done. "Wow! Where have I been that I missed all this? You guys have been keeping me in the dark."

"It's not like we've been withholding info from you," Claire said, always the one to try make people feel better. "We just figured this out and hadn't seen you since then. Not where we could talk privately, anyway."

"And the private talk is going to end again, because here comes your and Claire's first appointments," I said. "I'm going in the back to call Detective Wescott before my next one comes in."

Chapter 30

AS IT HAPPENED, IT was well into the afternoon before I had time to string together two minutes to call Detective Wescott. I went to the office to get my phone and saw I had a missed call from his number and a voice mail. I called him back. At this rate, it may serve me well to put his number on speed dial. My cynicism returned, following the well-worn path, grooves too deep to escape.

"Wescott," he answered gruffly on the first ring.

"Detective? I'm beginning to think my calls irritate you."

"Hi, Melanie. I didn't know it was you, sorry."

"You called?"

"Did you listen to my voice mail?"

"No. It was easier to just call you back. I had to talk to you anyway."

"About?"

"You first."

"I'd like to talk in person. Can you come to the station?"

"Not right now, but later I can." I thought about my promise to my grandmother that I'd be there after work, and that she was going to have dinner ready. "Actually," I added quickly, "I have to be somewhere after work. It will have to be tomorrow sometime."

"What news did you have for me?"

"I can tell you tomorrow when we meet."

"I tell you what. It sounds like you have dinner plans for this evening—"

"Cole said you were a good detective, but that's exceptional. Or was it a guess?"

"You said you had to be somewhere, and when you get off work at dinnertime it's not too hard to put two and two together."

"Alrighty then," I murmured, taken aback by his abruptness. He was one tough guy to figure out.

"If you can drop by the station when you're done, I'll go grab a bite myself and come back here and meet you."

"I guess I could do that."

"Eight?"

"Sure."

I hung up and went out to get the last leg of my day underway. I felt somewhat off my game the last few hours and couldn't shake the feeling that something was going to come along that I wouldn't like. I don't necessarily believe in premonitions, but if there was such a thing, I was having one. It felt like my gut was warning me about impending news.

"Melanie, you okay?" Claire asked. Apparently I wasn't the only one who noticed I was a bit off.

I stopped sweeping the hair from my last haircut long enough to look at her, those brown eyes filled with concern. I finished sweeping the hair, scooped it in the dustpan, leaned the broom against my chair and began walking to the office, nodding my head for her to follow me. Rubie still had a customer in her chair and this wasn't something I wanted to discuss in front of a stranger.

Once in the office I leaned back against the large oak cabinet that lined the wall, and Claire came in and closed the door behind her, leaving it ajar in case Rubie needed something from one of us.

"What's wrong? Did something happen? What did Detective Wescott tell you?"

"He didn't tell me anything, because he said he wants to tell me in person. It sounds big though. In fact he's coming in later this evening for me to meet him after I'm done with dinner at my grandmother's house. He didn't want to wait until tomorrow."

"Want me to come with you?"

"I'll leave that up to you. I don't need you to hold my hand, but I sure wouldn't object to you being there."

"Okay, then, it's settled. I'll meet you at the precinct. Just call me as you're leaving your grandmother's. I'll leave at the same time and we should get there about the same time."

"Thanks, Claire. For everything."

"Do you have any idea whatsoever what it might be about?"

"I don't. But—do you believe in premonitions?"

"Yes."

"Hmmm." I pondered her quick response.

"Why?"

"I just have this gut feeling that something is—that I won't like what he has to tell me. I can't help but feel like my world is going to completely change, but I can't put my finger on why I'm feeling that way or if it's going to be bad or good. Because it's such an uneasy feeling, my guess is it's going to be bad."

"Do you want Cole to meet us there?"

"You may want him there so you're not alone in case they arrest me." I looked at her, the concern in her eyes mirroring what I felt in my own. "I honestly don't know what I'm walking into."

"Maybe you should go there first. Before you go to your grandmother's."

I shook my head vehemently. "I need to see Nana first. Just in case."

"In case of what?"

"In case I'm not able to see her afterward." I was hoping she'd be able to read between the lines so I wouldn't have to spell it out for her. I didn't want to hear it said out loud. "I need to check in with her to be sure she's okay. I told her before I left this morning that I wanted to talk to her this evening. She's going to have dinner ready." I looked at Claire as she reached for her phone, presumably to call Cole. "I sure hope this isn't the Last Supper." My attempt at humor felt misplaced, even to me. But that's how I always got through a difficult time. Those around me didn't always appreciate it. My memory flashed back to Detective Wescott when he was swabbing for DNA and dusting for prints. I looked at Claire, her frown spoke louder than words.

"Melanie, that was just plain awful."

"Sorry." And this time I was.

It was five-thirty when I left the salon. Claire was finishing up her last customer of the day and Rubie was studying the appointment book, passing time while she waited for Claire. We made an agreement that none of us would be alone at the salon in the evenings past dark, unless the one working the latest knew their last customer well and knew they would wait for us to close up. Even if Rubie was involved in the shenanigans going on, I was confident she wouldn't hurt Claire or me. Then again, if she was involved, she's letting me take the fall. Maybe I need to re-think my trust in anyone other than Claire, Jack, and Nana.

I drove to my grandmother's so deep in thought that I was at her driveway before I even realized I'd gotten there. That I was so zoned out in my head that I didn't remember the drive was unsettling to say the least. What in the world was this feeling? Where was it coming from? I needed a good swift kick in the pants to get my mind off of me and make this about Nana.

I used my key to let myself in, slipped off my boots, and rounded the corner into the kitchen where I saw her standing at the sink, her long silver braid lying over her shoulder. "Hi Nana," I said softly, not wanting to startle her. Mission not accomplished successfully.

"Oh good heavens, dear!" She turned to face me, her cheeks flushed. "I didn't hear you."

"I gathered." I crossed the room and gave her a hug. "Whatcha thinkin' about so intently?"

"Not a thing, so don't you worry." She pulled back from me, her hands holding my forearms, and she looked deep into my eyes. "What's wrong, dear?"

"Why would you ask that? I've only been here two seconds."

"A mother—and grandmother—can tell."

I attempted a smile, failing miserably. "I didn't come here to talk about me. I want to talk about you."

"I'm not that interesting," she said.

"I beg to differ."

"Do you want to talk before we eat or during dinner?"

"How about during. I can't stay long. I have to meet Detective Wescott."

"Tonight?" Her eyebrows shot up.

"Yeah. Said he has some news for me."

"Did he say what about?"

"Now, Nana, don't you go worrying. I can see it in your eyes and hear it in your voice, despite trying to hide it from me. If it were bad, he wouldn't have waited until tonight. He would have come to the salon or had me come in earlier today." I was trying to decide whether I was attempting to convince her or myself. Perhaps both. Hopefully I was more successful at convincing her, because I wasn't feeling it. Maybe it had to do with the fact that he *had* asked me to come in earlier.

We put dinner on the table and each took our seats, bowing our heads to say grace before we spoke another word. That was one rule in her house she would never waiver on.

"What did you want to talk about?" she finally asked.

"I'm worried about you."

Again her eyebrows shot up and her fork stopped in mid-motion. "Why would you be worried about me?"

"Nana, you've been looking tired. And your smile that I used to swear was fixed to your face during all my years of growing up has given way to—let's just say it's been absent more often. When was the last time you had a checkup with the doctor?"

"I'm a retired RN, dear. I know when I need to see the doctor."

"Don't go getting stubborn on me. Doctors and nurses make the worst patients. Just like the barber's kids have the longest hair and the psychiatrist's kids are the most ill-behaved. It's easy to neglect ourselves and those we love trying to take care of the rest of the world."

"Who taught you that bit of wisdom?"

"You did." I smiled and placed my hand over hers.

"Really, you don't need to worry about me. You want to help me?"

"More than anything in the world."

"Then make sure you take care of yourself and keep yourself safe. That, sweetheart, would be the greatest gift you could ever give me."

"I love you so much, Nana. Do you know that?"

"I do."

The warmth of her smile, the merry twinkle back in her eye, erased any sense of ill-feeling I had earlier that day. At least until I got in the car and began my drive to see Detective Wescott.

Chapter 31

WHEN I GOT TO the precinct, Claire's car was already in the parking lot. I could see the silhouette of her sitting in the dark under the streetlights that lined the parking lot. I walked up to her window to find her talking on her phone. She hung up when she saw me.

She opened her car door and gave me a hug. "You scared me half to death standing there. I saw something out of the corner of my eye and turned to see a person inches from my face."

"You're in a police department parking lot. What could happen?" I tried to use Wescott's rationale he'd used on me.

"That's why you scare me. You're way too casual in your surroundings."

"Nothing's happened to me yet." I knew I wasn't convincing her, but it was worth a shot.

"Let's keep it that way, huh?"

We walked to the glass front doors as three officers were walking out. One of them held the door for us, and then continued walking without missing a beat in the conversation with his cohorts. Their laughter and jesting were disconcerting at this exact moment. It was a reminder that in light of whatever I was about to hear, or rather whatever my head was afraid it might hear, the lives of other people remained untouched and life carried on as usual.

I walked up to the front desk, the officer sitting on the other side of the thick glass enclosure smiling, something I tried, but failed, to return. "Could you let Detective Wescott know Melanie is here?"

"Sure thing, young lady." His jovial attitude grated on my nerves.

I stood there while he went in the back, saying loud enough for me to hear, "Wescott! A hot woman is here to see you! New girlfriend?"

I rolled my eyes at his apparent immaturity. If I weren't so preoccupied I just might have given him a piece of my mind. I went to sit down by Claire. Not five minutes later, Detective Wescott came through the door, holding it open for me to get back into the secure area. Claire was right behind me. He gestured toward the one chair, other than his desk chair, that was in his office and dragged another in.

"New girlfriend, huh?" I said. "You might want to tell the desk officer that his voice carries a long ways."

"I'll let him know." If I didn't know better, I would swear I saw a glimmer of amusement cross his face. Again. Amused is not how I would describe Detective Wescott, except when it's at my expense. He reached across the desk to shake Claire's hand. "Nice to see you again, Ms. Davis."

"You as well, Detective," Claire answered in her voice that sounded kind as always. "I hope you don't mind that I came with Melanie."

"Not at all. Glad you did."

My heart picked up its pace. Why was he glad she came with me? Was he about to give me bad news and thought it would be a good idea to have someone here with me when I crumbled?

"What is you needed to tell me that couldn't wait until tomorrow?" I asked, hearing the tension in my voice.

"It's not that it couldn't wait, but it's something I assumed you would want to know as soon as possible."

"So this is for my benefit?"

"Mostly."

"By all means, fill me in then." Out of the corner of my eye, I saw Claire looking at me. I averted my eyes from her afraid of what I would see there.

"Coffee?"

"No."

"Bottle of water?"

"No."

"Actually, I would love a bottle of water," Claire said.

"I'll get you something better when we leave, like tequila," I said, glancing quickly at her and then back at Detective Procrastination.

"I can get a bottle of water now," he said. "It won't take but a minute."

As soon as he left the room Claire turned toward me. "Melanie, you've got to get a hold of yourself. You're not doing yourself any favors by getting yourself all riled up."

"I just want to get this over with. Whatever *this* is going to be."

"Well, this will be much easier if you calm your nerves. Take a drink of my water as soon as he brings it in."

"Yes, mother."

Detective Wescott walked casually back through the door and handed Claire a bottle of water, who immediately handed it to me.

"Drink," she said. As much as it was intended to be an order, her kindness softened it to a helpful suggestion.

I took the bottle, struggled with unscrewing the cap, feeling like a child with a childproof bottle. I finally got it open and took a good long drink. I handed it back to her. "Happy?"

"Yes, thank you," she smiled winningly.

"Yes, thank you," the detective repeated as he looked at her.

"Okay, okay, okay." I looked at Claire, at the detective, back at Claire, and sighed. "I'm sorry. I truly am. I'm not myself these days. I feel like my emotions and nerves are all over the board, and that's unfamiliar territory for me."

"It's okay, Mel. Really." She turned to Detective Wescott. "Detective, I can see the toll this has taken on her. I hope it's good news you have so she can take a breath and relax a little. She's earned it."

I took Claire's hand in my own and hung onto it. "Thank you. Detective? What have you got for me?"

"We got a match on the DNA and fingerprint testing. The DNA from your nightstand drawer and that on the glove was a match. To your moth—Violet."

I heard a sharp inhale and realized after a beat that it was mine. I felt the color drain from my face, could hear the blood pulsing in my ears.

"That means—"

"That Violet shot Gina and set me up to take the fall," I said, interrupting him. A flood of emotions swept through me like a current surging through a river. "I'm not sure if I feel betrayed, confused, relieved, or ticked off. Or all of the above." I stared at Detective Wescott who was watching me closely, his eyes gentle for a change. I fought the tears stinging my eyelids as they threatened to overflow. "What kind of a mother does that?" I whispered. A tear escaped, trickling its way down my cheek. I furiously swiped at it and willed them away. I wasn't about to let him, or anyone, see the deep, raw pain of a child not only abandoned by her mother like a piece of trash, but used and stomped on. Part of me felt so little, insignificant, and unworthy.

"Not one anyone deserves." His answer was laced with anger.

"Why would she shoot Gina? What could be her motive? Do you think it's tied to California?"

"Sometimes there isn't a motive, Melanie." Somewhere in the back of my mind it registered that he called me Melanie, rather than Ms. Hogan. A rarity since this complete nightmare began. "But if there is one, I guarantee I'll find out so you can find some peace. As much as you can, anyway."

"Were her prints on the gun?"

"We found a partial, but not enough to make a direct or solid connection."

"Will that matter?"

"The nexus is still there between the nightstand drawer, the glove, and the GSR on the glove."

I stared over his shoulder at the wall behind him, seeing nothing but images of Violet. "What happens now?" My voice sounded like I was hearing someone else speak from off in the distance.

"We'll notify the police agency out in LA to bring her in and she will be extradited here."

"What if she has an alibi? She didn't have a car and was with my grandmother or me—oh wait!" I suddenly remembered. "How could I have forgotten? She used my grandmother's car to go get a nail fixed. She'd just had them done that day, broke one, and needed to get it fixed right at that moment. However, when she came back home, she didn't get it done. Of course, she had some excuse, but she probably didn't go to the nail salon at all."

"That would be my guess. And that information was exactly what I needed."

"In fact, what if she went to Gina's house and Gina is the one who did her nails to begin with?" I looked over at Claire who had been so quiet I had forgotten she was even in the room. My mind was spinning so fast I could hardly see straight. I felt dizzy. I reached for the water bottle and took a long swig, draining the last of it. I absently handed the empty bottle back to Claire. "Detective, how did you know they belong to Violet? Wouldn't you have needed her prints or DNA in a database to compare them to?"

"Yes."

He said nothing more. He didn't need to. "She has a criminal history." It was a statement, not a question.

"She was arrested for drug distribution and gambling."

I was mentally fitting the pieces together, and the last one clicked into place. "I think the questions about the shot through my window have just been answered."

Chapter 32

THE NEXT EVENING RUBIE and I were sitting in the booth at Grizzley's Tap house, talking as we waited for Claire to get there. I was doing my best at licking my wounds from what Violet did to me, yet celebrating at the same time. Rubie was still in the dark about the details of what had gone down at Detective Wescott's office the night before; she tried to get the low-down from Claire, but Claire told her she would have to wait to hear it from me, letting her know it wasn't her story to tell, but mine. Bless her kind heart. I love that girl. I took that day off, the girls graciously offering to reschedule whatever appointments I had that they couldn't fit in themselves. I needed the day to spend with Nana, to explain as best I could what happened. I knew it would be anything but easy for her to hear about Violet and I needed to stay and keep an eye on her. She had taken it better than I expected, but I stayed for a while anyway. When I left she was enjoying a cup of licorice tea and watching a pair of Cardinals and a scattering of Black-capped Chickadees flit about outside the bay window.

I listened now as Rubie was knee deep in a story about one of her male clients who had asked her out. When she told him she had a boyfriend, he told her he would just wait until she was free, because he wasn't giving up.

"Melanie, it was creepy. I mean, can we say stalker?"

I shuddered at the word that had become too much a part of my life. Nevertheless, I smiled at her eyes that were bright with the adrenaline of telling the story, her blond curls up in a ponytail, lips shiny and pink with gloss. I was sick over the fact that I had suspected her of murdering Gina. I stunk at being a sleuth. Next time I'd have to be sure and be better. *Next time?* The words popped into my head as if it was a certainty that there would be a next time. I realized Rubie was waiting for me to answer and snapped my attention back to her.

"Yeah, that is kind of stalkerish."

"You calling me a stalker?" I heard the familiar voice behind me.

"Jack!" I bolted up and out of the booth and threw myself at him, nearly knocking him over.

"Careful!" he laughed. "You may be little, but you pack a powerful punch."

I saw Claire right behind him, beaming from ear to ear. I winked at her.

"I'm buying. Drinks on me." I giggled, feeling joy I hadn't felt in all too long.

"Oh, I almost forgot something," Claire said with a mischievous twinkle in her eye. "I'll be right back."

I began talking to Jack when I looked over and saw Claire, one hand behind her holding onto someone hidden by her height. When I finally saw who it was, tears sprang to my eyes. This time I didn't even attempt to stop them. I just let them come. Jack stood up so I could slide out of the booth. I wrapped Nana in a hug, clinging onto her, feeling like a child who'd just found her mother.

"Nana," I whispered in her ear. "Thank you so much for coming." That she didn't leave her house to go out to eat, much less ever stepping foot in a bar, spoke volumes to me she was here now. I sniffed. "Do you know how grateful I am for you?"

"As grateful as I am for you, dear." Her eyes twinkled, her cheeks pink and soft like the velvet from a rose. As out of place a she looked in here, she was the most beautiful sight to behold.

I slid back in the booth as far as I could, Nana slid in next to me, and Jack took the end, Claire and Rubie on the other side. I signaled the server over.

"Hi folks," she said. "My name is Sharon. What can I get you?" She laid a napkin down on the table in front of each of us.

"Margarita, please," Claire and I said simultaneously.

"Mine on the rocks," I said.

Rubie ordered a Tom Collins and Jack a microbrew beer.

"And I'll have a Shirley Temple," Nana said, proud as could be.

"So Melanie," Rubie said, "spill everything. I feel like I've been living on a different planet than everyone else the past couple of days."

"I'm on the same planet as you, Rubie," Jack said. He looked at me expectantly.

I took a deep breath, drained my first margarita before my second arrived, paying attention to Nana watching me as I did so. I put my arm around her. "Don't worry, I won't drive home. I promise."

"I'll drive her home and stay there," Jack said. "That way she can stay in her own home and still be safe."

I choked on my drink. "We know how well that worked out last summer when you said that."

"Yeah, not so well," Claire said, laughing.

"It wasn't funny back then, though," he said.

"Melanie!" Rubie's voice rose above the others. "Talk."

"Yes, Melanie," Jack said, looking around my grandmother at me, "talk."

"Okay." I took another deep breath before delving into the story. "I'll start at the beginning from what I know. Whatever is before that and led up to what we know now I don't know yet. That being said, Gina and Violet knew each other back in L.A.—I told you that. Well, Violet's involved in drug distribution and betting on horses, not a good combination. We think the person who shot through my window was actually someone from L.A. who followed Violet here and was after her, not me. Another detail I'd already suspected. Unless he was trying to use me to scare her. Either way, she was the one who was the ultimate target. Violet's bookie, Lenny, called and tracked her up here. She arranged to meet Gina by my house, took my gun with her, which she found while she was snooping through my room on her first day at my house, or when she was hiding out in my room after the shot through my window. She took my gloves, and whatever led to the argument, she shot Gina. When she found out Lenny had called my grandmother looking for her, she hightailed it out of here and went back home. Well, I think she went home anyway. For all I know, she's hiding somewhere trying to lose Lenny's tail. Oh yeah, and I should use a disclaimer here. Some of this is what we believe happened but we aren't 100 percent certain. We won't know for sure until Violet is caught and brought in."

"Oh, my hell!" Rubie exclaimed.

"Actually, it's Violet's hell." I reached for Nana's hand under the table and squeezed it. "The part that's the hardest for me to digest is that a mother would actually frame her own daughter for a murder."

"A mother wouldn't," Claire said. "She's no mother." She looked over at my grandmother. "I'm sorry, Rose. I shouldn't have said that."

"The truth is what it is." She sighed and looked at me, giving me a small smile. Her eyes looked tired, and worry tugged at my chest.

Despite intimating he didn't know anything, Jack's lack of questions made me wonder if Claire filled him in on some of the shenanigans on the way over there. Which wouldn't have surprised me, since the three of us were partners in crime. Or rather trying to avoid it. Maybe he was afraid to know more and thought if he didn't ask, he wouldn't have to know. Not Rubie, though. She wanted to know. It was killing her I wasn't getting to the answers quick enough. The answers she wanted anyway.

"Ladies!" I heard behind me and saw Claire light up like she'd just seen Santa Claus. I turned to find Cole and smiled. When Detective Wescott's bald head appeared behind him, it surprised me, to say the least.

"Cole, nice to see you. Detective? To what do we owe the honor? Mixing business with pleasure? Hardly seems your style." I felt a smile tug at the corners of my lips.

"You're no longer a person of interest. That means there's no conflict of interest in having a drink with friends."

My head cocked to the side as I watched Cole pull up a couple of chairs at the end of our booth. The smile won out and I grinned. Jack signaled for Sharon, our server, who came much faster than when I called her over earlier. Jack had a certain charm with the ladies, too. "I think a table would better accommodate our growing number of guests."

She was all too happy to grant his request and had a table cleared off instantly, with a special smile for Jack.

I elbowed him. "Quit flirting."

"It's harmless."

"I know that and you know that. But she doesn't," I said, laughing.

We all got settled at our new table, Nana on one side of me, Jack on the other, Cole and Claire directly across from us. Rubie and Detective Wescott each took an end. Sharon brought Nana a re-fill on her Shirley Temple.

"Designated driver gets free re-fills," Sharon said.

Nana grinned and popped the cherry in her mouth, leaving the stem on the edge of her napkin.

"So, Detective," I said, raising my glass, my smile relaxed. "Thank you for everything you did."

"And here you doubted me."

"I wouldn't exactly say I doubted you, it's just—"

"There's no need to thank me. I was just doing my job."

I looked at Jack in mock hurt. "I'm just a job."

"Yeah, a nut job," he smiled. He put an arm around me and squeezed. "You know I'm kidding."

"Detective," I said, "it really is nice you could make it. These people sitting at this table are everything and anything that matters in my life." I looked over at the bar where the servers were hanging out. I waved as nonchalantly as I could at them, getting the nod from one of them showing they saw me. I swallowed the giddiness that bubbled to the surface as I looked over at Claire. With all the chatter at our table, the group of servers circled around her before she noticed anything out of the ordinary. They began clapping, making poor Nana jump a mile, and they broke out into a cheery and slightly off-tune rendition of the birthday song. One of them carried a vanilla cupcake with bright pink icing and matching pink candle, the flame reflecting in Claire's eyes and the tears that began forming there.

"Happy Birthday," I mouthed to her. I watched as Cole wrapped his arm around her and squeezed, then kissed the top of her head.

When the singing and clapping were done and we could hear each other talk once more, I said, "You thought I forgot, didn't you?"

"With everything that has been going on, I would have understood if you had."

"There's no forgiving someone who would forget her best friend's birthday."

I pulled a card and a small wrapped gift from my bag at the same time Rubie and Jack produced theirs. Fresh tears glistened in Claire's eyes.

"You guys are too much," she choked.

"You seriously didn't think this gathering was on my account, did you?" I said.

"Yes, actually I did," she said with a giggle. "After what you've been through you deserve this to be all about you."

She opened each card slowly then began on the gifts, peeling the paper carefully on the first one.

"Just open the darn thing," Jack said. "We're going to be here until morning otherwise."

Claire ripped the gold glittered paper off the tiny box she cradled in her hands, leaving glitter on the table, her shirt, and even some sparkles on her cheek.

As soon as Claire finished opening the last gift and gave the appropriate thanks, Nana drained the last of her Shirley Temple, grimacing as she swallowed the last of the syrupy sweetness, and said, "Well, kids, I'd like to stay but I turn into a pumpkin at midnight."

"There're hours to go for that," Cole teased. He had been engaging her in a conversation for much of the time.

"Not for this old woman," she smiled at him. "Jack, perhaps you could take me home?"

"It would be my pleasure."

I placed my hand on his arm, "Be sure she gets in the house, okay? And that she locks the door when you leave," I said to Jack but looked pointedly at my grandmother.

"I will the lock the door. I promise." She said.

"And, Jack, don't forget to come back for me. There are two officers here. I can't be seen getting behind the wheel of a car tonight."

"We can bring you home," Claire said.

"I can as well." Detective Wescott's voice.

"Thanks, guys, but Jack's staying at my house tonight anyway."

"Yeah," he grinned. "Someone has to keep her safe. From herself." He looked at Detective Wescott. "This girl can get herself in more trouble than anyone I know. And she doesn't even have to do anything to get there. It finds her."

"It's the company I keep," I said gently, loving every single person around the table right now. Well, almost everyone. "Detective—"

"Levi," he corrected me. "We're in a social setting, not work."

"Wait!" Rubie exclaimed and stood up so quickly her knee hit the bottom of the table, the last untouched Shirley Temple Sharon brought Nana sloshed over onto the table, the cherry toppling to the floor. "Before Jack takes Rose home we need to have a toast! And I get to do it!"

A round of laughter erupted around the table. Of course she would get to do it. Who other than Rubie? She clinked the side of her near empty glass with a knife and we all silenced, our attention on Rubie. The noise from the rest of the pub seemed to fade in the background as I looked at each of these dear people who surrounded me. Suddenly tears burned the backs of my eyelids again. It was such a happy time, and yet I was feeling overwhelmed and even somewhat—melancholy. So much love surrounded me. I would walk on burning coals for every one of these people.

I tuned back in to Rubie who was in mid-speech.

"—thank Melanie for accepting me into her circle. She's probably one of the most private people I know, but once she lets you in, you're in. Her loyalty to the people she loves is to be admired and something I'm grateful for. I know, without a doubt, that if I ever needed her, she'd be there in a heartbeat, as well as for any person at this table. Here's to her innocence and to many more evenings of getting together. Exactly like this."

I felt a sharp stab of guilt. If she only knew. Glasses raised and clinked together all around the table. There were a lot of "here here's" and laughter. Jack pushed his chair out and took my grandmother's coat off the back of her chair to help her into it once she finished hugging me close. I watched them as they headed for the door, Jack's hand lightly on her elbow.

"So how about the story behind why you call your mother Violet?" Levi asked, his voice bringing me back to the present.

"Another time maybe. Why ruin a fun evening." I smiled, despite sadness tugging at my heartstrings as he reminded me of the ultimate betrayal and deception. That of a mother betraying her daughter.

"Another time then." He said. "I'll hold you to that."

Not quite a half an hour after Jack left with my grandmother the screen on my cell phone lit up. I plugged one ear and pressed the phone to the other.

"Jack? Where are you?" I struggled to hear above the noise all around me. Rubie, of course, was telling yet another story that had everyone laughing. "Guys, hush for just a minute," I told them.

"That's so rude to tell the people who are with you to hush so you can take a phone call," Rubie teased. The rest of the table laughed above the background noise. It all faded to nothing while I heard what Jack had told me.

When I hung up I saw them all staring at me.

"What is it, Mel?" Claire asked. "It looks like you've seen a ghost."

"Claire," I said, struggling to breathe, looking from her to Cole, "can you guys take me to the hospital? Something's happened to my grandmother."

Chapter 33

MY MIND TRAVELED A thousand miles an hour faster than the car as we sped toward St. Joseph's Hospital. Jack's words kept replaying in my head. *Your grandmother is in the hospital, looks like it was a heart attack. I called 9-1-1. We're at the hospital.* I thought I remembered him telling me she's going to be okay, but I wasn't sure. I couldn't get past the part that she stopped breathing. Everything he said after that was a blur. If anything ever happened to her—well, I couldn't even fathom what I would do.

When we pulled up to the emergency room entrance, I opened my door before we came to a complete stop. I had been beating myself up until my psyche was black and blue wishing I'd taken my grandmother's fatigue more seriously and insisted she go to the doctor rather than take her word for it she was okay.

"We'll park and meet you inside," Claire shouted.

I ran up to the front desk, my breathing a tell-tale sign I hadn't run for far too long.

"I'm looking for my grandmother," I gasped.

"Her name?" Her casualness irritated me.

"Na—Rose. Rose Donnelly."

"Are you a relative?"

"Yes. I just told you she's my—"

"Melanie?" Jack's voice said from around the corner. "We're back here." He looked at the woman. "This is my sister. Rose Donnelly is our grandmother."

Before the receptionist could utter a word I was next to Jack, following him.

"Smooth."

"It was quicker than waiting for approval."

"What's going on? What happened?"

"As I told you when I called—"

"Thanks to our loud and entertaining friend Rubie, I couldn't hear everything you were saying on the phone." I walked beside him, my stride matching his.

"We were almost to her house when she started having chest pains."

"Did she tell you she was having them?"

He cast a sideways glance at me. "What do you think?"

"No. Of course, she didn't," I muttered. I took a deep breath, hoping to alleviate the dizziness I felt. "So how did you know she was having chest pains?"

"Because she kept touching her chest and she was breathing rapidly. It seemed like she wanted to get a deep breath but couldn't. I asked if she was okay. She started saying she was fine, just a little nauseous. Then I saw her face scrunch up like she was in pain. She said she was just feeling a little weak and I told her we were going to the hospital. She said she was fine, she was just having a bit of indigestion. I turned around to take her to the hospital, even though she didn't want to go, and then I heard her breathing sound odd, then she was unconscious."

"You kids can come in you know," I heard her sweet voice say.

It was only then I realized we'd reached her room and were standing outside her doorway as Jack continued to fill me in. I reached up and gave Jack a quick peck on the cheek.

"Thank you," I whispered to him. I crossed the tiny room in three steps and leaned over my grandmother to give her a hug, trying to be as gentle as I could. A nurse was inspecting a couple of fluid-filled bags that hung on a pole beside the bed. "What's wrong with her?" I asked the nurse.

"Looks like it was probably her heart."

"Probably?" I asked. "That's not good enough."

"Melanie Rose Hogan," Nana scolded.

"Nana, probably doesn't cut it. If it's your heart, we need to know for sure so we can do what needs to be done." I looked at the nurse, her eyes kind, making me feel ashamed of my behavior. "I'm sorry," I said and sighed. "I know it's no excuse, but this has really rattled me."

"No apology necessary," she said, her gentle smile reaching her eyes. "If it were my grandmother, it would rattle me too. These things are never easy. The doctor will be in to talk to her as soon as we get the results back from the tests."

"What tests did he run?" I asked, my hand resting on my grandmother's shoulder.

"So far we've done an ECG and a blood draw. Depending on the results of those she may decide to do—"

She was stopped short by another nurse poking her head in the door.

"I'm supposed to tell you your friends are in the waiting room," she said and then disappeared.

"Which friends did you bring?"

"I didn't bring any friends. They brought me," I said. "Claire and Cole."

"I'll go out there and let them know what's going on and what we know so far," Jack said."

"Which is pretty much nothing," I said looking from my grandmother back to the nurse.

As soon as Jack left, a woman in a white coat and a clipboard came in, stethoscope looped around her neck. She reached her hand out.

"You must be Melanie."

"I am. How did you—"

"Your brother Jack told me you would be here."

"Of course. My brother. What did you find out?"

"We know it wasn't a heart attack. Her enzymes are good." She turned to my grandmother. "Mrs. Donnelly, do you live alone?"

"Yes."

"Do you have a social worker that visits you in your home?" She edged up to the bed and placed her hand on my grandmother's.

"I don't need a social worker. I do just fine."

"Have you had any episodes where you were confused or found yourself someplace and didn't know how you got there?"

I looked at my grandmother, my eyebrows knit in confusion.

"Of course not," she said. "I'm not senile."

"Where are you going with this, Doctor?" I asked. "What did you find?"

She smiled at me, a sentiment she most likely meant to bring me comfort but did the opposite. She looked at my grandmother.

"Who makes your meals?"

"She's an exceptional cook," I said.

"Anyone else?" she asked as if I hadn't said anything at all.

"Melanie cooks with me sometimes."

"Doctor," I said, getting impatient. "What did you find?"

"Her blood work showed chemicals found in antifreeze," she answered without looking at me, studying my grandmother. "Who made your last meal and when was that?"

"What kind of chemicals?" Nana asked, her voice weak. "I made my last meal, and that was at about...oh, I'd say about three o'clock this afternoon. And then Jack—my grandson—made me a snack about six o'clock before he took me to a party at the Grizzley's place."

"Does Jack have any reason to be upset with—"

"No!" I said, abruptly standing up from where I had sat down beside my grandmother on the edge of the bed a moment earlier. Anger flared like lighter fluid thrown on a fire. "Jack would never hurt my grandmother. *Our* grandmother."

The doctor turned toward me, carefully studying my every move. "At this point we can't rule anything out, Ms. Hogan. Right now we need to look at everything and take every precaution. Someone tried to harm my patient."

"Your patient is my grandmother. Jack would never hurt her." It was a battle of the wills and I was determined to win.

"I took an oath to protect my patients, Ms. Hogan. What you think doesn't change that oath. I've contacted the authorities. In the meantime, no one is allowed near my patient."

"I'm not leaving her room."

"The authorities will be here any minute. You can take it up with them."

She was pushing back at me, but I would not budge. Not even an inch. I looked down at my grandmother who had drifted off.

"Nana?" I said, panic rising.

"I had the nurse give her something to help her relax. She's been through quite an ordeal."

"What about being awake when the police get here?"

"By the time we're finished talking with them she'll be awake and able to speak with them."

She motioned to someone on the other side of the curtain that closed off my grandmother's room, beckoning them over. She checked my grandmother's chart that hung at the foot of her bed, lingering there until a man in uniform who I recognized as one of my clients at the salon stood outside the door. He'd told me he was a security guard somewhere, I just didn't know where until now.

I sat beside my grandmother's bedside and held her hand against my cheek, watching as she slept. I stretched my brain every which way trying to figure out how she would have gotten antifreeze in her system. I couldn't come up with anything logical. Anything I came up with was so far off in left field that that it wasn't even possible.

I looked up as the security guard poked his head in the room.

"Melanie," he said as surprise registered on his face.

"Hey Sean," I said. "I see you're charged with babysitting until the police arrive."

"Yup."

"What do you know about this?" He looked down, averting his eyes from mine. "I'm not the enemy here. You know me, Sean."

He looked over his shoulder, then down the hall to his left, his right and back to his left again, resting his sights on me.

"I heard someone tried to kill her," he said, his voice a low rumble, "and that the suspect is probably still in this hospital."

"Did you hear the name of this suspect?"

"Jack somethin' or other. My partner is keepin' an eye on him in the lobby. Sounds like it's her grandson. How pathetic is that. That SOB, trying to kill an old woman."

My blood was close to boiling again, and I glanced down at my grandmother to be sure she was still sleeping. I looked up at Sean.

"First of all, Sean," I said, my voice a steady, low, eerily calm tone, "don't believe everything you hear from people who don't know what they're talking about. Jack would never hurt this woman. Second, she's not old."

"I—I—I just meant—" he stammered, his cheeks flushing.

"I'm just saying don't believe what you don't know to be the truth." I stood up and walked to the door. "Could you please monitor her while I step out of the room for a minute?"

"Of course, of course," he said, all too eager to make me happy with him.

"I'll be back in a minute."

"Okay." He tipped his hat and put his hands in his pockets while he puffed out his chest.

I rolled my eyes and walked out. The thought that he was in charge of my grandmother's safety made me a little uneasy. I had to hurry back.

As I walked out of the room and around the corner I came face-to-face with two police officers walking through the double doors that opened up into the hallway lined with rooms on both sides. I turned and watched as they walked to the desk halfway down the hall. The tall one stood with his elbow on the counter, the hand of his other arm resting on the butt of his gun. The other officer, at least a foot shorter, stood to the left, hands on his hips as they talked with the staff behind the desk. I saw my grandmother's doctor lean over the desk and look down the hallway just as I turned back around. I had to find out what happened before they arrested Jack for something I knew he didn't do. And yet, the slightest suspicion niggled at me. If Jack was the last one to give my grandmother something to eat...

When I went into the Emergency Room lobby, an officer was stationed at the only exit door, other than the one I'd just come through that led back to the patient rooms. Claire, Cole, and Jack were sitting in a corner. Claire and Jack were deep in conversation while Cole got up and approached the officer.

"Anderson?" I heard Cole say. I strained to hear more but they kept their voices so low I couldn't make out anything that was being said. Lip reading wasn't my strong suit.

I heaved my weight down next to Claire. She put her arm around my shoulders and the tears started trickling. When Jack sat on the other side of me and put his arm around me, too, the trickle turned into a downpour. When I finally pulled myself together, I pulled a sandpaper-like tissue from the box in front of me and blew my nose.

"Where's Rubie?"

"She and Levi were still at Grizzley's last I heard," Claire said. "'Course that was right after we left there with you. She texted me on the way to the hospital and asked us to keep her posted."

I watched the guy Cole was talking with as he kept staring at Jack, watching his every move. I could tell it was getting on Jack's last nerve.

"If that guy doesn't stop giving me the eyeball I'm going to give him the eyeball back," Jack said. "And maybe a ball of the fist."

"Jack," I said, looking at him, my eyes burning from the buckets I'd just cried, "someone gave my grandmother something with antifreeze. They're looking at you as the possible—"

"That's crazy!" He said, his dark eyes wide. Johnson looked over at him, his eyes piercing with suspicion. Jack lowered his voice to a harsh whisper. "That's why Bruno over there is standing there watching me like a hawk? Why are they looking at me? And why would anyone ever want to hurt Rose? That's the equivalent of wanting to hurt a puppy."

"You were the last one to get her something to eat or drink." I patted his knee. "I'm going to go back to her room for a little bit."

"Take Bruno over there with you," he grumbled.

"Seems he wants to stick by you." I gave him a quick peck on the cheek and turned to leave.

My grandmother was barely awake when I went to stand beside the bed. I took one small, frail hand and held it in my own. She smiled as she squeezed my hand slightly.

"How are you doing?" she whispered, trying to moisten her lips with her tongue. Her long silver braid lay over her shoulder and down her chest.

I reached for the plastic water glass on the bed tray and gently placed the straw between her lips. "How am I doing?" I shook my head. "Nana, I'm not the one lying in a hospital bed." After she finished taking a sip of water I set the glass back down on the tray and sat on the edge of the bed. I smoothed a wiry tendril of hair back from her cheek. "Claire asked if she could come and see you but I told her maybe later. Only one of us is allowed in at a time. And you know me. I'm kind of selfish." Nana chuckled and squeezed her eyes shut briefly. "Are you in pain Nana?" I can get a nurse to give you something.

"What's going on? There seems to be quite a ruckus going on out there."

"Are they keeping you awake? I can ask them to keep it down."

"Good heavens, no. I need to get home, don't cha know."

I leaned over and touched my cheek against hers. "You will go home soon enough. First we need to get you well."

"I'm fine, dear."

"Your voice says otherwise, Nana." My voice sounded deep and husky as I tried to hold back a few tears that threatened to escape. "You sound tired and a teensy bit weak."

"I'm not a weak woman."

"That's not even close to what I said, Nana. I know better than that. We all do." Except she looked all too frail at the moment. I laid my right hand on top of her hand that covered my left one, making a hand sandwich.

"Something is going on, Melanie. I don't need protecting. Tell me straight up what's going on."

I sighed. "Someone put what appears to be antifreeze in something you ate or drank. You don't remember the doctor saying that?"

Rose squinted and made a face. "Well—no, I don't. Why would they do that?"

"None of us has the answer to that."

"Who do they have in mind would do such a thing?"

I hesitated before answering. I didn't want to worry her, but I also didn't want to experience the wrath of Rose Donnelly should she find out that I was keeping the truth from her. I decided she deserved the truth.

"Since Jack was the last one who gave you something to eat they're looking at him."

"That's ridiculous," she said, her voice stronger. She struggled to sit up, and I gently eased her back down. "That boy wouldn't hurt me and you know it."

"I do, Nana. We all do."

"Someone needs to tell the police that. Now tell them to stop giving me this stuff that makes me so sleepy so I can set them straight. And I need to speak to Jack."

"They won't let him back here or anywhere near you."

"You can sneak him, can't you?"

I chuckled at her fierce determination. "I can't, Nana. That would do nothing but get him in even more trouble. And me. If that were possible," I mumbled.

Her muscles relaxed as she sighed and lay back against her pillows. "Oh, I suppose you're right." She patted my hand. "You need to go sit with him, don't cha know. He shouldn't be alone at a time like this."

"Nana, you're the one who shouldn't be alone. It's you someone tried to harm."

"Well, they didn't. I'm stronger than that. Besides, I'm not alone. There's people in and outta here. It's like grand central station in this place."

I chuckled again. This woman was a pistol. "I'll go sit with him." I leaned over and gave her tiny frame a hug, surprised at how strong her grasp was when she hugged me back.

When I opened the curtain and entered the hallway, the officer charged with my grandmother was standing across the hall speaking with a nurse. He stood with one elbow leaning on the counter, laughing at something he'd just heard. It was a little disheartening to see that the one who's in charge of keeping my grandmother safe was more interested in flirting with the staff than doing his job. At least he was an actual officer and not Sean.

When I rounded the corner into the waiting room, Cole was sitting on Jack's right, Claire standing beside Cole, her hand resting on the back of his neck. To Cole's left, partially hidden behind an artificial palm tree, was someone else. When I got closer, I was surprised to see that it was Levi.

"How's Rose?" Claire asked.

"Feisty. Wants to go home. Any news out here?"

"No," Jack said, clearly not happy.

"For what it's worth, my grandmother thinks it's absolutely ridiculous that they would think you did something to her."

"You told her?" He asked, the color draining from his face.

"She wanted to know what was going on. And you know my grandmother, Jack. There's no keeping anything from her. I swear she could get the truth out of a turnip. We'll find out who did this, Jack. I promise."

"Don't you go digging to get to the bottom of one of your hunches," Levi said. "We all know where that's gotten you in the past."

"If the police do their job then I won't have to," I said, winking at Jack. "We'll get you out of this. Don't worry."

"You're not worried?" he asked as he straightened the cuff on his jeans. I could tell he didn't know what to do with his nervous energy. It was unfamiliar territory for Jack.

"I didn't say that at all. I'm worried sick." I sighed and sat down next to him, resting my arm around his shoulders. I looked at Levi. "You're not the investigator on this case?"

"No. Not yet, anyway." The words were no sooner out of his mouth when his cell phone rang. He looked at the display and held it up. "Looks like saying *yet* was the kiss of death. The captain is calling as we speak." He touched a button on the screen, said, "Hey Captain," stood and walked over toward the door where Officer Johnson resumed his post. They all watched as he pushed through the door and disappeared.

Jack sat back and absently stared at the television screen. I reached for my phone to call Rubie but set it back down, deciding to wait until I had some answers before calling her. Just when things were getting back to normal. Whatever normal was these days.

Claire stood from where she had been sitting on Cole's leg, reached for her shoulder bag from the chair next to them and fished out her phone, looked at it, then set it back down. It was as if we were all trapped in our own circle of helplessness.

I looked at Johnson just as Levi came back in from outside, a frown causing deep creases between his brows. He looked at Cole and they exchanged a secret

232

unspoken message. Except it wasn't a secret. I could sense what it was before it happened. I looked at Jack.

Levi walked over to us, more sober than he even normally was, and said, "Jack Dancy, you're needed at the station for questioning in the attempted murder of Rose Donnelly."

Claire gasped and looked at Cole. I felt like I might vomit. I watched Jack's expression shift from disbelief to defeat in a nanosecond. I couldn't remember a time I'd ever seen him look so lost.

"Do I have time to call Bryce first?" he asked Levi.

"Yes. You're not being arrested. Just wanted for questioning."

"Looking at the big picture, it's the same thing," he mumbled as he retrieved his phone from his jacket pocket. I knew exactly what he meant.

"I'll be waiting for you outside," Levi said. "Take your time."

Claire sank down into a chair, fighting back tears. We watched as Levi disappeared through the door and into the night. She reached up for Cole's hand and said to no one in particular, "Who'd have thought a few short hours ago that we would be here going through this? This has been the worst birthday ever."

"Technically it's not your birthday anymore, babe. It's well past midnight." Cole rubbed her neck with his free hand. "Not the way I had planned to celebrate your birthday." He slipped his hand into his pocket.

"One minute we're toasting Melanie, and the next..."

As I watched and listened, it felt like it was all a terrible dream. I desperately wished I could wake up, open my eyes and see the sun shining through the skylight above my bed.

"Melanie," I heard Jack say, "you have to know I didn't do it. I need you to know—"

I put my hand on his knee and leaned my head on his shoulder. "I know you didn't do it, Jack. I know it wasn't you." Did I though? Did I really know, without a shadow of a doubt, that he didn't? But that was crazy. Of course, I did. Didn't I?

Chapter 34

JACK, CLAIRE AND I sat huddled on the sofa for one last moment, lost in the deafening silence of our own thoughts as we each tried to fit the pieces together. I watched as Cole stood talking to Johnson again, Johnson's stance showing dominance with his feet hip-width apart, arms crossed in front of him as the conversation began getting somewhat heated. Johnson was impatiently explaining something to Cole, but Cole remained unaffected by his co-worker's ruffled demeanor. Cole unwrapped a piece of round red candy, dropping it on the floor before he got it to his mouth. He bent over to pick it up, looked at it, and tossed it in the garbage can behind him.

In a split second a vivid image of hours before flashed through my mind. I bolted upright and drew in a sharp breath.

"Melanie, what is it?" Claire asked. I felt both of them looking at me.

"Claire, can you see if you can get Cole to get you back to my grandmother's room somehow? I need you to stay with her for a few minutes."

"Where are you going?"

"Out to Jack's car. I'll be back in a sec." I looked at Jack. "Can I have your keys? You'll be riding with Wescott anyway, right?"

"I wasn't planning on it. What do you need? I'll go get it for you before I leave."

"Thanks, but I'll go. I need some fresh air anyway."

"Let me come with you then. It's midnight. You shouldn't be going out there by yourself."

"I'll be fine." I heard the edge in my voice and felt a stab of guilt. But more than that I felt the need to flee. And fast. "Why don't you ride with Wescott, and I'll come and pick you up with your car. Please?" I held out my hand waiting for him to hand me his keys. "Please, Jack? There are lights all over out there. It's lit up like a Christmas tree. Besides, security cars are driving around the parking lot all the time." He finally, but reluctantly, dropped the keys in my hand. I reached over and pecked his cheek. "Thanks, Jack. I'll meet you at the station."

I forced myself to walk away from them until I was positive I was out their line of sight. Levi stood a few feet from the door, his back toward me as he held his phone to his ear. I tiptoed as quietly as I could in my black boots until I rounded the corner of the building and then made a run for the car. If I was right, I had to get there fast.

I started Jack's car and tore out of the parking lot, the tires squealing as I turned the corner onto the street that ran parallel to the parking lot. I stepped on the gas, slowing slightly at a stop sign, and glanced on all sides for any flashing lights to appear. That was the last thing I needed right now. Between the officers that were inside the hospital and the fact that it was the night shift, I couldn't imagine there would be anyone on the force driving on the streets right now. Or I could hope that would be the case.

I reached Oak Avenue, one of the three main streets that runs from one side of Birch Haven to the other, and made a fast right, speeding up as fast as I dared, heading to the edge of town. I stopped breathing and my heart skipped several beats when I glanced up in my rearview mirror and saw red and blue lights coming up too fast. Instinctively I slowed down, knowing it was too late, he would have had me clocked on his radar already. I pulled over, hoping he would just give me the ticket and get it over with. I had someplace I had to be. I closed my eyes, sending up a quick prayer. When I opened them the siren screamed by my window as it passed and the lights were now in front of me speeding off to some other unfortunate car. I let out the breath I'd been holding and began toward my destination, pressing my luck as much as I dared but keeping my speedometer to no more than five miles per hour over the limit. I once heard that five miles over the speed limit was safe and a cop wouldn't stop someone for that. I hoped with all my might that it was true.

A mere ten minutes later I turned into the parking lot of Grizzley's Tap House. There were only a handful of cars left. I scanned them to see if I could guess which one was the suspect vehicle. In between episodes of fearing I would get stopped for speeding or running stop signs, more of the pieces fell into place as I replayed the events in my head. I knew what happened, the only part I didn't know was the why. But I would find out in a matter of minutes. And there would be a price to pay for the poor soul who messed with my grandmother.

I slammed my car door shut, pushing the button on the key fob until I heard the beep, letting me know it was locked. A habit that cost me an extra five seconds I didn't have. I jogged to the front door and pulled it open just as someone was pushing the door open to come out. Had I not been so rigid and firm in my stance, all of my energy propelling me forward at a rate faster than the door opened, I would have toppled over from the woman who fell into me. I helped right her back to a standing position and walked around her and through the door.

I walked around the restaurant looking for what Levi would call a person of interest, what I would call nothing other than a suspect in an attempted murder. Unable to spot her in the restaurant, I pushed open the swinging doors that led to the kitchen and looked around.

"Help you?" asked the man who was scrubbing the steel surface of the grill with a grill brick. It reeked of burned something or other.

"I'm looking for Sharon."

"Ain't here." He went back to putting his weight into pushing the brick back and forth on the grill.

"Where is she?"

"Don't know," he said over his shoulder, less than interested. "Tonight was her first night on the job. Her last, too. Couldn't handle it, I guess. She left her tables a mess and took off."

"What time was that?"

"Prob'ly about—I couldn't even guess. Gus might know. Go ask 'im."

"Where would I find Gus?"

He stopped long enough to shrug and say over his shoulder. "Behind the bar'd be my guess. If he ain't workin' he's drinkin' back there."

Without another word I went back through the swinging doors to find Gus. There was one person counting money in the register behind the chest-high bar. Rows and rows of stemmed glassware hung over his head, the entire length of the bar.

"Are you Gus?" I asked as I bellied up to the bar. A man perched on the stool at the end looked up.

"Wasn't you in here earlier? I 'member you."

"That was a few hours ago. Sounds like you've been in here too long. Not driving I hope." He answered with a shrug.

"I'm Gus," the bartender said. "What can I do ya for?"

"I'm looking for Sharon."

"Left about two hours ago. Left her phone here though so I imagine she'll be back."

"Tonight was her first night?"

"Yup." He closed the till, jotted down something on a pad of paper that lay on the counter, and looked up at me as he grabbed a towel and began wiping the top of the bar.

"The guy in the kitchen said she left early?"

"Yup. Guess she decided this job wasn't for her." He finished with the wet towel and grabbed a dry one, picking up a glass and methodically wiping it. I had all I could do not to rip the towel from his hands so I could get his full attention.

"Who hired her?"

"I did."

"From where?"

"Couldn't tell ya where she came from, miss. I had a server not show up for her shift tonight, Sharon walked in needing a job so I hired her. Lotta good that did."

I looked around the room and saw the last of the customers had left. Except for the guy at the end of the bar who sat so still looking at the bottom of his glass I somewhat wondered if he was still alive. I didn't have time to check right now, though. Just in case he wasn't.

The table we'd sat at hours earlier remained untouched, our glasses, straws, and napkins still littered the table. Thank the good Lord for small miracles.

"Gus, would you have a plastic bag of some sort?"

"Sure I have one somewhere 'round here. Whatcha need it for?"

"I need to put something in it." *Duh!*

I strode over to the table we'd been sitting at in the corner, swiping a napkin from a clean table as I passed. I wiped up my grandmother's spilled Shirley Temple from when Rubie hit her knee on the table when she stood to do her toast. I brought the napkin up to my nose and took a whiff, recoiling as it confirmed my suspicions.

I went back up to the bar where Gus was still wiping glasses and looked around for the plastic bag. Not seeing one, I held up the napkin.

"Gus, a bag?"

"Oh, yeah. I didn't know you needed it right now. Hold on and I'll go in the back and getcha one."

Taking his sweet time, he disappeared behind the swinging doors of the kitchen. Each minute felt like an hour. Just as I was going to go see what was taking so long, he came back out.

"Sorry 'bout that. Sharon came in to get her phone."

My phone buzzed in the side pocket of my shoulder bag, the same pocket that held my shears. I let it continue buzzing until it eventually stopped. I didn't want to have to answer questions about where I was or what I was doing there. Not yet, anyway.

"When?"

"Just now."

My heart started beating wildly.

"Where is she now?"

"Leaving, I 'spose."

"I didn't see her come in. How did she get in here?"

He looked at me as if I had a screw loose somewhere. "Through the backdoor in the kitchen. It's the door all the employees use." He shook his head and tossed the baggie on the counter. "Here ya go."

Typically a sarcastic remark flies off the tip of my tongue but I didn't take the time to spew one right now. I threw the napkin with the evidence down alongside the bag. There was something I needed to take care of first. I bolted through the swinging doors of the kitchen, nearly plowing into the kid who'd been cleaning the grill as he crossed in front of the doors.

"Back door—where is it?"

"Thataway."

He pointed off to the left, and my legs hurtled in that direction. Just before I reached the back door, I slipped on some grease and caught myself on the metal bar across the steel door, pushing it open and stumbling into the parking lot. I hadn't expected the step and fell headlong into the damp gravel, cursing under my breath as the gravel bit into the palms of my hands. My phone went scattering into a patch of weeds to the side of the door. I frantically looked around the dark parking lot as I struggled to my feet, the only light being a weak beam from the front of the building that leaked around the side and one small sliver of the back. Suddenly I spotted the taillights light up on a car off to my right and took off at a run. I had to stop her.

Chapter 35

I TOOK OFF ON A dead run, the pain in my palms and knees forgotten as only one thought pulsed through my head. I had to stop her, and since she had a car and I didn't, I was already at a severe disadvantage. Just as Sharon was about to pull out of the parking lot, I reached the side of the car and pounded on the window. Sharon looked at me through her closed window, her lips twisting in a half smile. Her window began rolling down, stopping little more than half-way.

"Melanie, Melanie, Melanie," she sneered. "What do you need? Complaints about your service here? Go tell the management."

"Not the service, Sharon. Just you." I said, breathless. My lack of running the past months showed up again and I cursed my laziness.

"Looks like someone needs more exercise," she taunted and rolled down her window the rest of the way. "I tell you what, Miss High and Mighty, while you catch your breath, I'll just be going on my way. Give your grandmother my regards."

A surge of adrenaline came from out of nowhere and I lunged at her through the opened window to grab her keys. I heard her muffled scream against my torso and yelped in pain as I felt her teeth sink into my side. Instinctively I reached and elbowed her, catching her square on her jaw.

"What in the—who are you and why did you poison my grandmother?" I said. I balled my fist, keeping her keys secured so she couldn't get them back.

"Gimme my keys," she hissed, rubbing her jaw.

"I want some answers first."

Sharon attempted to open her door but I slammed it shut.

"Oh, please," she said, "holding your hip against the door could never stop me from getting out."

She pushed on the car door and I stumbled back. Stupid heels! My hand went over my shoulder and I threw her car keys as far as I could. She turned to run after them but I stuck my foot out and she went head over heels.

"Oops," I said, stifling a laugh. "Your white coat may never be white again."

"Lenny'll just buy me another one."

My heart just about leaped right out of my throat and my world stopped for a moment. *Lenny?* "Lenny who?"

"You know exactly who I'm talking about. If not, just ask your mother."

The wheels started spinning again and the last of the pieces fell into place. Now I knew the why. Sharon took off to search for her keys and I reached in my pocket, relief filling me it was only my phone that had fallen out.

"Hey, Sharon?" I called out after her. She squatted down, grasping around her in the dark as she searched for her missing keys. "You won't be needing those." I went to one tire, then the next, and the next, pausing before I shoved my shears into the last one, the air hissing its escape. She watched me, marvelously speechless. "Maybe Lenny can buy you a new car, too. But I'm pretty sure you won't need one where you're going."

"Noooo!" she screeched and came running over to me at the same time I heard car tires crunching on gravel and looked up to see Cole's car come around the building.

I grinned. "Your escort arrived."

"My—my—my escort?" she stammered.

I grinned at her discomfort. "No, silly, not that kind of escort. That's Lenny's business. This one is the one that will escort you to jail."

Her head swiveled to look at Cole as he got out of his car, his handcuffs at the ready as he ran over to her.

"I'll get you," she wailed at me. "I'll so get you for this. Lenny will see to it."

Claire came over to stand by me and circled her arm around my shoulders.

"Maybe you and Violet can share a cell," I called out to her as Cole led her to stand beside his car while he called for a patrol car. "Might be fun for the two of you to compare notes on Lenny."

Claire shook with held in laughter. "Good one."

"How did you guys know where I was?"

"I've known you long enough to know how your mind works."

I shuddered. "Now that's a scary thought."

"True story, my friend." She giggled, such a delightful sound compared to Sharon's screeching and wailing that continued. "Poor Cole. He has to stand there and listen to that. He's going to be deaf by the time backup gets here."

"I tried calling you. Why didn't you answer?"

"I felt my phone buzzing in my pocket but I was a little tied up."

"Why didn't you let us know where you were going?"

I leaned by rear end against Sharon's car and folded my arms in front of me, rubbing my upper arms for warmth. "I needed to do this on my own. For Nana."

"You could have gotten killed, Melanie. Then what would your grandmother have done?"

"But I didn't."

"Well, you could have." She sounded like a defiant child and I smiled to myself. "It was a bonehead move, you know."

"Yeah, probably. Have you heard from Jack?"

"He was still at the police station. I'm assuming he's been relieved of that duty since Cole called in about Sharon." I shivered. "Cold?" she asked me.

"This was too close, Claire. Not only did Violet leave me to take the fall for her in Gina's murder, but she's the reason my grandmother was almost killed." My voice quivered.

"From now on we're celebrating the fact that woman is out of your lives."

A squad car came around the building, red and blue lights on but thankfully he left his siren off. I had a splitting headache. "I'm probably going to need a rabies shot," I said drily. I felt Claire turn to look at me.

"A rabies shot?"

"You betcha. She bit me and I'm pretty sure she's rabid."

Claire's head tilted back and she laughed that glorious sound that reminded me of glass jars tinkling together in the warm summer sunshine. "If that's the worst thing that happened, Mel, consider yourself one lucky woman."

"Lenny's a punk, sending his girlfriend to do his dirty work."

"They deserve each other."

We watched as Officer Johnson got out of the police cruiser and led Sharon to his car.

"There's still something I don't understand. How did Gina and Violet know each other to begin with? And what brought Gina to Birch Haven?"

"Here's what I've pieced together. Both she and Violet worked for Lenny. Violet has been getting deeper and deeper in debt. Apparently Lenny found out where I was, knew Gina had been a manicurist before she started working for him, and planted her in our salon to keep an eye on me as collateral in case Violet didn't pay her debt."

Johnson began driving to the front of the building, Sharon still ranting, her voice carrying into the night through Johnson's open window. Another car pulled around the building. Levi and Jack got out.

"Bet this parking lot hasn't had this much action since—well, probably since never," I said. Jack walked over to me and wrapped me in a hug. "Ouch!" I flinched when his arm pressed against my side. "Sharon bit me," I explained.

"There's a name for female dogs like that," he said.

"Be nice, Jack." I chuckled.

Levi strode over to Cole, said something, and they both walked over to us.

"What?" I asked. "You two look like you have news to share."

"You haven't had enough for one night?" Levi said. I could see him smile as he stood at an angle that allowed the moon's beam to shine on him. "I hear you use your shears for more than just cutting hair. Bet it ruined 'em, though."

I shrugged and smiled. "Awe, it was worth it."

"We found the woman whose shift Sharon took at the pub tonight."

"Where was she?"

"In the hospital. She's sick."

"Let me guess," I said, dryly. "Antifreeze poisoning."

"You're good, Detective Hogan."

"All in a day's work, Detective Wescott."

Chapter 36

DETECTIVE WESCOTT CALLED ME the following day to let me know the authorities in L.A. located Violet with little trouble. At a racetrack of all places.

"I never said she was too bright," I told him when he showed up at the salon to deliver the details.

"Arrested for first-degree murder. Any chance at bail will be denied. Not only because of the serious offense but she's a high flight risk. They'll extradite her immediately."

"I want to talk to her." I wasn't sure what I was going to say, but I was very sure I had to talk to her.

"That's not a good idea," he said.

"Why?" I asked. "I have a hundred and one questions I need to ask her. Maybe even a hundred and two."

"But who's counting, right?" he grumbled.

I could tell he was backing down. "I have a right to know why she did what she did. Why she would frame her own daughter."

"She probably doesn't even recognize it as doing anything wrong. Are you sure you want to know that?"

"Even if she didn't realize it at the time, she left having to have known I would take the fall. She's selfish and self-centered, but she's not stupid."

He looked at me and was silent for a moment, as if trying to decide whether to say what he wanted to say. Apparently he wanted to. "Do you really believe she will tell you the truth? Be honest with yourself. Because I think you're expecting too much from someone who's unable to deliver."

"If there's the smallest chance, I have to try."

He exhaled long and slow and leaned back in the chair. He ran a hand over his bald head. "Fine. I need to interview her first. When I'm done you and I will talk more, okay?"

"You're not the one I need talk with, Detective. She's the one who holds the answers I need."

"Melanie," his voice was so soft, the gruffness diminished, "the answers you're looking for, you may never get. Why put yourself through that?"

I worked on the floor with the toe of my boot, trying to scrape something that wasn't there off the worn tile. "Fine. You talk to her first." As if he needed my permission to do his job. "But when you're done, I want a shot at her." My eyes darted up to meet his. "I mean at getting some answers," I quickly clarified. I expected him to disapprove of my unintended choice of words as he had in the past when I made a tasteless joke. But this time, he shook his head slowly and chuckled. I breathed with relief.

"I get the first shot," he said and winked, a friendly gesture that brought me comfort, if even the smallest bit.

"I know you have those one-way mirrors because when I was considered a suspect—"

"A person of interest," he corrected.

"Call it what you want, but I was a suspect. Admit it."

"I won't."

"Only because you're being stubborn." I met his eyes with mine in a challenge. "As I was saying, those one-way mirrors aren't only in the movies. I want to watch while you question Violet. I need to."

"I'll see what I can do."

"Detective, please."

"Melanie, I said I'll see what I can do. I know you don't trust people, but you have to trust me here." His voice pleaded with me to understand his position.

"I'll work on it."

True to his word, Violet was extradited to Birch Haven the following day. By the time she was brought in and Detective Wescott was ready to question her, he had worked it out for me to sit behind the glass, but only under the condition that I agreed to someone else being there with me. It surprised him when I had agreed so readily. Was I really that difficult? I didn't have to ponder that question too long, though, before I knew the answer. Of course, I was. Or at least lately I had been. Desperate times call for desperate measures. And desperation reared its ugly head in this whole debacle.

I stood behind the glass despite the chair they placed there for me. The last thing I could do at that moment was to sit down or to be still. My feet and fingers were moving continually as if I had a bad case of the jitters. The jitterbugs were more like it. It felt like my skin was crawling as I looked at her through the glass.

I watched Violet sitting there looking every bit the victim as she waited for someone to come in and talk with her. That someone being Detective Wescott. I closely studied her every move, the few that there were.

She mostly stayed so still, so poised, every move so controlled, that I wondered if she was capable of being real at all. Life was just one big stage for her, and that had been her biggest role. It was the one she excelled at and the one she didn't even realize she'd landed.

I watched as she appeared to suddenly become agitated, thrumming her fingernails on the top of the metal table, her handcuffs still in place. She looked at her nails and cursed. She'd broken one, obviously. I looked at her hair, the most disheveled I'd ever remembered seeing it.

She began squirming in her chair, sliding down, then sitting up straight. She tried crossing her legs, only to be stopped by the shackles that held her feet in place, close together.

"Somebody get in here!" She yelled. "This is inhumane!" She looked around and then straight at the one-way glass, as if she were looking directly at me. I felt a shiver down my spine. "You can't keep me here like some caged animal!" she screamed. "Do you hear me?"

And as quickly as she'd gotten angry, she calmed back down again, looked at her nails and then folded her hands in her lap as if she didn't have a care in the world. It was then I realized that not only did she not have a conscious, was conniving, and manipulative, she was a woman with a clear mental illness. Would she even remember she killed someone?

Finally Detective Wescott entered the room, every bit the calm, cool-headed, good cop. He turned a chair around and casually sat down on it backward, his arms leaning on the back of the chair in front of him as he faced her.

She sat forward, tilting her head down slightly as she looked up at him, batting her eyelashes. "Detective," she purred seductively. "You don't really think I did anything wrong, do you?" She continued batting her lashes at him. Always an act. Her whole stinking life has been an act. One big production of which she was the star.

"What I think doesn't really matter, now, does it? It's what we both know. That's what we're really here for, isn't it?"

"Tell me what you know, Detective." Ever the flirt, she was. And it made my skin crawl some more.

"Why don't you tell me what you know, Violet."

Despite his back being toward me, I could sense him smiling at her, daring her to try hiding the truth that he was determined to find out.

"I know if you let me out of these cuffs I would be a very good girl," she purred.

My cheeks flushed with embarrassment for her. Embarrassment for me, related by blood to this woman making such a complete fool of herself.

"Naw," he said, sounding like he had a slight drawl. "You're not really my type."

Her eyes glinted steal and then became seductive again. "You never know unless you try."

"Try being honest with me. How did you know Gina?"

"Gina who?"

The cat and mouse game continued until I thought I would scream and break through the window that separated us, wrapping my hands around her scrawny, lying neck, squeezing the truth out of her. And still she sat there, enjoying the game just as much now as she did when it first began. And Detective Wescott kept his cool the entire time, not letting on for an instant that he was thinking anything other than boredom with her game.

"He'll get her to crack. Just you wait and see."

I startled at the voice behind me. I had been so wrapped up in the live stage performance in the next room that I had forgotten someone was in this room with me.

"What makes you so sure?"

"He always does."

He seemed to enjoy the show, just waiting for the expected outcome. I wasn't as confident as he was, though. Patience never had been my strong suit. I was just beginning to think it would never happen when she turned into what seemed like another person, her eyes turning hard, her voice like steel.

"You really want to know, Detective?"

The voice behind me said victoriously, "Aanndd here it goes."

I pressed my face closer to the glass as if it would make me hear better.

Violet continued. "I had big dreams and aspirations for my life. When I got knocked up those dreams vanished. For a while, anyway. I did that girl a favor by leaving her with my mother and my pops, and she has always treated me like crap for doing it. I did her a favor!" Beads of spittle scattered through the air in front of her.

"Yes, you did," I whispered to myself, tears burning hot behind my eyelids.

"So when she acts like the ungrateful child she always has, well, I didn't have to put up with that. She ruined my chances of becoming a star, so I did what I had to do."

"Where does Gina fit in the picture?"

I wanted to hear more, to have my questions answered, but I had a feeling Detective Wescott was steering her in another direction. Manipulating the interrogation to get exactly what he needed, including

253

hearing Violet confess to details we had already figured out. But he wasn't working to get a thing more than what he needed.

"Gina was the one that introduced me to quick money. She introduced me to a bookie."

"Lenny?"

She looked at him, eyes hard, then continued. "Yes, Lenny. That son-of-a—well he tracked me down like a dog. When he found out Gina lived in the town where my daughter worked, he planted her in that little playhouse Melanie calls a business. That—that—girl," she stammered, "Gina was just waiting for me. Says he knew I would go there, and he said I owed him money. I didn't owe him nothing. Not. A. Single. Cent." She stabbed her finger at the table with each word. "Besides, I offered to work it off, ya know. But no. He was being a jerk."

"So why did you shoot Gina?"

I sucked in my breath.

"She threatened me. She was going to kill me."

"We didn't find a gun on Gina, Violet."

"She called me and asked to meet. I thought it was for old time's sake. To catch up, you know?"

"If that's what you thought, why would you bring a gun?"

"I told you I didn't. Gina did."

"But we didn't find a gun on Gina."

She tipped her head back and groaned, a sound that was a combination of boredom and frustration. "Okay, fine. I'll be straight with you." She looked at him again, her eyes now dull and devoid of any emotion at all. "When Gina wanted to meet me at Melanie's house I knew something was up. I told her I would meet with her, but not at the house. On my way to the meeting spot, I stopped to get something to protect myself with. Surely you can understand that. I wasn't about to walk into an ambush. That would be just stupid."

"But I told you, there wasn't a gun on Gina."

"Well, there was probably one around there somewhere. What could she have done with it when she was dead?"

"Bingo!" the voice said behind me, sending me up in the air a foot.

Geez! This guy has got to stop that!

"There was a gun, Violet, but it didn't belong to Gina. It was registered to your daughter. Gina didn't have access to the gun. But you did. See, what I can't figure out is why you would set your daughter up to take the fall and then just leave her. Sounds like you've gotten to be an expert at leaving when the going gets tough."

"You don't know a thing about me, Detective," she spat, eyes glinting steel again. She tipped her head back ever so slightly. "You sit there all cool, the world by the tail, using your charm and good looks to get what you want. My daughter," she spat the word, so full of contempt. "She has the picture-perfect life. I gave her that life and what has she ever given me? Nothing but rejection. She needs to learn that life isn't always a party." She sat back and smiled an evil smile. "Detective," she said quietly, "Have I hit a nerve?" She laughed loud. "Oh, I have! You have the hots for my daughter."

I blushed, not sure if I was more embarrassed for Violet making such an idiot of herself or for Detective Wescott that he had to deal with it.

"This isn't about me, Violet, it's about what a rotten excuse of a mother you are. And a cold-blooded killer." His answer was quiet, controlled, but his tone spoke volumes.

"It was self-defense. I had to shoot her or she would have shot me." Her eyes almost pleaded for him to believe her. "Lenny's goons shot through Melanie's window at me for Pete's sake. What better proof do you need?"

"None at all, Violet. None at all."

He stood, turned the chair around and pushed it in like he was leaving from an ordinary visit with a friend. When he reached the door he stopped and turned back to face her, but I could see his face now. And I could see contempt in his eyes as he looked at her. "Just one more thing."

"I seem to be the one doing all the giving here, Detective. What's in it for me?"

"A clear conscience." Violet snorted at that. "I agree," He said. "That's a comical thought, isn't it?"

"And I ask again, why should I help you with anything else?"

"You're not helping me, you're helping yourself. What about the attempt on Rose Donnelly's life?"

"What about it?"

"What do you know about it? Were you in on it?"

We'd talked about that before and we both knew Violet couldn't have been in on it. I wondered where he was going with this.

"Of course I wasn't in on it," she said. It enraged me she had the nerve to look insulted that he would ask her that after what she'd already done. "That was Lenny's woman who did that. He said he was going to make me pay one way or another. I figured he would finally come to his senses and let me work it off in his other business. I didn't know he was going to punish my mother for it. That just goes to show what kind a man he is. He isn't a man at all. He's a coward who hides behind his goons, one of his goons being his woman, to do his dirty work for him."

"Do you know how it happened?"

"Of course. Lenny told me about it. He said Sharon, Karen—whatever her name was—put antifreeze in her drink. He's the one you should be after, not me. I did nothing wrong but defend myself."

I looked at her, incredulous at how she could be so casual about it. Her own mother could have died and she was acting like it was nothing more than a mere hangnail. Could she really be that cold? Or was she that sick?

"And you didn't think to mention that when you found out?"

"What for? It's not like it would have done any good. The only thing it would have accomplished is to get me in trouble. It had already gone down and she was safe in the hospital."

For a moment, I feared for Violet's life. I swear Levi's eyes were spraying bullets. His cheeks got red and a vein protruded in his temple. Without saying a single word, he turned and left the room.

And I was left in awe of the many faces of one person I had just witnessed in Violet. I felt empty, yet full. Sad, but not so much angry anymore. Confused, but the bitterness melted away. There was no other way to explain it other than she was just a very sick woman.

Chapter 37

I DECIDED NOT TO tell Nana about the interrogation of Violet by Detective Wescott. That plan became easier to carry out when I got to her house and found she had turned in for the night. If she heard me and woke up, Plan B was to let her know I was too exhausted to stay up a second more, and tell her we could catch up in the morning. That would give me ample time throughout the night to think about how best to handle it. It's not like there was a high likelihood I would sleep much anyway. There was a fine line between causing her unneeded worry and keeping something from her she would want to know. I needed to find the best way to walk that line. Also, that she'd just gotten home from the hospital earlier that day cemented my decision to wait.

Once again I brushed my teeth and washed my face in the kitchen sink so she wouldn't waken by the sound of the water running through the pipes so close to her room. Before all of the latest drama played out, she had insisted on me staying with her until the killer, and the hit man—or woman—who had shot through my window, were caught. The only thug left to catch was

Lenny, and I thought there was a pretty good chance it wouldn't be long. After the past couple of days, I wasn't only staying because of my grandmother's request, but to keep watch and help as she regained her strength. Not only was it the least I could do, I was grateful to not have to stay at my house by myself yet. Jack left back to Minneapolis as soon as he was free to leave, but he would come back over the weekend. I desperately hoped Lenny would be behind bars with Violet and Sharon by then. I was dying to be back in my house, getting it back to the sanctuary I'd created it to be before all this chaos ensued. I could almost envision a long hot bath in my antique claw foot bathtub, followed by lighting a fire in my fireplace, curling up with a good book, a blanket, and a cup of tea. I couldn't wait to sit on the deck at night looking over the lake, the moonbeams dancing on the water, and watching the night sky, wishing on a shooting star. My wishes were going to be so different than in the past.

When I pulled the towel away after drying my face, I expected to see Nana standing behind me, grateful when I didn't. She needed a good night's rest. If staying here for a few extra nights gave her the peace of mind to make that happen, then it was more than worth it.

I went into my room, quietly closed the door, and lay down in bed, pulling the covers snuggly around me and up to my chin. I lay staring at the ceiling and listened to the sound of cars passing by on the street, far enough away to be muffled, yet close enough to cast a dim light through the window of my room as they turned the corner.

So much had changed in so little time and I didn't know what to make of it. What does one do knowing that her mother, the woman who gave her life, didn't care one way or another what happened with that life? A woman who disregarded that life as so insignificant because it ruined her own dreams?

The thought crossed my mind—again—that maybe that's why I wasn't able to have children of my own. Maybe it was God's way of telling me I would be just like her, despite Nana telling me every time I voiced that fear that God isn't a vengeful God and that I would be a wonderful mother someday because of Violet. That irony was lost on me until today. Someday if I adopted a child, God willing, I would make certain I would never do to them what Violet did to me. I would make double sure they felt loved, no matter what, and that they came first. I would strive to be the mother Claire was and thrilled to be even half the mother Nana had been to me.

I turned my head to look at the clock just as the numbers rolled over to midnight. My eyelids were feeling heavy, and I fell into a fitful sleep, waking several times. I was grateful when I finally woke to the sound of my alarm. I had been having a horrible dream that I was outside in my front yard, and I saw a car coming up the drive. The car was going fast, kicking up dust behind it. I didn't know who it was, but my gut told me they were bad people. I tried with all my might to get to my front door, but my legs would only move in slow motion. The car kept getting closer but I couldn't move except for mere inches. I had almost reached the front door when two men wielding guns got out of the car, the driver and one from the passenger side. They aimed at me just as I put my hand on the doorknob and turned it to find it locked. I had a sense that maybe it was a dream and all I had to do was wake up, and fast, before I was dead and couldn't wake up ever again. One man morphed into Violet and the other into Detective Wescott, who turned and shot Violet. At the same time the shot rang out, my alarm rang and woke me up, drenched in sweat.

I jumped out of bed, stripped out of my sweat-drenched t-shirt and into the shower. After slathering on mahogany-scented body lotion, I dressed in faded jeans, my black boots, a long-sleeved white t-shirt with a scoop neck, dried my hair, applied some lip balm, and left a note for Nana on the kitchen table before I rushed out the door. I wasn't in any shape to have a conversation with her this morning. I just knew she'd see right through me and do nothing but worry the rest of the day. One thing my grandmother had was a strong faith in God, and she entrusted me to Him daily, but lately she'd struggled a bit more with that. My bad, I knew.

I stopped for coffee on my way to the salon. Today called for something strong. A double espresso later and I was out the door of the coffee shop, looked down to find my keys and smacked right into someone solid. I looked up into familiar eyes, my cheeks flushing.

"Detective Wescott, I'm so sorry."

"How about I buy you another of whatever you're drinking since I'm wearing the one that was in your hand." He was brushing lightly at his tweed jacket with one hand, an amused smile played on his lips.

"I'm so terribly sorry."

"I know. You already said that. Really, it's no problem. Come on, I'll buy you a replacement." He placed his large hand on the small of my back, leading me back into the coffee shop. "What were you drinking?"

"I wasn't drinking anything yet, but I was about to drink a double espresso."

His hand remained on the small of my back as I went back through the coffee shop doors, his other hand holding the door for me. It felt strangely comfortable. My stomach twirled and I skirted around and out of his reach. He strolled up to the counter, all of three steps with his long legs, while I stood back against the wall, pulling out my phone to check if I had any calls. I half expected Violet to have called me with some sob story since she was unaware that I'd heard the entire exchange with Wescott the evening before. I wasn't sure if I was relieved or disappointed when there was nothing that indicated a missed call.

"Do you have a moment to sit?" He was standing at my side holding my espresso toward me.

"I should really get to the salon. I have paperwork to do."

"Just ten minutes is all I'm asking for." I sat down at the table I had just been standing by, and he took the chair next to mine. "How are you doing?"

"Fabulous, thank you."

"Yeah? You sure?"

"As well as can be expected for someone whose mother thinks of her daughter as yesterday's trash."

"I would give anything to make it so you wouldn't have heard that yesterday. I shouldn't have agreed to let you watch."

His voice reminded me of a black velvet sky – soft, tender, yet mysterious. I placed my hand on his arm and looked into his eyes. "No, Detective, I had to hear it. I needed answers and though they weren't the ones I wanted to hear, I needed to hear them." I pulled my hand back and took a sip of my espresso. "Thank you."

"For what?"

"For the coffee. What do you think?" I smiled at my attempt at lightening the mood.

"You don't have to be so tough, you know. For such a tiny lady, you're probably the strongest woman I know."

"I've heard that before. What got my attention though is that you called me a lady and a woman in the same sentence. I've been called a lot of things, but those two aren't typically it." I chuckled and looked out the window, looking at really nothing at all, just needing to focus on something other than that moment. "Listen, Detective—"

"You've got to stop calling me that. It sounds so formal."

"You don't like formal?" I asked, teasing. I already knew the answer to that. For the short time I've known him, formal was the last word I would use to describe him.

"Tell you what, if you keep calling me that, I'll start calling you ma'am. We both know how well you like that."

I genuinely laughed for what felt like the first time in too long. "Yeah, not very." I stood and pushed my chair in. "I'm afraid I have to go. It's been longer than ten minutes." I smiled at him. "Thank you again, Detec—Levi."

He stood immediately after I did. "I'll walk you to your car."

We walked the short distance in silence. I pressed the button on my key fob to unlock the door and Levi opened it for me. Peace was finally finding its way back after my restless night. "It really was nice running into you this morning. Literally," I laughed again. Man, it felt good.

"Maybe sometime you could tell me about how Melanie got to be who Melanie is. Over a beer."

I smiled at him. "Maybe sometime I will."

Chapter 38

WHEN I GOT TO the salon, Claire and Rubie were already there. Claire was doing the books that she hated doing so much, and Rubie was folding the towels from the dryer.

"Hey, ladies!" I called to them as I walked in feeling rejuvenated after my morning coffee chat.

Rubie looked up from the dryer and Claire poked her head around the corner.

"Don't you look like Ms. Happy Pants this morning," Claire said. "Share."

"Can't," I said. "Your first customer of the day is walking up to the door." I nodded my head toward the window where Sam Nelson strolled up the sidewalk. "Good thing you don't have a jealous boyfriend. Oh, that's right, he is." I laughed.

"Eww! The guy's like 50 years old!" Rubie said, nose wrinkled.

"Careful there, my friend, you're treading on thin ice. My birthday this month brought me one year closer." I thought about how my birthday seemed like months ago, not mere days.

"You're still a decade away," she returned.

I finished the bookwork where Claire left off, while she attended to Sam. I had just finished when my cell phone rang. I looked at caller ID and saw an unfamiliar number.

"Hello?"

"Hi, Melanie." The caller said, voice raspy as if he were a two-pack-a-day smoker.

"Who's this?"

"That doesn't matter."

A chill went through me. "I beg to differ. Who is this?" I asked, my voice steady.

"The only thing that matters is I know who you are. And you are going to give me what your mother owes me."

"And what would that be, Lenny?" My voice was barely a whisper.

"Twenty-five thousand dollars."

"Why would I do that?"

"Because next time when you're standing at your window I might not miss."

My blood turned cold at his threat. "I'm not afraid of you, Lenny. It's you who's making my life better by eliminating the threats from it. First Violet, then Sharon...it's only a matter of time before you're eliminated as a threat, too."

An ugly chuckle came across the line. "You don't know what you're talking about. Get me money by midnight or I kill your mother."

"Well, now, that would be interesting, to say the least." Now it was my turn to have the upper hand. I would not be a victim of these people, including Violet, for another second. "You go ahead and try, Lenny. And good luck with that. Because she's in jail for murder. In fact, she and Sharon are probably comparing notes. You knew Sharon was arrested, too, right?"

The line went dead.

Good thing Levi's number was on speed-dial because it was the quickest I'd made a phone call in my entire life. I hung up from Levi after a brief relay of events, including the number Lenny was calling from, knowing I was well on my way to reclaiming my life. There was just one more thing I had to do.

"You look like you're a million miles away." Claire's voice brought me back to reality. "Who was that you were talking to?"

I smiled at her. "That, my friend, was exactly what I needed to go back home." I gave her a hug. "Claire, I hate to ask you this, but I have a huge favor."

"Of course, anything."

"Can you, Rubie, and Connie reschedule my appointments for this morning? By the time this is through, I might lose half my clientele."

"Of course. Are you okay?"

"I will be. I have somewhere I have to go."

"For the record," she said as I stood up, "your clients are as loyal to you as you are to your family and friends. They would never go to anyone else."

I hugged her and walked out the door to reclaim the rest of my life.

When I walked into the jail, the heavy steel door clanked shut behind me. My heart was beating so loudly I was sure anyone within fifty feet of me could hear it. The blood pulsed in my head, throbbing, and the tips of my ears felt like they were on fire.

I walked to the desk, told the security guard why I was there. She picked up the telephone, spoke a few grunts, and told me to have a seat.

"Do you know how long it will be?"

"Nope."

She went back to reading a magazine that lay open in front of her. "Alrighty then," I whispered through an exhale and turned to have a seat in a grimy puke green chair. For a moment, I almost felt sorry for Violet. But only for a moment. In fact, it was so quick I wondered if I even felt it at all.

I reached over to the little wobbly table beside me and picked up a brochure not really caring what it was about. I had no plans of actually reading anything, I just needed to keep my hands busy. I wondered if this was what it felt like for someone trying to quit smoking.

My head snapped up when I heard a harsh, "Melanie!" I saw an officer brusquely motion for me to follow. Like an obedient child (Nana would be so proud), I stood on heavy wooden legs and followed her through a set of heavy metal doors and back to the visiting area. For a moment, I thought I was going to be sick as years of culminating emotions bubbled to the surface. I wanted to bolt out of there but honestly didn't know if I could move a muscle.

And then I saw her. She came through the doors, met my eyes, and smiled! She sat in front of me, picked up the phone from the wall beside her and I picked up the receiver on my side.

"You came to see me," she purred into the phone.

"It would appear so." I couldn't seem to do anything but study her. When I was a little girl I used to think she was so beautiful. I didn't see that anymore. Pity tried to stir in me once again and I pushed it away.

"Melanie, you believe I didn't do this on purpose, don't you?"

"I don't know what I believe."

"Honey—"

"It's Melanie. You've lost the right to call me any terms of endearment." I thought I saw sadness flicker in her eyes. Was she even capable of feeling that? I didn't think so.

"Melanie," she said, then hesitated before going on. "I wish you wouldn't be so angry with me."

"Violet—"

"I'm your mother. Call me mom."

"No, you're not, and no, I won't. You may have given birth to me but that's as far as you took your role of mother."

"Give me another chance. Please."

I studied her eyes, trying to see what was there. Desperately hoping I didn't see any part of me in there. "I can't do that."

"Can't or won't?" she asked, accusation lacing her words, her eyes turning hard. "Then why are you here? To gloat?"

I shook my head slowly and looked down as a tear threatened to escape. I sniffed. "No, Violet. I came to tell you I forgive you."

"For what?"

Disbelief seized me and I thought I was going to go crazy and begin laughing hysterically. She seriously had no idea. Instead, I took a deep breath and said. "For everything." I could see the question in her eyes. "I don't expect you to understand."

"Will you come to my trial? Because I'm going to get out of here you know. And then I can be the mother you always thought you needed."

This time, I let the pity flow through me and touch my heart. I really felt sorry for her. "I'm sure you think that's true." I looked down and then back up at her. "But no. I won't be going to your trial."

"I thought you said you were forgiving me. Will you, at least, come visit me then?"

I opened my mouth to say maybe in thirty-six years, but out came, instead, "No. But I forgive you."

I looked at the sad, pathetic woman on the other side, the one who bore me and was part of the first four years of my life. I touched my hand to the glass, wiped a tear, hung up the receiver and turned to walk away. The last thing I saw was my mother angrily shouting what looked like my name as a guard came and took her away.

I walked out of the jail and into the freshness of the spring air. The gray cloudy skies had given way to the bluest sky I could ever remember in a very long time. I was sure others could see the bounce in my step that I could feel. The blanket of fear, the heaviness of rejection and self-pity I'd carried on my shoulders, the resentment, and bitterness that shrouded my heart for so many years, had melted away like the snow melting furiously before me as I walked to my car. This is what Nana must have meant when she said forgiveness sets free the forgiver, not the one being forgiven. She said whether or not the person accepts that forgiveness is not in our control. She said forgiveness allows us to set free the ghosts of the past, and that allows more room for joy and peace.

I sat in the silence of my car for a moment and lay my forehead against my hands on the steering wheel. I felt my jeans absorb fallen tears. Tears of joy. I felt so light and burden free, and peace enveloped me.

I sat up, brushed the palms of my hands across my cheeks, looked up to the heavens and whispered, *Thank You*. I started my car and pulled out of the parking lot, leaving behind my past and all the demons it once held. I had a life to live. One that included the people I loved more than anything in the world - Nana, Claire, Sydney, and Jack.

Seven-Layer Lasagna

One box lasagna noodles
One pound sweet Italian sausage
½ onion – chopped
2 jars roasted red pepper spaghetti sauce
1 can tomato paste
1 can water
1 can sliced black olives
1 small container cottage cheese
1 small container ricotta cheese
1 bag shredded Italian five-cheese

Combine chopped onion into a pound of hamburger and brown. Drain.

Cook one box lasagna noodles. Drain.

To the drained hamburger, add the spaghetti sauce, tomato paste, water, and black olives.

Spray bottom of 12x9 pan with cooking spray

Spread a small amount of the hamburger mixture on the bottom of the pan.

Place a layer of noodles on top of that.

Next, cover the noodles with the hamburger mixture.

Sprinkle dollops of cottage cheese and ricotta cheese.

Sprinkle shredded cheese over the top.

Repeat by placing another layer of noodles, followed by the cottage and ricotta cheeses, and more shredded cheese.

Sprinkle garlic powder over the top.

Cover with foil and bake at 350 degrees for 50 minutes. Remove foil and bake for another 10-15 minutes, until cheese is golden brown.

Dear Reader,

Word of mouth is the best promotion for an author. Please consider leaving a review on up your favorite retail site(s). A sentence or two is all that is needed. By doing this, it helps me, as the author, as well as other readers.

I would love for you to connect with me at:

Website
www.rhondablackhurst.com

Email
rhondablackhurst@gmail.com

Facebook
www.facebook.com/rjblackhurst

Rhonda's Rockin' Readers Facebook Group
www.facebook.com/groups/1089643708616600

Instagram
www.instagram.com/rhonda.blackhurst/

Newsletter Sign-Up
https://shorturl.at/aiOX9

Best,
Rhonda

ABOUT THE AUTHOR

Rhonda lives in Colorado but frequently escapes to her Arizona home. She is an avid reader, writer, lover of words, and dark chocolate connoisseur. Her writing career began at the tender age of four when she began writing with crayons on the knotty pine walls of the family home. She has 10 published novels: The Inheritance, a contemporary fiction novel; Shear Madness, Shear Deception, Shear Malice, Shear Murder, Shear Holiday Mayhem, Shear Fear, Shear Misfortune, and Shear Camping Caper--A Short Story, in the Melanie Hogan Mysteries; and Finding Abby and Abby's Redemption in the Whispering Pines Romantic Suspense duology. She has a non-fiction book, Finding Peace Through Gratitude, under the pen name Alexandra Benn. She is also an indie author consultant and awarded the 2022 Master of Literary Arts Award from the Brighton Chamber.

She can be found at her online home at
www.rhondablackhurst.com.